Prodigal Son

Prodigal Son

The Second Book in the Sword Trilogy

A Novel

Tom Teal

iUniverse, Inc.
New York Lincoln Shanghai

Prodigal Son
The Second Book in the Sword Trilogy

Copyright © 2007 by Tom Teal

All rights reserved. No part of this book may be used or reproduced by any means, graphic, electronic, or mechanical, including photocopying, recording, taping or by any information storage retrieval system without the written permission of the publisher except in the case of brief quotations embodied in critical articles and reviews.

iUniverse books may be ordered through booksellers or by contacting:

iUniverse
2021 Pine Lake Road, Suite 100
Lincoln, NE 68512
www.iuniverse.com
1-800-Authors (1-800-288-4677)

This is a work of fiction. All of the characters, names, incidents, organizations, and dialogue in this novel are either the products of the author's imagination or are used fictitiously.

ISBN: 978-0-595-45113-5 (pbk)
ISBN: 978-0-595-89426-0 (ebk)

Printed in the United States of America

Chapter 1

The sea breeze carried a different scent. Gone was the sting of salt that had stuck in the back of Hernando's throat. Now the calm night air hinted at fruit and spice, but he could not place this new sensation that tickled his nose.

For weeks he had stood at this spot in the bow of the ship, hoping to glimpse land. Now his despair left him and his heart rose a little from the pit of his stomach, where it had sunk with the weight of life and living. Life had been bad for so long, he had forgotten what it was like to hope or even smile. "Hernando Diaz," he said to himself, just under his breath. The name stuck in his throat as he said it, and the old shame rose with the name to shove his heart back down to where it belonged.

Pink streaked the sky behind him, heralding daylight, but he looked ahead, anticipating landfall. Sensing land was near, the crew went about their business in the predawn gloom, tightening the sheets against the breeze. Hernando made out the backs of porpoises riding the pressure wave on either side of the bow as it split the waters with greater speed. Behind him, more sailors took their places in the growing light.

The sky above paled to a velvety blue, dotted with virgin white clouds of billowy consistency. Still he could see no New World shores, only the flotsam of tropical foliage and seaweed coasting on the azure sea. He knew they were close. As he turned he could see it in the men's faces, a release of the tension that had tightened their expressions during these last few weeks of the crossing. Beyond the stern, a red spot on the horizon grew rapidly as the rising sun leapt from the indigo Atlantic, throwing the faces of the officers on the bridge into shadow, their figures into silhouettes.

"Land ho!"

Tears came to his eyes as the lookout in the crow's nest shouted. He spun so hard, his sword slapped his side. It was not the regulation issue of the Spanish soldier, but a prize of battle taken from a Moorish sultan by his great-great-grandfather. His mother had given it to him at the docks, just before he departed. He knew what the sword meant to her, and to his nation.

The crewman shouted again, "Land ho, port side, ten degrees."

The first mate barked orders and sent for the captain. Immediately the ship tacked to starboard. Some of the crew not busy with their duties, and even some who should have been, ran to the gunwales, looking for land.

"Captain on deck!"

The warning sent most of the men back to their posts, but two lingered without even a glance over their shoulders. That pair, although part of the crew, took their orders from a higher authority. He moved over beside one of the two Jesuits. "Do you think we will be in port by nightfall, Father?"

"Most certainly, Hernando," said the older of the two robed figures, then added, "if God is willing."

Hernando thought of his older brother Ignatius who, two years before, had made this same journey. He had not heard from his brother, although his exploits in the wild lands of New Spain were trickling back and exciting the church. Ignatius had left the rest of the family to deal with the tragedy of their father's death, a death Ignatius could have prevented, if he had not turned his back. As Hernando thought about it, the sick feeling rose in the pit of his stomach, and blood pumped into his face, reddening his cheeks.

"There! There is land," someone called, and the sailors cheered. Hernando could plainly see land now, and seabirds floated on the humid air around the ship. The officers issued orders in steady succession as the ship entered the dangerous waters around Hispaniola. A bosun sounded from the bow, calling out the fathoms he read from the weighted string as he retrieved it from the depths. Lush tropical beaches slid by, far off to port, as the ship paralleled the coast, looking for Port Santo Domingo. The reading the navigator was making put the town to the north.

The voice of the ship's boy at his elbow pulled Hernando from his trance. Complying with the request, he made his way to the captain.

"Commander Diaz." The captain spoke without taking his gaze off the port bow. "I trust you are pleased to see New Spain exactly where I said it would be."

It was an obvious reference to the extra ten days the voyage had taken, which Hernando had mentioned at dinner three days ago. Careful to keep his expression bland, Hernando replied, "I never doubted your sailing prowess, Captain. I only made mention of how badly the winds had treated you on the voyage."

Captain Colius Menindez turned to study him, trying to detect sarcasm in his voice or eyes, but Hernando's face betrayed not a hint of anything but respect. He knew the captain had worked his way up the ranks, and disliked all officers who bought their commissions looking for fame, winning their glory on the backs of common soldiers. But the captain tended to forget the prize ship bounty with which he had bought his first commission. True enough, it was his great skill at sea that had caught the Admiralty's eye and brought him to the command of the *Alva Cordova* ... Hernando's eyes swept the deck of the war galleon, armed to the teeth and spoiling for a fight.

"Your orders are to be opened at the first sight of Hispaniola, I believe, Commander?" Menindez didn't hide his hatred of the secrecy surrounding his young passenger.

Only when they saw Hispaniola could his sealed orders be opened; only then would Menindez know where he was to deliver the young commander and his two hundred soldiers. Hernando hesitated, wondering if he should ask if this was indeed the Spanish island of Hispaniola, but decided not to push the captain. Instead he reached inside his leather jacket and produced an ivory envelope sealed with bright red wax. Hernando broke the seal, which was quite obviously from the court of Charles V, and handed the orders to the captain.

"We are to proceed with all haste to Villa Rica de la Vera Cruz," the captain read. "There, I'm to off-load you and your men." He looked up. "It says nothing of what you are to do there."

Hernando met the captain's eyes. "That I already know, sir."

The captain grumbled at the continuing mystery. "You're dismissed," he said, as if he had more authority over Hernando than he did.

Hernando returned to the ship's rail to ponder his next step. He'd been charged by the Duke of Aragon—"with the highest authority," he'd been told—to find Cortez and make sure that the lands he had conquered were being taken in the name of Charles V of Spain. The conflicting reports coming back to Spain had the court worried. The governor of Havana had insisted that Cortez was a rebel who countermanded his orders to establish a beachhead, instead running off on some wild chase, looking for a mythical golden city. But Cortez himself had sent one of his own ships home to Spain with unimaginable treasure: gold necklaces, richly coloured robes adorned with long green bird feathers, gold and silver ornaments, and, most impressive of all, disks of hammered gold as large as cart wheels. The treasure caused an instant stir in the king's court, nearly bankrupt from its long wars with England and France.

"Sail off starboard." The cry came from the crow's nest. The bridge officers raised their brace of telescopes. The sun glinted off their slender casings, for Menindez was a stickler for neatness and none of the junior officers wanted to give him reason to look their way.

"What is she, Mr. Higuero?"

"A brigantine, sir. Not flying her colours, though."

"Run out our call, Mr. Higuero."

The first mate called the orders to raise the Royal Spanish flags which, by the laws of the sea, should elicit the same response from the smaller ship. As if the sleek ship and her crew could not tell she was Spanish from the huge red cross in the middle of the sails, Hernando thought wryly.

"She's started to run, sir," Higuero announced. "Shall we give chase?"

Menindez hesitated, no doubt pondering his orders. "Steady as she goes," he said.

The junior officers looked at each other. The standing orders were to give chase to all privateers they encountered at sea. Eyeing the other ship, Hernando realized the wind was stronger farther out; Menindez knew she had too much lead on them.

"Mr. Higuero!" the captain barked.

"Sir?"

"Make for Santo Domingo. Call me as we make the harbour."

"Aye, sir!"

The captain turned to go below. Hernando intercepted him before he had taken three steps. "Captain, the orders are to make all haste to Villa Rica de la Vera Cruz."

"Yes, Commander," Menindez said mildly. "If you can point it out on the chart to the navigator, we will indeed sail straight there."

The two stood looking at each other, Hernando a full six inches taller and massively built, Menindez slighter and older, but with an inner strength that exuded confidence.

With a flush of embarrassment, Hernando realized the new villa would not be marked on their charts yet. He stepped back. "Of course, Captain."

The captain whirled triumphantly and disappeared belowdecks. Hernando turned in time to see the officers on watch, who had been listening, look away. His hand found the hilt of his sword, as if seeking security. As they went about their business, he strode down the ship's walks to the bow.

His two officers were there, watching the land slide slowly by. "I thought we'd never see it again, sir," Luis, the younger of the two, said to Hernando.

"Neither did I," agreed José.

The brothers came from the same region of Spain as Hernando. He had picked them for their family name, recognizing one of the noble families who, along with his mother's family, had defended Christendom from the Moors along the Duero River some eighty years earlier, turning the tide of the war against the infidels. They were from the same stock as the warrior knights that had been bred in that harsh valley, the same knights the pope had compelled to crusade in the Holy Land. Hernando had a premonition that he might have to count on their valour, sometime soon. The other soldiers were conscripted professional men from the duke's personal army—hard, well-trained men. Hernando had no way of knowing whether he would be fighting natives or Spaniards, and if it came to that, Cortez's men were battle-hardened indeed.

"I want the men drilled on the docks," he told them. "If there's not room, break them up into smaller groups and set sentries. I don't want any man jumping ship."

"No leave, sir?" Luis looked incredulous. "The men will be in quite a mood when we ship out."

Hernando thought for a moment. "Don't give the order until we tie up."

As Hernando moved farther toward the bow, Luis leaned toward his brother. "He's going to be a hard-ass, this one. We'll see if he lives up to the legend of his name."

Chapter 2

▼

The captain returned to his spot behind the wheel man just after supper. The sun was low, dipping behind the land, but there was still adequate light to enter the harbour and drop anchor. An air of excitement hung over the deck as the sailors made fast the sails and rigging, knowing that in just a few hours, they would be embraced in the arms of rum, a lover, or both.

Hernando went below to the cramped quarters he shared with the large chest he had brought from Spain. Kneeling before it, he pulled an ornate key from his breast pocket. It slid easily into the lock, and the tumblers fell into place with a click. As he opened the curved lid, the hinges creaked from the assault of salt air on metal.

Pushing his hand past the bright red shirt lying on top of the clothing inside, he retrieved two silver-filigreed pistols. These were obviously not built for war, but duelling. Placing them on the table alongside a pouch and powder horn, he dug some more and found a small framed set of paintings. He unfolded the hinged frame and stared at the portraits of his mother and father. *How could life have changed so quickly?* He thought as his mind raced back to his father's dark, wood-panelled office.

In his mind's eye, he was a boy of fourteen again, his gangly frame already heading for the heavens as he stood in front of the man seated at the desk.

His father looked up from his paperwork. Juan Gregory Calsonia was a large, impressive man, quick to frown and slow to smile. What is this your brother has told me?"

All day, Hernando had waited for the punishment that would surely come when his father returned from his work in the vineyard. He shuffled from foot to foot.

"What is this I've heard about you not finishing your chores, and using one of the ponies without permission?"

Hernando considered telling his father that he had quarrelled with Ignatius about doing more than his share of work. Ignatius, three years older than Hernando and accorded an older brother's responsibilities, handed them down to Hernando with relish. He had taken one of the ponies into the hills without permission because he'd been angry at his brother. He'd known Ignatius would tell Father, but he just had to get away, and the hills behind the house were ideal for losing himself and healing injustices.

He thought of four or five excuses he could use, and discarded each one. "Sorry, Father," he finally said.

Hernando was unsure why Ignatius hated him, but hate him he did. He thought it might be because Ignatius' own mother had died giving him life, and that their father had married Hernando's mother. She was good to Ignatius and treated him as her own son, even taking his side in disputes with Hernando sometimes, and indeed, Hernando had thought she was Ignatius' mother as well, until Ignatius had revealed the truth during one of their squabbles.

"Hernando! Are you listening to me?" his father demanded. He shook his head, scowling. "You're just like your mother, daydreaming the day away. Look, there's a lot of work to running an estate this large. Why can't you be more like your brother?"

"I do most of Ignatius' work as well as my own," Hernando blurted without thinking.

"You boastful little whelp! What kind of behaviour is this, blaming your brother for your transgressions?" his father growled, surging to his feet and stalking toward Hernando. "On your knees, and ask God for forgiveness!"

His father's large hand forced Hernando to his knees. "Oh God, please do not despise my lazy and blasphemous son, Hernando," he intoned. "Please do not burn him in the lake of fire for his lying ways. Oh God Almighty, put your redeeming hands upon my wicked son and correct the error of his ways." The hand lifted. "Now, Hernando, you stay on your knees and ask God to forgive you until bedtime. I will send for you then." Juan Calsonia left the room.

Hernando did talk to God then, but he didn't ask forgiveness. Instead he gave thanks for being spared his father's strap, his usual punishment. Then his thoughts turned from God to his father, who seemed distracted these days, and sterner than usual. Still on his knees, Hernando looked around his father's office, filled with so many books that they'd overflowed the shelves to sit in piles on the ends of the desk, on the floor, and even on the leather couch.

At bedtime, Ignatius came into the office. "Well, Hernando," he slurred, as though he had a speech impediment, "I guess you'll do as I say tomorrow, won't you."

Hernando stood, but said nothing to him, which infuriated Ignatius. As Hernando passed him to go upstairs, Ignatius stuck out his foot and tripped him. Hernando fell hard, then quickly jumped to his feet and whirled on Ignatius. His brother had already balled his hands into fists.

Hernando stopped. "You won't always be bigger than me," he said, and left the room.

It had been around that time, Hernando recalled, that Father had sent Ignatius to the village monastery to study with the Jesuits. He had a head start, for their father had taught them from classical Latin and Greek books from a very early age. The family saw less and less of Ignatius as time went by. But time did not heal the rift between Hernando and his brother.

"Sir," Luis called from outside the cabin door, "we've made harbour."

Hernando hadn't realized how long he had been lost in remembering the past. He closed the framed portraits and tucked them back into the chest. "I'll be up directly."

When Hernando came on deck, officers were shouting orders and sailors balanced on the yardarms, taking in the sails. Only one sail was still to the wind and even that had been loosened, to let some of the breeze spill out the sides and slow the creaking ship. On shore, activity on the wharf seemed to be picking up. The captain stood silently at his place behind the helmsman. Hernando watched for a moment, impressed with the crew's efficiency as they brought the huge ship quietly into port.

"Drop anchor, Mr. Higuero!" Captain Menindez ordered. As he spun to head below, he added, "Full uniforms, Mr. Higuero."

"Aye, sir." Higuero wore a large smile as he relayed the orders to the other officers, for he knew they were going ashore.

Hernando watched his men as they came on deck, and José quietly told them they were to be drilled, with no shore leave. As the men grumbled loudly, Hernando stepped into view. "Is there a problem, Lieutenant?" he asked José.

The master sergeant boldly voiced their disgust at being denied shore leave. "The men gotta have leave, sir. We've been cramped up in the holds the whole crossin'."

Hernando stepped close to the sergeant. "What's your name, Sergeant?"

The soldier drew himself up. "Wells, sir; Master Sergeant Wells."

"That's not very Spanish, is it, Master Sergeant Wells," Hernando said, his voice inaudible to the rest of the company.

"My mother's Spanish, sir," Wells replied in a flip and equally quiet voice, as if seeing how far he could push his commander.

Hernando put some bite in his voice. "Are you always this familiar with your commanding officers, Wells?"

"You're the one who wanted to talk, sir," Wells replied, his voice still light, still pushing.

Hernando leaned in even closer. He knew he had to gain the respect of his men, and he planned to secure that respect here and now. He'd already taken note that Captain Menindez and his officers were rowing toward shore in the cutter, their dress uniforms sparkling in the last rays of the sun. "Can you fight as well as you talk, Sergeant Wells?" Hernando said, his voice now loud enough to carry to every soldier on board.

"Yes, sir, I can," Wells replied, his voice just as loud. His face split in a big, silly grin.

"Do you think you could take me?" Hernando asked.

"With or without that fancy toad-sticker at yer side?" Wells jerked his chin at the Saracen sword belted at Hernando's waist.

Hernando pulled his two pistols from within his jacket and handed them to Luis. "Shoot the first man who interferes, Lieutenant," he said calmly.

Luis gaped at him as he accepted the pistols. "Sir, what are you doing?" he hissed. "These men have fought all their lives."

Ignoring him, Hernando unbuckled the legendary sword and handed the jewel-encrusted hilt to José.

Wells started to unbuckle his sword and armoured breastplate, then stopped. "It's a hanging offence to strike an officer."

Hernando turned back to his two lieutenants. "Your word as knights that not a word of this will leave this ship, ever."

"Sir, I must protest—" Luis stopped when he saw the warning in Hernando's eyes. "Yes, sir," he muttered, and José echoed him.

Hernando turned back to Wells, who was already stripped to the waist, revealing a heavily muscled torso. Wells started to speak, but Hernando cut him off. "Just as I thought, the bark's worse than the dog's bite."

Wells lunged. Hernando sidestepped, tripping Wells as he went by. Wells hit the deck hard, and the other men jeered at him.

"Get that pretty boy, Wells," someone yelled from the back as Wells leapt to his feet.

Wells, angry now, rushed for Hernando, who again sidestepped. This time, though, he sent out his fist, landing a noisy blow to the side of Wells' head that again sent him to the deck. It had to be a good one, Hernando thought, because his fist hurt like hell.

Wells got up slower this time, and shook his head. "All right," he growled, "that's yer game."

He came in slower, bobbing and weaving. Still Hernando sidestepped and connected with Wells' face every time. Wells' nose trickled blood, and his anger grew as he realized he was quite obviously outclassed in a boxing match. The other men got louder, crowding closer. Luis levelled the two pistols, now cocked, at them.

Wells jumped at Hernando, taking two more jabs, the last splitting his lip—but he got his big arms around Hernando and started crushing him. The men cheered him on. Hernando could feel his backbone cracking as the air was forced out of him. Then Wells drew back his head like a green heron fishing for sardines and smashed Hernando in the nose with enough force to knock him down.

"Now we got a fight," Wells mocked as Hernando wiped the blood from his nose.

Hernando stood, a little shaken. Wells came in and they exchanged blow for blow, neither giving an inch. Eventually, bloody and winded, they fell together onto the deck, still striking each other, although their punches were now ineffective. Finally they sat looking at each other. Hernando's tongue probed a loose tooth.

"This old dog's still got a lot of bite," he commented. The men, who had fallen quiet, broke into laughter. He knew they had half-expected him to order Wells flogged for putting up such a good fight. Pushing to his feet, Hernando extended his hand to Wells, who took it. As Hernando hauled him to his feet, the men cheered.

"Drill the men, Lieutenants," Hernando said. The cheering stopped. He turned to Wells. "Master Sergeant, get yourself cleaned up, or the ladies of Santo Domingo won't give you a second look." Then he raised his voice and said to the men, "After you've been properly drilled, shore leave for the night—and you have Master Sergeant Wells to thank for it. But mark this well, any man who doesn't make ship in the morning will have to answer to the Master Sergeant and me!"

The soldiers cheered, and the two officers saluted Hernando.

"My pistols and sword, if you please; the men are yours." Hernando turned to go below, careful to conceal the pain of his battered body.

Chapter 3

▼

Cleaned up and impressive in his dress uniform, Hernando was rowed ashore in the other cutter, watching as his lieutenants bellowed orders at the drilling men. The cutter nudged against a wharf that was deserted except for a few workers and the youngest naval officer he'd ever seen.

"Commander Diaz?" the young ensign queried, peering down at him.

"Yes," Hernando replied as he climbed the ladder to the young man's side. "And who do I have the pleasure of speaking to?"

"Ensign Averra, sir," the young man replied crisply, snapping to attention.

"Don't salute me, Ensign, I'm not navy!" Hernando chuckled, sticking out his hand. The youngster shook it energetically.

"Are you really the grandson of El Cid?" he asked.

"Great-great-great-grandson, I think," Hernando replied, wondering how the young man could be so knowledgeable.

"My father, the governor of Hispaniola, wanted to be here personally," Averra admitted, "but I'm glad he sent me instead." He flashed a grin. "Everyone has been taken to the governor's palace. I have a carriage waiting."

Hernando glanced out at the *Alva Cordova*. The drilling was over, and his men were coming ashore. The young Averra followed his gaze; his jaw sagged in awe. "It looks like you mean to invade us."

"Invade the brothels, more like it," Hernando said wryly, but he had to admit they made an impressive sight.

* * * *

At the governor's house, he was introduced to all the local royalty before the governor, a student of history, rested his hand on Hernando's shoulder and described to his guests the feats of Hernando's great-great-grandfather, including chasing the Moors out of Spain and reclaiming Spain for Christ. Hernando knew the stories, but he was a little embarrassed by the attention. He glimpsed Captain Menindez, listening with an ill-concealed scowl at the back of the crowd. *He thinks they should be crowding around him,* he realized.

With a twinge of envy, Hernando's thoughts turned to his men. They would be revelling in the company of honest, unpretentious soldiers. Even the harlots, who would be swarming the new arrivals like bees at a broken hive by now, were at least honestly plying their trade. Here, the bewigged and powdered strutted like bantam roosters and peafowl. The wives wore so many petticoats, he could not tell where woman left off and clothes began. Only their shoulders were bare—and the pale, powdered tops of their breasts, squeezed together so hard within their bodices, they looked like two tomcats squaring off nose to nose. And each woman had a little black mole in exactly the same spot on her left breast, apparently the latest bit of vanity, back in the Spanish court.

He began thinking of ways to excuse himself. Smiling, Hernando eased from the governor's proprietary grip and attempted to fade back into anonymity, but the young ensign dogged his every step, beckoning to have his wine glass topped up with claret every time Hernando took a sip. Finally he could take no more.

"Ensign Averra."

The ensign snapped to attention. "Yes, sir!"

"I have to see to my men. Is there some way to excuse myself without making a fuss?"

"You want to leave?" Averra looked astonished. "But, the party is really in your honour!" He looked into Hernando's pleading face. "Let me speak to my father," he said quietly, and hurried away.

He returned so soon that Hernando expected excuses and pleas from the governor to stay. "We can go," the ensign said, and escorted Hernando to the palace entrance. "I made your excuses to my father, and the captain seemed relieved that you were leaving. I think he's jealous of the attention the ladies were giving you." The young ensign smiled.

The carriage was waiting. Hernando climbed in, then turned to the ensign. "I should be able to get back to the ship by myself."

"No, no," Averra quickly interjected. "My father said I must accompany you—commanded me, even. You see, I did not know what to tell him, so I said you had some secret business to attend to. So he said I must accompany you and keep you safe from harm, here in Porto Santo Domingo."

Hernando could make out his scarlet cheeks even in the half-light of the carriage lanterns. "All right, Ensign Averra," he sighed. "Do you have any idea where my men would be?"

"I do indeed, but you don't want to go down to that part of town!"

"That's exactly where I'm headed," Hernando told him.

Not fifteen minutes later, Hernando ducked under the lintel as he opened a door built for dwarves. The inn beyond was noisy and smoky and stank of rum already filtered through some sailor's kidneys. Recognizing some of his men, singing and carrying on in the back, Hernando wove through the crowd toward them with Averra hot on his heels, his face pinched with concern.

A burly, bearded man with a large gold earring in his right ear stepped into Hernando's path. "I thinks yer outta place, aren't ya cap'n?"

Hernando wordlessly tried to dodge the rum-soaked sailor, but another grabbed his shoulder and spun him around. In a blink, Hernando had grabbed the man's wrist and twisted his arm up behind his back. The sailor squealed in pain.

"I don't think you've had enough to drink," he hissed in the sailor's ear. "Let me buy you a grog." As Hernando pushed him to the floor, three other sailors stood and charged for Hernando, but before they got close, Wells rose up behind them and slammed all three together like a giant playing dominoes with their bodies.

The bar erupted into a chaos of soldiers punching sailors and whores punching whores. Wells snatched his drink from a table as a brawler sprawled across it, and the battered trestle collapsed under his weight. "A little lost, are ya, sir?" he asked Hernando conversationally.

"No, I was looking for you." Hernando leaned back as a bottle flew between them. "Let's get out of here; I need to talk to you."

"Yes, sir, but first, do ya think we should save the little dandy that followed ya in here?" He nodded past Hernando's shoulder.

Feet dangling, Averra hung in a boatswain's grip. Clasped firmly by the neck, the young ensign was looking straight at the man's fist, which was cocked back for another punch. Hernando caught his arm before he could deliver the blow, and Wells clubbed him a good one on his cheek. Averra slumped to the floor with his dance partner as the man crumpled. Red-faced with anger, he kicked the unconscious sailor in the head with the heel of his boot.

Hernando helped the lad to his feet. "You're supposed to do that *before* he gets you by the throat."

The three moved outside. Sounds of destruction followed them from the inn. The driver had pulled the carriage close to the door and had his pistol cocked and ready. They climbed in, and the matched pair of bays lurched down the street.

"What about the men?" the young ensign asked, absently rubbing his neck.

Hernando twisted his head to look back at the bar. "I don't think you should be worried about the men, but you might say a small prayer for the locals." He leaned forward. "Driver, take us to the Cathedral de Santo Domingo." The driver nodded, snapped the reins, and the carriage clattered down the street.

Hernando entered the cathedral with Wells at his side and the young Averra bringing up the rear. "What in God's name are we doing here, sir?" Wells asked, looking uncomfortable about entering this place with so much rum in him.

"I need to talk to the priest," Hernando said, looking around. He hesitated before asking, "Do you think the men would fight their own, if commanded to?"

Wells stopped and turned to Hernando. "I don't understand, sir."

Hernando came right to the point. "If commanded, could they kill other Spanish soldiers?"

"I would say they would follow you without question in a good cause, sir," Wells hedged.

"Cut the crap, Wells!" Hernando snapped. "Tell me what you think!"

"They like you, sir, but … fight their own? No way to tell."

Wells turned at the sound of a door opening. Hernando's eyes also followed the sound, and saw a priest come out of the vestry.

"Let's hope it doesn't come to that. Stay here for a moment," Hernando said, and strode toward the priest.

"Good evening, Father." Hernando paused to bow deeply at the altar before he passed.

"Hello, my son," the older man intoned as Hernando straightened. "What can I do for you?"

"Do you happen to know a Jesuit who was stationed here about two years ago? His name is Ignatius Calsonia."

"Yes, there was a Jesuit of the Alpha Order here for a while, but he went on to Havana. He is a relation of yours?"

"No, no." Hernando stuttered a bit, but recovered. "Just an acquaintance. I was trained in the classics at the same monastery. Thank you." He turned to leave, then turned back politely as the priest spoke.

"I'm sorry I couldn't be of more help. Maybe you would like to speak with the Bishop of Hispaniola in the morning."

"No, thank you. I was just curious, that's all." Hernando turned, bowed more deeply to the altar this time, and went to gather his comrades.

"Looking for someone?" Wells asked as they left.

"Yes, but he's gone on to Havana. I guess I won't be seeing him on this trip." Hernando sighed with relief. He hadn't known how he would react at the sight of his brother, but he suspected it wouldn't have been pleasantly—he felt the old anger rising in his throat.

* * * *

Two days later, as those on the *Alva Cordova* gathered up her crew from the bawdy houses and hurried to restock her provisions, Hernando was called to the governor's palace. He smiled at the term as he was ushered into an anteroom with two walls lined with padded, straight-backed chairs, their frames and feet carved with birds and large cats in jungle scenes. It wasn't a palace, really, but merely the fanciest house in the port, situated atop a hill overlooking Santo Domingo.

Hernando was admiring the carvings when young Averra emerged through a large wooden door also ornately carved with unfamiliar animals and birds. "Commander Diaz. My father will see you now." His right eye was puffy and purple.

"Nice eye," Hernando whispered as he passed. The ensign broke into a smile, then looked toward the governor and quickly removed it.

"Ah, here you are, Commander. I must apologize for my son. I hope he didn't get you into too much trouble the other night. I expressly told him to look after you, and I apologize if we have failed you." The governor looked sick, as though Hernando had already written unfavourable dispatches to the king of Spain.

"No, on the contrary; if your son had not been there to lend a hand, I fear those ruffians would have gotten the better of us." Hernando winked at the younger Averra, careful not let his father see. The smile returned faintly to his face.

A smile also came to the governor's face. "Is there anything we can do for you while you are in our fair city?"

"No, I think the restocking of our provisions is going well," Hernando replied, wondering when the man would get to the point. There had to be more to the visit than cordial chit-chat.

"I hear you next make for Villa Rica de la Vera Cruz." The governor lowered his voice, as if to protect the secret.

Hernando hid his surprise. "News travels fast in New Spain."

"Not much goes on in this little city of mine that I do not know about." The governor leaned forward in his chair. "That's Cortez's landfall, isn't it?"

"Yes," Hernando admitted. "I go to join him in his conquest of this new land."

"His Majesty must be very interested in the souls of the Indians, to send another soldier to help with the conquest—especially one with such an illustrious name as Diaz."

Hernando also leaned toward the governor. "Things are rather delicate back home, what with the wars and the king's enemies on all sides. He needs some trustworthy men such as yourself to look after his interests." They both were thinking about the treasure Cortez had sent back to Charles' court, but neither said it out loud. "What can you tell me about the governor of Havana?"

"Yes, Don Francisco Barbaro." The governor paused. "I think he does well in the converting of pagans. I hear Cortez disobeyed his order and burned ships so his men could not mutiny and return to Havana."

"This is what I've heard, also."

The young Averra interrupted, offering, "Madeira?" as he pushed a glass into Hernando's hand.

After another glass and polite conversation that bordered on gossip, Hernando excused himself and returned to the ship.

As he climbed up the rope ladder and through the entry port, the ship's boy asked him to see the captain.

"Aye, there you are, Commander Diaz," Menindez said as Hernando joined him on the bridge. "Your supplies will be loaded by noon tomorrow. We should be able to sail shortly thereafter; then I can return and refit the ship with my own provisions."

Hernando inclined his head in acknowledgement. "Thank you, Captain. I appreciate the speed at which your men completed the task."

"We would have been making way by dawn if your men hadn't done so much damage to mine, that first night of shore leave," the captain retorted.

Hernando bit back an angry reply. "I've already apologized for my men, sir. If there is something else I can do—"

Menindez cut him off. "I'll be glad to see you off at Villa Rica de la Vera Cruz." He turned to go below, leaving Hernando in the midst of the junior officers, who eyed Hernando haughtily.

He went below in search of Wells.

"Sergeant Wells, please relay to the men my pleasure that the captain is still complaining about the hurtin' your boys put on his sailors," he said when he found the master sergeant. They both laughed, then Hernando settled down to business. "We set sail at noon. Everyone accounted for?"

"Yes, sir. No one jumped ship. They must like you, sir!" Wells pulled his big grin out of his bag of looks. "The men will be happy to get onshore for a longer spell, sir."

Hernando paused before he spoke. "They might not like it so much when we get there."

"Don't worry, you have the men's support, Commander."

"Thank you, Wells; good night."

Hernando returned to his quarters. He heard the watch bell and decided to skip dinner, instead lying on his bunk, which was about two feet too short, and imagining that he was lying on the hilltop just behind their house in Spain. He conjured the green grass, the shepherd whistling his dogs to move the sheep, the pale blue sky dotted with grey clouds that just hinted of rain ... that and the gentle rocking of the *Alva Cordova* slowly lulled him to sleep.

Hernando awoke with a start, noted groggily that it was dawn, and that there was a commotion on deck. He had slept late! He splashed a little fresh water on his face, then headed above.

When Hernando came on deck, he saw horses being craned onto the ship.

"A gift from the governor of Hispaniola," the captain informed him when Hernando joined him on the bridge, where Menindez surveyed the activity with his hands behind his back and a scowl on his face. "Six Iberian warhorses for you, Commander Diaz."

"Honestly, Captain, I had no idea these animals were coming."

"Well, you've delayed us again! I'll make deep water by dusk, if I have to drown your damn war ponies." The captain stomped away to see to the new cargo. Hernando could only shake his head in disbelief.

Chapter 4

They were away by dusk, and with no equines swimming for shore. It felt good to be on the move again. And as the days passed, Hernando got to know one of the horses, a large, black stallion with a white face and an intelligent look in his eye. After a while, the horse seemed to look forward to Hernando's visits. Of course, the cane sugar lumps he brought with him helped the friendship along. He spent many hours grooming the beast, recalling wryly how he'd hated caring for the horses in their own stable, back in Spain.

Remembering that, as he pulled the brush over the horse's coat, Hernando imagined he heard his mother calling his name, as she'd called when he arrived for Christmas break from the San Cristobal Nositary School—when? He would have been just eighteen, two years into his serious schooling, as his father called it, with one year left. He had surveyed every inch of her face as they embraced. His mother, although as beautiful as ever, looked tired and worn out. Dark circles shadowed her eyes, and there were wrinkles and little lines in her face that Hernando had not seen before. Her bright blue eyes seemed to have dimmed a bit.

* * * *

"Is there something wrong, Mother?" he'd asked, drawing back and peering at her, his brows pinched together in concern.

She looked startled, then sidestepped the question. "Hurry, or you'll miss dinner," she said, and they hurried through the great double doors of the house so Hernando could clean up in time to eat.

"Where is father?" he asked when he entered the dining room, looking at the empty chair at the end of the table.

"He is in an important meeting," his mother said, not meeting his eyes. She began passing great bowls of food in his direction, and Hernando noted that the servants had retired early, which he thought particularly strange, with guests in the house. "Your father has been under stress lately," she elaborated vaguely. "His friends are here to try to help."

Hernando waited for further explanation, but when she offered none, he asked bluntly, "Is it money, Mother? Is the estate in some sort of trouble?"

"No, no nothing like that." His mother hesitated. "Your father has been called to the capital to explain some statements he made, that's all."

Hernando set the bowl she'd passed to him carefully beside his plate. "Explain to whom, Mother?" he asked, his voice level. "What statements did he make?"

"Your father will explain tomorrow before he leaves."

He got no more from her, and Hernando retired after supper without seeing his father. He lay on his linen duvet, still dressed, his mind racing with possibilities.

What was happening?

When he could stand the scenarios his imagination conjured no more, he roused himself and headed downstairs to his father's study. The door stood ajar and light still burned within, casting a thin rectangle of candlelight on the floor and opposite wall. Hernando paused in the shadows when he heard voices. His father was speaking with his friend, Fausto Morales. Their voices were quiet, almost secretive, and Hernando could not make out the words. Hernando knew Fausto Morales well, for he had long been a family friend, and Hernando's godfather. But something in their voices kept Hernando in the shadows, unwilling to intrude.

When his father and Fausto paused at the door to shake hands and embrace, Hernando felt a bit sad that his father had never embraced him in the same way. He crept silently backward and returned to his room to await the morning.

Before the sun had peeked over the old oaks on the hills in the east, Hernando was in the kitchen, sampling the breakfast specials. The old cook, who had been old when Hernando was a boy, now seemed ancient. She still had enough fire in her, however, to chase Hernando from his pilfering of the sweetmeats, brandishing a pot. Hernando decided tactical retreat was better than wearing the pot, for the way the cook brandished it, she meant to use it.

The groom was preparing his father's horse as Hernando entered the stables on his early morning rounds of the estate. Everything there was pretty much as he had left it six months ago, when he'd last visited from school. Satisfied everything was as it should be, he made for the dining room, where he was sure his father would explain everything to him.

His father and mother were already seated at the table, waiting for him, when he entered.

"Ah, Hernando." His father rose and came forward to seize his hand in his mighty paw and shake it heartily. Hernando hoped for a moment he would receive an embrace, but his father stepped back, and Hernando felt a wave of disappointment flow over him.

"Sit and eat. I'm in a hurry this morning, but I need to speak with you," the older Calsonia said as he sat back down at his place. "Son, one more year and you'll be finished school. We'd be having this talk then, but God has seen fit to push matters along faster than I had wished."

He looked at his wife, and Hernando saw the love that passed between them. And more—was that a tear welling in his father's eye? No; it must be a trick of the early morning light now streaming through the tall, arched windows overlooking the central courtyard.

"Hernando," his father started again, "someday you will have the care and control of the estates, and you must promise me to carry on the way I've taught you—to be fair and honest in your dealings with men, and to treat the workers well and not like animals, as some of our noble neighbours do."

Hernando wanted to ask why he was giving him this speech now, since he had heard it a hundred times before, but he sat quietly and listened. Something seemed different this time.

"In all your problems, trust in God; if you're unsure what course of action to take, imitate Christ, and do as He would do." The speech went on, his father going through how he should carry himself in all aspects of life. Then his father stopped, as if realizing his sermon was too long.

"Hernando," he said, staring into his son's eyes, "if things go badly for our family, trust Fausto Morales to get you through. There is nothing he would not do for you and your mother."

The suggestion of doom in his father's voice set Hernando's nerves on edge. He could remain silent no longer. "What is going on, Father?"

Juan Gregory looked at his wife and she gave him a small nod. "Son, I am a knight in an old order, as were your mother's father and my father before me." Seeing the confusion in Hernando's eyes, he elaborated. "The order has been condemned, deemed unlawful for hundreds of years by the pope and the Holy Roman Church. Our families, as well as others in Spain and France, have secretly kept alive the sacred order all these years. At nineteen you were to be initiated into the order—the order of the Knights Templar."

Hernando frowned. "Why have I never heard of this before, Father? Not even in school do they teach the history of this order."

The senior Calsonia drew a deep breath before he spoke. "The church has sought to expunge any trace of the order; it confiscated the lands and the gold the Knights Templar had amassed, tortured most of the knights to death, and persecuted any members of their families it could find. In this way, King Philippe of France secured his power over the state, and Pope Clement V secured his over the church. Someday, history will be rewritten, and the truth told," his father said, his voice hard.

Hernando looked at his mother, who sat with a serene smile on her lips. "But what does this have to do with Father going to the capital?"

"Your father thinks he's been betrayed by someone close," she replied.

"You mean someone in the order?" Hernando blurted.

"Not exactly." She paused and looked to her husband for support.

Juan spoke quietly now. "I have reason to believe your brother has brought my affiliation with the brotherhood to the attention of the church."

Hernando was struck dumb. No one spoke for several minutes. The three of them stared into the middle distance, considering the enormity of what Juan Gregory had said. Hernando, putting aside his own hatred for his brother, spoke first. "This can't be. There must be some mistake. Ignatius would never do that to you, Father."

Juan looked down at his unfinished breakfast. "When Ignatius turned nineteen, your brother turned down the invitation to become a Knight Templar. Now he is an ordained member of the Alpha Order of the Jesuits, accomplished without a cent coming from our bank accounts, and at a very young age."

"During the last couple of years, your father has been brought before the cardinal three times," his mother went on. "He was questioned about friends and acquaintances, some of them Templars. Now the cardinal has called him in for statements he made years ago, at a public meeting about the mixing of state and church. Someone is digging hard into your father's life."

* * * *

Hernando was jerked back to the present by the incessant pounding on his cabin door.

"Sir! Sir—" the voice outside was that of Sergeant Wells "—we have made Villa Rica de la Vera Cruz!"

Hernando blinked. His eyes felt dry, as if he'd stared at the wall all night. He could hear orders being relayed up and down the deck, and then he heard the great anchor rope being played out.

When he stepped out on deck, the light blinded him with its strength. He shaded his eyes and squinted in the direction the other sailors were looking. The waves rolled onto a beach that stretched as far as the eye could see to the north, and miles to the south, where a headland of dark rock could be seen.

"Your landfall, Commander Diaz." Captain Menindez had moved soundlessly up beside Hernando, startling him when he spoke. "You want to go ashore, I assume?"

"Yes, thank you, Captain." Though taken off guard by the captain, he was now back in charge. "Sergeant Wells!" he called, and when the master sergeant presented himself, added, "Get the men and supplies off-loaded and safely ashore."

"Yes, sir!" Wells was already heading for the fo'c'sle, and the men below.

"Mr. Higuero, you have the deck," the captain announced. "Let's get these soldiers cleared away!"

"Aye, sir!" Higuero barked back. The captain turned back to Hernando. "If you wish, we can supper together tonight."

"Thank you, Captain, but tonight I'll spend with my men in New Spain, if you don't mind." He noted the captain's sigh of relief.

"As you wish, Commander," Menindez left Hernando with his duties.

The men were jubilant at the sight of land, and attacked their work as though tackling an enemy. Hernando stood in the bow of the first cutter with the two Jesuits, studying the strange shoreline, where the surf swelled and crashed on the beach. "It's beautiful, isn't it, Father."

The older Jesuit replied without taking his eyes off the jungle, "Looks like the Devil's own playground."

Hernando wondered how the same sight could be so different when viewed through religious eyes. Then the longboat surged through the surf and was propelled high onto the sand, where it suddenly thudded to a stop, throwing everyone forward.

"You see? The Devil starts his work already," the old Jesuit said as he hoisted up his robe and jumped for the sand.

Hernando and his lieutenants clambered onto dry land and went down on one knee. As the standard of Spain unfurled, Hernando announced, "We claim this land for His Most Gracious Highness, King Charles V of Spain!" He was taking no chances. Cortez's letters spoke only of mysterious cities of gold, and announced that he had resigned his commission. Hernando had no idea if Cortez had affirmed Charles' right to the new land.

As the Jesuits said prayers and blessed the expedition, Hernando looked about. The land was lush and green, the waves foaming up the beach a crystalline azure. He grinned, forgetting the Jesuits, who had to raise their voices so God could hear them as the men started unloading the cutter.

All that day, the stores and weapons and men came ashore. The beach looked like a siege area at the base of some great, green castle. As his men set up an encampment of tents and lean-to shelters, Hernando and his lieutenant walked to the beachhead and stopped at a tangled mass of trees and undergrowth. It looked impenetrable.

Luis had lagged behind. Hernando called his lieutenant to him.

"Yes, sir?" Luis gasped, his breathing laboured in the stifling heat.

"Get the armour off your men. You're going to kill them in this heat. And where is that interpreter the governor lent us?"

"Yes, sir." Luis turned to survey the beach. Hernando turned to gaze back the way they'd come as well. "There he is—the fellow being accosted by the Jesuits, sir."

Hernando nodded, smirking, and Luis grinned as his commander took off to save the interpreter from being saved.

"Father, could I speak with our interpreter for a moment?" Hernando said as he jogged up to the trio. He didn't wait for an answer, cutting the man out of the group like a shepherd culling a ewe.

"You speak Spanish?" he asked the little brown man.

"Yes, most good, sir." The man flashed a big smile.

"What is your name?" Hernando asked as he sized up the stoutly built man. His black hair was blunt-cut like that of a squire, and his black eyes shone with the cast of black obsidian. Hernando stood head and shoulders over him.

"My Christian name is Juan, sir." He bowed his head slightly in a subservient fashion.

"How long have you been a Christian?"

"For two Christian calendar years, sir," Juan answered.

Hernando thought about questioning his conversion, but then thought that if there were any problems, the Jesuits would have already brought it to his attention. He wasn't worried about the man's faith, but about his loyalties. "I need to know which way a man named Cortez went. Are there Indians hereabout?" Hernando swept his arm toward the hills beyond the beach to make certain the interpreter understood.

"Yes, most certainly; they watch us now. Soon they will come."

Hernando heard this with dismay. He didn't need hostiles coming into his camp. "Do you mean they will send a force against us to repel us from the beach?" he asked, nervously peering over Juan's head, choosing places for fortifications.

"No, sir." Juan read Hernando's concern perfectly. "They will send a small party to counsel with you."

Hernando felt relief, but still shouted an order to José to set up a guard at the perimeter. "How do you know they will come to talk?" he asked Juan.

"It is our way. We counsel with the enemy before we make plans to do battle," Juan said simply. Hernando was astonished at Juan's apparent grasp at the situation. Juan stood for a minute and then offered without being asked, "These are my people. I know their ways."

Juan's head suddenly turned toward the beach as shouting men and wild-eyed horses broke the surf and pawed ashore. They'd swum the horses ashore; it was the only efficient way of bringing them to land, but now they were spooked. As they gained a footing, the animals were surrounded by soldiers with their arms raised to corral and calm the great beasts. Hernando noticed the effect the horses had on Juan; even after two years of living among white men, the sight of horses still astounded him. Hernando filed that piece of information away for later.

"Then we just wait?" he asked, bringing Juan's head back around.

"Yes. It will not be long," Juan replied.

Hernando dismissed him and called for Sergeant Wells.

"Yes, sir?" he said, snapping to attention as he stopped before Hernando.

"Give me some cover from the sun here, where I can watch the beach and the jungle."

"Yes, sir!"

"And keep your eye on our interpreter," he added.

"Yes, sir," he said again, but this time he turned his head to eyeball the brown man.

"That's all." Hernando's attention turned to his great chest as two men struggled through the soft sand to set it at his feet. And as Wells hurried away, he raised his voice so that the men nearby could hear: "Very efficient landfall, Sergeant Wells."

Wells turned on his heels in the soft sand. "Thank you, sir." He sketched a salute, then continued down the beach.

Chapter 5

▼

The captain of the *Alva Cordova* came ashore with the last load of the day to speak to Hernando. They sat in the shade of Hernando's newly built hut, drinking wine and talking in vague generalities about Hernando's mission, for the captain's curiosity was still not satisfied.

A movement in the green curtain before Hernando's hut drew his attention, but before he could react, a brightly coloured procession of Indians emerged from the jungle. Hernando and Menindez leapt to their feet. Soldiers immediately ran between the officers and the procession, shouting warnings. The procession stopped short of the soldiers' weapons, its members staring calmly past the armed men at Hernando and his guest.

Hernando stared back for a moment, shocked both by the ease with which the procession had walked into the camp, and their regalia. The Indians wore headdresses of bird feathers in a rainbow of brilliant hues, and more gold and jewelry than he had seen at all the fancy parties back in Spain. He counted ten of them, each more dazzling to the eye than the next.

"Juan!" Hernando yelled, then realized the interpreter had been at his side the whole time.

"Yes, sir," Juan said as he smiled at the procession, but the visitors' faces remained solemn. Standing between the two senior officers, Juan waited calmly until they'd regained their composure before supplying, "They are the Toltecs, the people of the land north of this beach." He raised his hand. "Shall I talk to them, sir?"

"Yes, by all means do." Hernando had had the presence of mind to snatch up his steel helmet and jam it on his head, but his half-armour hung on one of the hut's support posts. He eyed it as Juan spoke to the Toltecs, wondering if he should put it on. Abandoning the idea, he listened as Juan spoke to the visitors, who then returned his greeting. The language sounded harsh to Hernando's ear. As they talked quickly back and forth, Hernando realized he should have prepared a speech for Juan to interpret for him.

Two of the Indians strode forward from the back of the procession, and Juan appeared to be introducing Hernando and the captain. He turned to Hernando. "I told them you are from the east, where the sun sleeps at night." At Hernando's puzzled look, Juan quickly elaborated. "We—they," Juan stumbled in his Spanish, "worship the Sun god as their most sacred god. So they see you now as their god's emissaries."

Hernando and Captain Menindez looked at each other. Hernando was trying to grasp the significance of what had just been said. "They think we are gods?" he asked.

"No," Juan said, "just friends of gods. They have already seen that you can be killed, like them."

Hernando looked into the eyes of the older of the two patiently waiting Indians. "Bid them come in, out of the sun, Juan."

A smaller group, the two leaders among them, stepped from the procession and moved under the shelter. They sat with obvious discomfort on the hard wooden chairs Hernando had brought from the ship. "The chief's name is Paynala Chak-mool," Juan added.

"Ask them about Cortez, Juan."

"I have already; they say that Cortez is their brother and that they have a treaty with your people." Juan smiled, pleased at being one step ahead of Hernando's questions.

Hernando glanced at the two Indians, again taken aback. He saw Captain Menindez smile at his poor control of the situation. Refusing to react, he looked back at the interpreter. "Explain what you mean by 'a treaty,' Juan."

"Is that not the right word, sir?" Juan thought for a second. "When two sides join against another?"

"Yes, yes, but who are we joined against?" Hernando persisted.

"The Aztecs, sir." The other Indians stirred at the mention of the name.

"Ask them—" Hernando began, but Juan interrupted.

"The chief and his high priest wish to make presentations to you, sir. They are waiting patiently. This is our custom, and they are starting to wonder why they haven't been allowed to proceed." Juan looked at the chief and then added, "These people live by ceremony, sir."

"Yes. All right, then—Juan, you proceed, as you know their customs."

Obviously relieved, Juan spoke to the chieftain, then bowed his head to the great old man, whose face cracked in the first smile since he'd arrived on the beach. A young Indian who seemed to be more resplendent in bird feathers of various colours jumped up so quickly, he startled the soldiers, some of whom reached for their swords. Hernando gestured for calm.

The young Indian shouted to the others, and most of them disappeared back into the jungle. Minutes later, they reappeared with more of their fellows, bearing glorious gifts of animal skins, feathers, vegetables and fruits, tame parrots, and wooden boxes carried lightly in the hands of half-naked girls. Hernando immediately felt ill at ease, as religious teachings rumbled in the back of his mind. He felt his face flush with embarrassment, or excitement—he didn't dwell on which—as each of these supple young maidens brought forth her treasure and laid it at his feet.

"What is happening, Juan?" Hernando said out of the corner of his mouth, his eyes on the next beautiful little brown girl as she placed a black pelt complete with a large feline head, its fangs bared, at his feet.

"This is a jaguar, the most fearsome beast in our jungles," Juan told him, looking more delighted than the old chief, who was smiling from ear to ear now, delighted with the greatness of his gifts. "This is a great honour, sir."

The last young lady straightened and looked into Hernando's eyes, which none of the other maidens had done. Her eyes were like dark pools, and her brown lips were full and proud. They curved in a demure little smile, then she inclined her head and backed away.

Juan spoke again to the chief, who was waiting anxiously for Hernando's response, then turned when Hernando spoke.

"Thank the great chief of the Toltec peoples," Hernando said, then paused. Juan jabbered to the old Indian. "That the great king from the east thanks him for his splendid gifts. I would like to repay his kindness."

Juan stopped. "Be careful not to outdo his gifts," he cautioned Hernando, "for it will embarrass Paynala Chak-mool, and he will have to make war on you."

Hernando thought about that. "You can tell the lieutenant what would be proper to offer from our stores," he said.

Juan asked for steel axes, cloth, pots, and a few caskets of dry sea biscuits. Smiling, Hernando gestured for the gifts to be brought, and they returned to the intricacies of the ceremony.

It lasted the rest of the day. When the chief suddenly turned to leave, Hernando realized he hadn't gotten any important information. Jumping to his feet, he blurted, "Wait a minute!"

Startled, Paynala Chak-mool turned back to him, his eyes wide. Hernando immediately knew he had made a mistake. Unsure how to recover, he thrust out his hand for a traditional handshake. Juan looked ill. Hernando tensed, expecting danger.

The old chief looked at Hernando's hand for a long moment, then slowly took it. Hernando smiled, slowly exhaling his pent breath as the chief addressed his people. They also released grasps. Without another word to Hernando, Paynala strode back into the jungle, followed by his retinue.

Juan gazed after them, slumping with relief. Finally he looked at Hernando and explained, "It is death to even touch the cloak of a chief."

Hernando breathed normally for the first time since realizing he had made an egregious error in the encounter. "What did he say, Juan?"

"He said that the Great Sun God's helper wanted to touch such a great chief so he would have stories for the little ones when he returned east."

Hernando nodded his appreciation. The old chief was as great a politician as any lord or noble back in King Charles' court.

All the Toltecs had left except two young ladies and a broad-chested man. The interpreter was already heading toward them. "Juan, why are they still here?" Hernando asked.

"They are yours, sir; they were also gifts from the chief to you."

Hernando gaped in shock. "No, no! We'll send them back."

Juan stopped and turned to him, his face grave. "Then you risk war with the Toltec's," he said. "They are his to give, and now they are yours. Besides, it is from them that you will find out what you want to know."

Hernando, who'd been about to complain further, closed his mouth and tried to figure out what he could do with the new arrivals.

Captain Menindez spoke for the first time that afternoon, drawing Hernando's attention from the pretty girl who'd been left by the chief. "I need to be away before darkness sets in, Commander."

"Yes, I understand," Hernando replied, his mind elsewhere. "Thank you for delivering us safely to the shores of this strange land. When will the *Alva Cordova* sail back to Spain, Captain?"

"We are to patrol the waters here for Spain, and teach the privateers that Spain will no longer put up with the taking of His Majesty's ships. A job I strain at the bit to take up," Menindez added.

Hernando ignored his acid tone. "Yes, I understand, Captain. Would you be so kind as to deliver these tributes to our king on your next sailing to Spain?" He indicated the treasures the Toltecs had left.

"Yes, of course, Commander."

"I will send them aboard immediately, so as to not delay your sailing."

Hernando also sent a letter, stitched into a canvas bag and sealed with red wax and the crest of his mother's family. In it was a letter for the Duke of Aragon, describing what had transpired so far.

As the great warship turned on the wind and made for open sea, Hernando watched until the fading light and distance made the sails indistinguishable from the cumulus clouds rising from the horizon.

"Juan," he shouted, but the man was right behind him, standing quietly in the shadows. He stepped forward. "What have our guests told you about Cortez?" Hernando asked him.

"Nothing, sir. They will only talk to you."

"What do you mean, only talk to me? How am I going to talk to them?" Hernando blurted, perplexed.

"They will talk to you through me, but not to me," Juan began, but Hernando held up his hand to stop him. The long day was wearing his patience thin.

"Bring them here," Hernando said.

A few minutes later, Juan showed the three Toltecs under the roof that made up Hernando's hut. Hernando stood as they entered and stopped before him, looking like a small flock of migrating ducks, the pretty little woman in front and the other two a step behind her on either side. The two in the rear knelt with one knee on the sand floor, and the young woman bowed her head without looking at Hernando.

He motioned to Juan to ask her to sit. As Juan translated, she looked into Hernando's eyes. He could not make out her expression, but the reflected light from the fires still revealed her beauty. Her black hair shone with carefully applied oils. He could smell her, too; the scent of flowers and spices hung in the air around her as she sat down at the crude table.

"Ask her name, Juan," Hernando said softly, trying not to look down at her plump breasts, but he was painfully aware that they were round and firm, each mounted with a black jewel for a nipple.

Juan did not speak to her. He instantly replied, "She is called Laocan. She is the great chief's daughter."

Hernando looked from her to Juan, startled. "You mean to say the chief gave away his daughter?"

"Yes. You are bound now in a treaty with Paynala Chak-mool."

Chapter 6

When Commander Diaz urged Juan to tell Laocan his name and why they had come to this land, Juan said to her in Toltec, "This is Hernando Diaz, a great soldier from the land where the Sun god lives. He comes to find the other white man who went to the golden city of the Aztecs."

Laocan's eyes were on Hernando when she spoke. "He is a beautiful creature. His eyes look like the emerald stone artisans use for the eyes of the stone gods. Surely he is one of them. Tell him I will happily obey my father's wishes. And tell him this Cortez is far ahead of him, but we will find him."

Juan turned to Hernando, who was staring at her, and switched to Spanish. "She says the man Cortez is far ahead of you, but that she can lead you to him." He smiled, knowing this was what Hernando wanted to hear.

Hernando's eyes dropped to Laocan's slender neck, where a heavy gold and emerald necklace rested, the emerald pendant hanging down between the mounds of her breasts drawing his eye down between them. Laocan's lips curved in a slight smile. Hernando looked back up to Laocan's eyes. "Ask her if her father will give us guides and bearers for our supplies."

Juan started to ask, but Laocan interrupted in a musing voice, "He looks at me with desire in his eyes. This is a good sign." Juan did not comment. He finished the question Hernando had asked and Laocan replied, her voice harder, "My father will give two hundred warriors to fight the Aztecs. The Toltecs have broken their treaty with the Aztecs. They subjugate us no longer."

Juan nodded, and said to Hernando in Spanish, "Yes."

Hernando frowned, hearing much too many words spoken for just "yes" and realizing that Juan was not translating exactly what the maiden was saying.

Watching the commander's frown disappear as his eyes strayed back to the beautiful young woman, Juan did not bother to elaborate.

"Tell her good night for me, Juan. Find her a place, and tell her that I would like to make an early start after Cortez tomorrow."

Juan turned to the chief's daughter. "The commander says good night. He would like to start after Cortez tomorrow. I'm to find a place for you and your servants."

Laocan looked at Juan and then back at Hernando. "I will sleep wherever the green-eyed giant wants. Does he not know I am his to command?"

"Yes," Juan answered, again without elaborating.

This time the skin between Laocan's fine black brows furrowed. "I think I please his eye; why do I not lie with him tonight?"

Juan shuffled his feet in the sand. "These people of the east have different customs than us. He does not mean to offend you."

"Then I will sleep in the corner of his house," she said imperiously. Her servants immediately started preparing her place.

* * * *

Hernando watched in confusion as the two Indians with Laocan began rearranging what few things were under his roof. "What is happening, Juan?" he demanded.

"She means to sleep here tonight, sir," the interpreter said, his expression and voice neutral.

Hernando stepped outside and looked about for the Jesuits, but most of the camp was quiet now, with only the odd cough or low voices murmuring in the darkness. "All right," he sighed. "Juan, be here at first light."

Juan left, and Hernando turned back inside. By now the pretty young lady was half hidden in shadows. Ignoring her, Hernando settled down to sleep. But sleep did not immediately come. He could still smell her scent, and lay still on his pallet, imagining he could hear her light breathing as she slept.

* * * *

But laocan did not sleep. She was happy and excited at the prospect of this new adventure. She too lay awake, half expecting Hernando to come to her in the darkness, then wondering if she should go to him. *No,* she decided. She would let him make the advance she knew must come. *Soon,* she hoped.

Chapter 7

▼

The next morning, Sergeant Wells had the men moving before Hernando had even washed his face. The young Toltec woman came back to the hut after looking after her personal toilet. While she'd been gone, her servants had prepared some fruits and cooked flatbread on the hot rocks rimming the fire.

"Wells," Hernando shouted.

The sergeant was at his side as quickly as a sheepdog. "Yes, sir!" he replied, but his eyes were on the pretty young woman, who ignored him.

Hernando glared. The possessive jealousy that surged through him when he saw where Wells' gaze had fallen surprised him. "Wells, I'm over here."

"Yes, sir; sorry, sir."

Hernando mastered his expression. "The Princess Laocan is my guest and under my personal protection," he said.

"Yes, sir." Wells winked. "I know what you mean, sir."

Anger destroyed his carefully constructed demeanour. "You're a pig, Wells!"

"Yes, sir, that I am, sir," Wells replied, unmoved by Hernando's outburst.

Hernando clamped his mouth tight, squelching another angry remark, and looked away. "I want half the men ready to march in one hour," he said evenly after a moment.

"Yes, sir. We can be ready in half that time, sir!" Wells said enthusiastically, as if sensing he'd pushed Hernando more than he should.

"No, one hour is fine."

"Yes, sir."

"And bring up my horse," Hernando added, then turned to his two lieutenants, who had trotted up. "José, you'll ride with me. Your brother has our back."

Luis looked disappointed. Like most of the men, he was looking for a fight and ready to seize fame and fortune. "Sir, I think I should accompany you, as well. You may have need of a good sword at your side."

Hernando smiled at his youthful exuberance. "I have need of a good sword at my back," he countered, and Luis inclined his head to acknowledge his authority.

Juan was at Hernando's elbow, a bowl in his hand. "Laocan wishes to have breakfast with you," he said.

He hesitated, not expecting this and uncertain how to respond. "Ask Laocan if she will accept a gift from me," he finally said.

Juan looked up from the food he had invited himself to eat and translated.

She smiled when she heard Hernando use her name and nodded her head like a little girl.

Hernando went to his great chest and dug through the clothing until he found the silk skirt his mother had placed in there—" for special occasions," she had said. He handed Laocan the folded garment and she took it in her hands and smiled in wonder at its softness. She held it to her cheek and grinned as it tickled her soft brown skin. She said something to Juan.

"Laocan thanks His Greatness," Juan said as the princess's maidservant took the garment from Laocan to wrap it carefully in a woven cloth.

"No, no!" Hernando blurted when he saw Laocan surrender the garment. He stammered an explanation, thinking about the incident with Wells. "She must wear it. It is a shirt."

Juan's voice when he translated went low, as if he were not used to speaking so to a person of higher status. But she immediately retrieved the shirt from her servant and slipped it over her head. It enveloped her slight frame. She looked like a mizzen mast with the wind let out, Hernando thought, and laughed. Laocan met his eyes and laughed as well. The joy Laocan seemed to bring him surprised Hernando, for he had not felt happy since his father was killed.

Laocan stopped laughing as the great black stallion was brought to Hernando's hut. She backed away in fear, and Hernando caught her as she backed into him; she felt firm and warm under his hands. He released her and caught her hand, then pulled her toward the stallion. She moved reluctantly, her eyes round with terror, but she followed Hernando. He placed her hand on the horse's neck and the stallion's great head came around and blew air on her. She pulled back, startled, and spoke to Juan.

"What did she say?" Hernando asked quietly when she returned her hand to the horse's neck. A smile formed on her warm brown lips, as if she liked the feel of the great beast.

"She asked if this beast obeys her lord," Juan said. "And I told her yes, as do we all."

The great creature's eye looked her over and she seemed to relax, as if she could see no evil in its gaze. Hernando placed her hand on its muzzle and she giggled like a little girl; the sound lightened Hernando's heart.

When Hernando mounted the great stallion, Laocan backed away, her lips parted in shock. Juan spoke to her and she replied.

"She says she had heard that Cortez has similar beasts, but she never dreamed they were so big," he told Hernando. "That the beast obeys you without you even saying a word must surely be magic like she has never seen."

Hernando had no time to deny her belief; a runner from Wells announced that the men were ready. It was time to set off.

With Laocan and her servants in front, leading the way, the ungainly procession pushed into the thick jungle at the edge of the beach. Hernando's doubts evaporated when the undergrowth gave way to a trail, and the band made better headway toward the hills that rose out of the jungle in the distance. Eventually the path widened and the land seemed drier, but a gentle breeze stirred the humid air and kept the heat bearable. Hernando worried about the men, who marched heavily laden with muskets, armour, and supplies.

Dismounting from the stallion, Hernando walked beside Juan and Laocan, asking her questions through Juan. "How far is it to the city of gold?" he asked as he looked back at his struggling army.

"Laocan is taking you to her father's city to get men and supplies," Juan told him.

Hernando asked about her people and about the Aztecs.

"My people, the Toltecs," she replied through Juan, "have lived along this coast since time began. The Aztecs came to the great city where they are now, in the middle of a large lake. The ground was swampy, but they fortified it and made it impervious to attack, except by way of narrow causeways built from the shore. They are a warlike nation; they subjugated us and many other peoples between here and their walled city."

Hernando frowned, apprehensive at the thought of going up against such a developed people.

They travelled and talked all day, stopping only for a meal near midday. Late in the afternoon, the path turned into a paved road. "We near the city of my father," Laocan said as Hernando looked in amazement at the squared stones making up the road surface. In the distance he could see large stone buildings—not the huts he'd been expecting.

As they drew nearer, an escort came out to lead the Spanish into the city. They passed cultivated fields with ditches or small canals moving the water from field to field. These people were more advanced that he had believed.

The whole town turned out for the entrance of the Spanish. Only the escort carried any kind of weapons—large clubs with blades of black volcanic glass bound to them; Hernando would note later that these stone axes were every bit as sharp as their own steel ones. The welcoming ceremonies lasted for hours. When they sat down to eat, Hernando made room beside him for Laocan, and the old chief smiled, pleased at this tie with these new peoples from the east. He informed Hernando that Cortez was holding the great Montezuma, king of the Aztecs, hostage and demanding a great ransom from the king's brother.

Hernando thought this strange, but listened intently as Paynala also revealed that some of the other tribes were revolting against the Aztecs who had been their lords. As they talked, Hernando grew satisfied that the chief was playing square with him. He turned his attention to the food, most of which he had never seen before. All he could tell was that it was mostly seafood, and mostly delicious.

He hesitated, however, when a great, steaming creature with spiny legs and a large, flat tail was placed before him. What was this? He had no idea how to eat it, or even if it was meant to be eaten. Laocan reached over and broke off the tail and handed it to Hernando. Watching her, he followed her lead as she broke apart hers and sucked the soft flesh from inside the bony shell. They washed it down with cups of sweet wine made from honey and spices which, Hernando was realizing, packed quite a punch.

When the chief excused himself for the night with two or three maidens under each arm, Hernando dismissed José and Wells, who had accompanied him to the feast. Laocan led him back to a hut which had been set aside for him. Her servants followed, as always, just behind them. Hernando looked around the room. A bed of freshly cut grass, covered with woven blankets of many colours, waited against the back wall. Just one. Hernando felt a moment of panic, then assumed the princess was instructing her servants to bring in another bed for her when she said a few words to them in Toltec. They left, but they did not return.

She looked up into his eyes and he thought she was the most beautiful thing he had ever seen. The soft lamplight glowed on her small hands as she fumbled with his half-armour and the belt holding his great sword. The buckles clinked in the silence and although he saw her struggling with these new fastening devices, Hernando stood unable to help her with the catches, his mind too numbed by her beauty and slowed by the quantity of wine he had consumed.

When she had plucked him out of his outerwear, he felt the cool night air through his linen shirt and the warmth beginning in his loins. His mind waded back toward reality and he stopped her hands as she was undoing the top buttons on his shirt. She began murmuring in her language, soft and reassuring to his ear.

* * * *

"Relax, you green-eyed god; relax and let Laocan fulfill her duty," she soothed. As if he'd understood her, he dropped his hands, and she began to unbutton his shirt again. She slid the white cloth off his massive shoulders and it fell to the hard earth floor. As she stooped to pick it up, she slid her hands down his back to his buttocks, pausing for the briefest moment before continuing down the backs of his legs to the floor. She saw his manhood straining against his breeches as she folded the shirt.

When she straightened and turned back to him, Hernando embraced her and pressed his mouth to hers, his lips hot and his tongue probing. Laocan was taken off guard, for she'd been taught a prolonged ritual of undressing and touching to stimulate the man she was raised to please. She felt weak in his arms, and knew she had lost control, for she desired him as much as he desired her. Her knees buckled as the long, hot kiss continued.

Hernando lifted her and placed her softly on the thick blankets. His hand slid up her side and lightly caressed her pert breast through the silk of the shirt. The touch electrified Laocan's body, raising goosebumps on her skin. "I'm supposed to be pleasing you, my master," she whispered into Hernando's ear. She pressed her breast into his palm, feeling the nipple harden under his touch.

He unbuttoned the shirt and she wiggled out of it. His fingers fumbled with the beaded strings of leather on her loincloth; Laocan reached down and moments later, it fell away. Hernando shrugged off the last of his clothes, and then they twined like two boa constrictors writhing in an ancient courting dance. His hands roved over her taut stomach, then moved downward, lingering to caress the delicate folds of flesh. Her body responded, and she wriggled under his touch. Laocan, who had been schooled in the arts of pleasing a man without ever actually being with one, was unprepared for her reaction to the touch of a male.

His lips pressed kisses down her neck, giving her a chance to breathe for the first time since their lips had met. He lingered at her nipple, sucking it into his mouth and gently tugging on it, like a newborn mouthing for milk. Then he kissed his way down her belly to her mound, where he touched her like she'd been taught to do to him. A sudden, violent spasm overtook her body. She shook uncontrollably, moaning.

*　　*　　*　　*

Hernando brought his head up to look at her, for the stable maid who had taught him the technique had never reacted in such a way. She was panting, but she smiled at him and pulled him up toward her. It took a second for him to realize that she wanted him to mount her. He moved up between her legs and thrust into her, and she squirmed to get away. He paused, thinking he was hurting her, but she gripped his buttocks with her heels and pulled him in closer. As they made love, Hernando was surprised at its quiet calmness, so unlike the riotous pounding the maid had given him in the stable on his father's estate.

Before he fell asleep in Laocan's arms, she kissed him gently on the lips and said something tenderly to him in her language. Hernando didn't know what she said, but he liked the way she said it.

The following morning, as they were preparing to march for the golden city, Hernando noticed a difference in Laocan. She was smiling and repeating his Spanish words as if trying to learn the language. Conscious of this, he kept his eyes on her when he spoke to her through Juan, and formed his words more slowly.

Paynala had placed two hundred of his finest warriors under Hernando's command, and they left the town amidst the cheering and crying of their women. Hernando noted that his soldiers had gotten their land legs back as Wells snapped them into formation.

As they prepared to leave, the two Jesuits approached Hernando and informed him that they were staying to convert the heathens into good Roman Catholics. "You will be missed on the march," Hernando told them as he signalled for José to leave a small guard with them.

The older man assured him his army not would be left bereft of spiritual guidance. "After all, Juan has told us that Cortez has his own priest with him. And we will follow when our work here is done."

Hernando nodded, feeling a bit saddened that these kind and happy people would soon have the strict and rigid morals of Rome forced upon them. *If Laocan had been a Christian,* he wondered, *would she have given so freely last night?*

The Jesuits again blessed the expedition, and Hernando's men departed. The extra warriors shared the burdens his soldiers had been carrying, which made the going easier; even the men pulling the small cannon had men to spell them off.

Still, even though they travelled a well-built road, the going was tough. The still air was hot and humid, making even breathing a chore. They walked the horses so as to not tire them. The Toltec warriors split their force in two, half marching at the front and the other in the rear, helping with the supplies. Hernando noted that the two warriors in the forefront never took a turn with the supplies and assumed they were the commanders. He asked Juan about them.

"Yes, warrior priests. They have never performed a labourer's duty," Juan replied quietly, as if they could understand Spanish. "The one on the right was betrothed to Laocan before she was given to you in treaty," Juan added.

Hernando was shocked by a custom that gave away someone else's potential wife, but when he looked at Laocan and she smiled at him, he was also happy that their custom had brought her to him. A few times, Hernando thought he glimpsed the solidly built warrior priest staring at him, but he decided it was just his imagination and left it at that.

Each day brought more of the same hardship, but Hernando's men were becoming lean and hardened under the tropical sun. On the fourth day the warriors in front stopped and the column ground to a halt while the pair conferred. Their leader came back and knelt in front of Laocan, directing his words to the ground at her feet. She replied in a curt voice, the tone quite obviously one of displeasure.

The young warrior stood and addressed Hernando through Juan. "The Almeimecs await an audience with the green-eyed god in the road ahead."

Hernando turned to Juan. "What did he say to Laocan?"

She looked at him when she heard her name. Juan looked at her and she nodded, as if giving permission to repeat the exchange. Juan turned back to Hernando. "The warrior priest was unwilling to talk to you and the princess said he must."

Hernando glanced at the young warrior, who looked impatient at having to wait for Hernando to talk to Juan. Hernando put his hand on Juan's shoulder and turned him so their backs were to the young warrior priest. "Juan, when you translate, you must tell me exactly what is said. Our very lives could depend on it."

Juan thought for a moment, then stated, "This man doesn't like you and doesn't believe you are a god."

Hernando smiled. "There, you see? That wasn't so hard, was it?" He turned back to the young priest. "Translate this, Juan: you may not think I'm a god, but my king has a thousand cities larger than the golden city and a thousand men for every one here who is not an ally. He will not hesitate to crush all who oppose his desires."

After Juan complied, the two men stood staring defiantly at each other. Laocan broke the tension. Juan translated her words to Hernando: "Go and set a meeting; we will follow." The warrior bowed deeply to her and left.

"Tell my god that a meeting will be set," Juan translated as she turned and spoke, but Hernando knew what had happened.

"Wells!" Hernando shouted, but Wells had moved to his side during the exchange with the warrior, and the "Yes, sir?" that came from beside him startled Hernando. "Wells, stop sneaking up on me."

"Yes, sir," Wells answered with a smile. Hernando sensed that the sergeant had grown to like him as much as he liked Wells.

"Wells, bring up the muskets, slow matches at the ready. And bring my armour and helmet. See if you can find some of those long green feathers the chief and the priests are so fond of."

Within minutes, twenty-five men with muskets in hand marched up through the column with José at their head. Wells returned with Hernando's armour. "We going to see action, sir?" Wells asked as he handed Hernando his half-armour and helmet, now resplendent with two long, green bird feathers.

"It's best to be prepared," Hernando muttered as he donned the armour.

"Yes, sir." Wells grinned at the thought of action.

Hernando took the lead with José beside him. Laocan and Juan followed close behind. They marched up the road to where the young priest and two of his warriors were waiting. After a short pause to stare at the quetzal feathers Hernando had placed on his helmet, the priest turned and led them to a party waiting farther up the road.

The Almeimecs seemed a poorer tribe than the Toltecs, for their costumes were not as resplendent as those in the old chief's retinue had been—but they looked fiercer, if that was possible. After introductions, Laocan led the proceedings. An hour passed, and still they jabbered away while Juan translated.

"They want a tribute to cross their land. They grow bold, now that Cortez has taken the golden city."

"How many men do they have, Juan?"

"It is uncertain, but there can be many hidden in the forest," Juan replied.

Hernando whirled. "José!"

"Yes, sir?"

"Fall back and bring us our horses." He turned to the sergeant. "Mr. Wells."

"Yes, sir?"

"When the horses get here, have three of your men fire over the heads of these fellows."

"Yes, sir." Wells nodded curtly and left.

Hernando strode forward toward the chief of the Almeimecs. "Juan," he said, interrupting the proceedings, "tell the chief that he holds up the great god of the east's men and he must move out of the way. We will pay no tribute; in fact, it is he who must honour the great eastern god's representative." Juan looked at him with fear in his eyes. "Tell him!" Hernando shouted, and took Laocan's arm.

As the horses came up, a thunderous volley of musketfire erupted. The old chief hit the ground, along with his retinue and the Toltec warriors standing nearby. Only the warrior priest held his ground. Hernando swung up into the saddle and lifted the little princess up behind him. He could feel her body tense against his back; she was more frightened by the great beast between her legs than by the commotion the rifle fire had caused.

"Wells?" Hernando called.

"Yes, sir."

"Bring the column through; be on guard—slow matches lit," Hernando cautioned.

"Yes, sir."

"Wells," he added, and the other man paused and looked back. "Don't shoot unless we are attacked."

"Yes, sir."

The Almeimecs had disappeared. The Toltec warriors cheered as the princess rode by behind Hernando. She'd slipped her arms around his waist to steady herself, and Hernando could only think of her loincloth pressed against his buttocks.

The procession marched on for many miles before Hernando called a halt at dusk. "Wells, large fires and double the guard," he said.

Juan interjected with, "Our people, like the Almeimecs, would not attack at night."

"Double the guard anyway, Sergeant!" Hernando barked.

"Yes, sir."

That night, Juan translated Laocan's words to Hernando, but already she was using some of his words when she spoke.

"What you did today will travel through the valleys and tribes," she told him through Juan. "This is good, for in a few days' travel, we will arrive at the walled city of the Beltecs, the traditional enemy of my people. We have had a forced alliance with them because of the Aztecs, but now I fear they may not let us pass, unless they hear of the way you ran off the Almeimecs. They might hesitate to attack such a fierce god."

Hernando listened intently to Laocan. He disliked Juan's presence. He wished he could tell her he longed to take her to bed, and tell her in her own language how beautiful he thought she was. But she started a story about an ancient legend that all the peoples of the region believed, and Hernando returned to reality.

"For hundreds of years, the downfall of the Aztecs has been foretold," she said, "even by their own priests. It is said that a people would come from the sun god in the east and destroy them. The Toltecs always thought a great leader would rise from our people and destroy the Aztecs, but when Cortez came over the water from the east, and the sun set a fire so great on the lagoon that it lit the night sky, we knew we were not the ones to fulfill the prophecy of Quetzalcoatl."

Hernando knew the fires had been set by Cortez—he'd burned the ships so his men had no way to get home if they mutinied—but the great ships burning in the bay of Vera Cruz must have seemed like a scene out of Dante's Inferno. But Hernando also wondered how Cortez had seemed to fulfill the Quetzalcoatl prophecy. Were the rumours that he and his conquistadors had taken the golden city true?

He wanted to explain to Laocan that he was just a man, but he decided he should not dissuade her from her current beliefs; they could still be used to tactical advantage. And, just maybe, she would reject him if she knew he was just a man.

He needn't have worried.

* * * *

Although he didn't realize it, Laocan was falling in love with Hernando the man. She also wished Juan would leave, so she could feel Hernando deep inside her again. Finally she dismissed Juan in the middle of one of his long speeches.

When he left, she came to Hernando and sat on his lap. She caressed his chin, its stubble prickly against her palm, and spoke softly to him. "My heart swelled with pride when you ran off the Almeimecs. I missed your kisses on my body today, and the movement of the great black beast between my legs made me long for you. Come to bed, my god."

Hernando, hearing the Toltec word for "god," assumed she was just fulfilling her duty as she pulled him to the corner of the tent, where her servants had placed a bed of fresh-cut grass. She undressed him and herself, then straddled him as if she were back on the great black beast. Hernando strained at the leads as she commanded him without words, riding him into the night.

* * * *

In two days they did indeed come to a narrow valley controlled by a walled city. A small procession of Beltec priests emerged through its gates and hurled insults at the green-eyed god, but stayed a respectful distance away. Juan, with obvious fear in his voice, reiterated what the priests were saying, adding, "They mean to make war. They say they're not afraid and will come in one hour to battle against your men."

"Wells!" Hernando shouted over his shoulder.

Wells materialized at his arm again. "Yes, sir."

Hernando gave him an irritated glance. "Will you stop doing that?"

"Yes, sir."

"Form up three lines right across the valley, in the narrow part there," Hernando ordered. "Juan, have the Toltec warriors stand behind the muskets. Explain that when we have fired twice, they should run by my men into the attacking army. Do you have that?"

"Yes, sir," Juan replied, and he took off toward the young Toltec priest.

"Do you think he understood you, sir?" Wells asked.

Hernando shrugged. "I don't know what these warriors will do, so save one volley of musketfire to repel a counterattack by the Indians. And have the pikes ready behind the Toltecs, in case they flee. If they do, have the pikes move in behind the gunners and keep the attackers off the musketeers until they've reloaded."

"Yes, sir."

Hernando gestured toward the heavy gun farther down the line. "And bring that cannon up, load it with grapeshot, and aim it at that noisy band of priests over there. I don't think I like their tone."

Wells smirked. "Yes, sir!"

The men waited in their positions for another hour. "José!" Hernando finally called. "Stay close to me. I may need to change orders and your horse will be the fastest line to the men."

"Yes, sir." José saluted for the first time in many days, obviously keyed up by the impending battle, as was everyone.

Hernando looked to the rear, where he had placed a small guard around the princess. Juan had already retreated to that position. "Ah, you piece of—"

Hernando didn't finish the thought, for the city gates opened and a great battle cry rose from the city. Beltec warriors marched out, chanting a war song and stamping their feet. The Toltec warriors answered them by chanting and stomping their feet as well, but they held their position. Black obsidian sparkled ominously in the sunlight—the Beltecs were armed with the same fearsome-looking war clubs as the Toltecs. Each warrior clutched a small buckler in his other hand, Hernando noted; the Toltecs wore their bucklers on their forearms, so they could swing their stone axes with both hands.

The Beltecs formed up in lines across from the gunners, ready to march across the short distance to the waiting musketeers.

Hernando mounted his stallion and drew his great curved Saracen sword. He kneed his horse forward, riding with José into the ranks of warriors, who gladly separated to allow them access to the front lines. "Sergeant Wells?" he called.

"Yes, sir."

"Wait until they are close. Watch my sword—when it drops, open up."

"Yes, sir!"

Hernando raised his sword as the priests' shouts reached a crescendo. Suddenly all was quiet. One of the priests threw his spear, which landed a few feet in front of Hernando's men. Then, with blood-curdling screams, the Beltecs attacked.

The Toltecs answered with their own war cry and moved closer behind the musketeers, eager to confront their attackers and restrained only by the shouts of the young priest. He obviously knew the danger they would be in if they attacked before the muskets had fired.

"Now, Sergeant—for King Charles and Spain!" Hernando yelled, and dropped his sword arm.

A great volley of musket fire belched forth, followed by clouds of smoke; the cannon roared, and a second volley filled the field with blue smoke that dissipated in the light breeze. Before it cleared, the cries of men who'd been cut down rose on the humid air. Hernando wasn't ready for the terrible destruction of life and limb that appeared before him. Men lay dying in heaps; others stood staring in disbelief at limbs torn off by musket balls or grapeshot. The Beltec priest who had thrown the spear had been completely blown up, his body caught square by the full force of the barrage; little remained.

Quiet fell on the valley except for the moans of men, then the Toltec warrior priest screamed and ran through the line of Spanish busily reloading their weapons. His warriors recovered their wits and followed. Receiving little opposition from the demoralized Beltecs, they hacked and chopped their way through the enemy ranks, not giving any quarter when one threw up his hands in surrender.

"Juan, for God's sake, stop those maniacs of yours!" Hernando yelled.

"It would be very dangerous to go out there until they have exhausted their bloodlust, sir." Juan said, staying as far away from Hernando's horse as possible.

The Toltecs ran on through the dead bodies and chased the fleeing Beltecs back to the gates of their city, which were closed so quickly, some of their own men were left outside, and to the mercy of the Toltecs. From the high stone walls, the Beltecs hurled rocks down on the Toltec warriors, forcing them back.

When they finally came to their senses, Hernando called to Sergeant Wells, "Take the men down to the gate, but keep them out of range of anything coming off the walls. We'll see if they want to parlay now."

Hernando rode down through the dead and dying to where his men had positioned the cannon. "Loaded with ball, sir, in case ya want to do some knocking on that great door of theirs," the soldier in charge reported, his face black from the powder and smoke.

"Juan, tell your warrior priest not to kill everyone in the town," Hernando said to his interpreter, who had trotted forward with him. "I need to talk to one or two of them." Juan looked sick at the idea of having to relay Hernando's order to the bloodstained man. Hernando ignored his squeamish expression. "And tell the people in the city to open the gates or we will open them ourselves."

Juan looked puzzled, but shouted the message to the men on the walls, who looked at each other but didn't reply.

"Sergeant, put some holes in that great door."

"Yes, sir."

The cannon erupted once, twice, and again; each time, a great hole appeared in the gates. Wood splinters flew high into the air with each crashing impact. The Toltecs cheered each shot. After five, one of the gates hung loosely on its hinges. The Toltecs rushed forward, pouring through the gates unopposed.

Hernando rode into the city after the noise had subsided a bit and his men had cleared the way. The Toltecs hadn't killed everyone; they had spared the old and young and most of the women. The people fell to their knees and pressed their foreheads to the ground as Hernando rode by.

In the central square, he dismounted. The Toltecs had rounded up the nobles, and they now knelt on the pale grey flagstones with ropes around their necks.

"Juan, ask them what they know of the Aztecs and of Cortez," Hernando instructed.

Juan moved forward and spoke to the gathered prisoners for a few moments, then turned back to Hernando. "They say Cortez passed through here under the protection of the Aztecs. The great King Montezuma is held in his city, and Cortez demands a large room filled with gold as his ransom."

"Tell them that the Toltecs are our allies, and any who fight against one fights against the other."

"They were not attacking the Toltecs, sir," Juan said before he translated. "They attacked the Spanish for what your brown robe did to their temple."

Brown robe? Aloud, Hernando said, "What do you mean, Juan?"

Juan asked a few more questions of the Beltec nobles, then turned back to Hernando. "Cortez's brown robe desecrated the temple and threw the altar down the side of the temple, where it still lies." He pointed to a broken altar lying in pieces at the bottom of a small pyramid.

Hernando belatedly realized they were referring to the Jesuit with Cortex. He moved to the base of the pyramid for a closer look. The altar looked more like a broken bathing tub than an altar, and the inside was painted dark red. "Why would he do this, Juan?"

"Cortez's brown robe didn't like the sacrifice the Beltec priest made to the gods in their honour."

"This is very strange." He frowned, then turned back to the prisoners. "But we don't have time for this. Ask them how far it is to the golden city of the Aztecs."

Juan relayed the question to the noble with whom he'd been speaking, then looked at Hernando. "About seven days' march from here, in the direction where the sun god sleeps."

West, Hernando mentally translated. "Sergeant Wells!" He didn't bother raising his voice; his guard dog sergeant had stayed very close during most of the conversation with the nobles.

"Yes, sir," Wells said from behind him.

"We can still make a few miles. Assemble the men."

"Yes, sir!"

Juan spoke up. "Sir, the Toltecs will want to stay here for the night, for the ceremony."

"What ceremony, Juan?"

"The victory ceremony over the Beltec, sir. The warrior priests will want to thank the gods of war."

"Thank the gods of Spanish technology, more like it," Hernando mumbled under his breath. "Sergeant Wells."

"Yes, sir?"

"Change in orders. Bring the men inside the walls. Find us a defendable position. No looting. The men are to be on guard."

"Yes, sir." Wells saluted and hurried off, shouting orders to his corporal.

Chapter 8

By the time evening set in, Hernando and Laocan were secure in a cool mudbrick building, its thick walls coated with white stucco and painted with geometric patterns. Laocan used a few Spanish words and a mixture of sign language and pantomime to tell Hernando how impressed she was with that afternoon's battle as they ate flat cornbread and a roasted meat that Hernando didn't recognize. He found it tasty, just the same.

When music started playing outside, Laocan took Hernando's hand and dragged him outside. He followed reluctantly; the last thing he wanted was to be around people. He had no desire to share Laocan with others.

She tugged him along until they entered the central square, where the warrior priest was sitting on a tall-backed wooden chair. The captured Beltecs huddled in a group, off to one side. One by one, the nobles and prisoners were brought to kneel in front of him, and he pronounced judgement with a wave of his hand. Some were spared; others were immediately decapitated from behind as they knelt before the priest. A great roar rose from the crowd of Toltecs and the Beltec women as each head was severed. The spectacle appalled Hernando, but Laocan seemed enthralled by the exhibition.

Hernando caught Juan's attention and demanded an explanation.

"The priest is removing all traces of the Beltec royalty, so they can never come back against the Toltecs," Juan replied.

Hernando knew of royal families similarly extinguished in European countries, but the Toltecs seemed to be really enjoying themselves. "Why does he save some of the nobles and kill others?"

Juan looked calmly at Hernando and simply stated, "They are all dead, sir, just in different ways. Those—" he pointed to the group of cowering nobles Hernando had thought the priest had spared "—will give their hearts to the gods of war."

Hernando's eyes swung back to the warrior priest in time to see him splashed with blood from the last victim. The young warrior stood at the final beheading and shouted with outstretched arms toward the night sky. The moon had just appeared, directly over the apex of the pyramid.

The first of the few he had spared were brought forward, a Toltec warrior clutching each arm. The priest stepped toward him with a chert knife raised in his right hand. Plunging it into the chest of the sacrifice, he ripped downward. Hernando heard the dull snap as the knife severed each rib within the man's chest. The man screamed and struggled, but he was held tight as the warrior priest jammed his hand into his chest and plucked out his still beating heart.

Hernando thought he was going to lose his dinner. He turned from the gruesome festivities and looked at Laocan, whose face was grim, but showed no signs of the revulsion that Hernando felt.

The hearts were taken one by one to the top of the pyramid and placed on a makeshift altar—and Hernando realized with a sickening jolt that the altar he'd seen earlier was not painted red, but stained with the blood of many such ceremonies. These people were as barbaric as the Toltecs, Hernando thought. He turned and retreated back to the bivouac.

"Sergeant, did you see what they're doing to these people?" he blurted when he encountered Sergeant Wells.

"Yes, sir." Wells seemed subdued, answering without his usual roguish enthusiasm.

"I've seen a lot of brutality in the wars and a lot of disgraceful things, but I guess this just about wins the first prize at the gruesome fair," Hernando muttered sourly.

"Are they going to kill all the men, sir?" Wells asked.

"At least the ones who could someday exact revenge for what is happening here tonight, I think," Hernando said. "It's something I will not soon forget."

Hernando retired to the stucco house and lay on the bed of cut grass that Laocan's servants had prepared. He could still hear the men's screams when exhaustion overtook him and he fell into a restless sleep.

* * * *

Hernando awoke with a start as he recognized the sound of his father's voice. He could hear only bits and pieces of a conversation that came from another room. Curious, Hernando rose and moved quietly down the corridor, his hand trailing along the rough, moisture-slick stones, until he saw a warm glow spilling from the next doorway. Hernando paused. His father's voice was denying some accusation being levelled against him. Hernando wanted to rush around the corner and rescue his father, who sounded as if he were in a lot of pain.

Another man spoke. *The Grand Inquisitor,* his mind supplied. Hernando's father hurled an insult back, then cried out in pain as a whip cracked, biting into flesh. Hernando forced his feet to move. He rounded the corner, then froze.

His father being racked. His joints bulged, the skin over them blackening under the force of the ropes. Pain contorted his face. His bare torso had been striped by the lash.

Hernando turned to the inquisitor, whose cold eyes peered back at him through two holes cut in the satin of his black pointed hood. The inquisitor spoke to Hernando, demanding that he leave, and this time Hernando recognized the voice: Ignatius!

Hernando yelled as a hand touched his cheek.

* * * *

He sat up so quickly that he startled Laocan and made her squawk. Quickly recovering, she mopped Hernando's brow with a piece of cloth and spoke to him, her voice calm and reassuring. "Lay back, my great king; let the night spirits run from your mind. Your great sun god will come in the morning and banish these demons. Lay back." She placed her hands on his chest and pushed him gently back onto the woven blankets.

Laocan rose and poured a cup of fruit juice, then brought it back to Hernando. He propped himself on one elbow and drank it, then set the cup aside and untied her long black hair from the thong holding it at the nape of her neck. She placed her lips to his and breathed into his mouth, "I will look after you Hernando."

It was the first time she had used his name. He pulled her down on top of him and the terror of his past slipped away.

* * * *

In the morning Hernando inspected his men, then he, José, and of course his loyal guard dog Wells marched a small contingent of men to the town square.

Half-burned bodies lay amidst a large bed of embers heaped up in the centre of the square. Sleeping Toltecs sprawled on the stones; apparently they had drunk every drop of the nobles' wine stores. Hernando stopped at one snoring body and kicked him in the side; although Juan was still alive, he was a long way from conscious, and he looked like he would not be anytime soon. "Tell these men to get up. We're leaving."

Juan groaned.

Hernando turned away angrily. "We should have left yesterday," he growled, and stormed back toward the bivouac with Wells shouting orders behind him.

As the men formed up around their sergeant, Hernando snapped, "Forced march, Sergeant. Leave everything unnecessary behind; each man is to carry seven days' rations and half powder and shot—leave everything else in this building." He indicated the stucco building that had served as his quarters.

Hernando took Laocan by the hand and led her to his horse, where he jumped into the saddle and pulled her aboard. "Sergeants, take the men on," he called out.

"Yes, sir!"

The column wound its way through the streets and out the smashed gates.

"Let's put some distance between us and the Toltecs," he growled to Wells. "If they are going to catch up, they will have to work at it."

With Laocan as their guide and the men making as many miles a day as possible, it was three days before the Toltec warriors caught up to the Spanish. Word came up from the rear of the column that the Toltecs were behind them, but Hernando told Wells, "Pick up the pace—double time, Sergeant. Let's see what these Toltecs are made of."

Late in the afternoon, Hernando called a halt. "Bivouac here, Sergeant."

Wells replied with his usual, "Yes, sir," mopping sweat off his brow.

By dusk, the Toltecs had reached the camp. Juan found his way to Hernando and stood before him, panting and complaining, "Eztli is not happy that you left him in the walled city. He marched us through the night, carrying the supplies you left behind. He even had us bring the cannon."

Hernando rounded on Juan. "He is here to serve me, not the other way around. I don't much care if the warrior priest is unhappy or not." He dismissed the interpreter with a wave of his hand.

Laocan smiled at him. "The great green-eyed god exerts his power over men," she cooed in his ear in the linguistic pastiche they had developed, brushing past him on her way to their tent.

Chapter 9

Later that night, Laocan sat with Hernando by the fire, with Hernando trying to find out more about Laocan, and Laocan trying to tell him she loved him.

Suddenly the warrior priest stepped into the circle of firelight. Instantly angered by the intrusion, Laocan stood. "Eztli! How dare you intrude on my time," she said, her voice harsh. "No one has summoned you here. Be gone!"

Eztli fell to one knee, but disapproval twisted his features, and he gestured disdainfully at Hernando. "How can you debase yourself with this pale creature?"

"How dare you judge your king," she snapped. Her voice rose. "How dare you judge *me*, the great Chief Paynala's daughter!"

"I demand the satisfaction that is due me." The warrior stood as he said this.

"No, I will not allow it," Laocan said firmly. "You have no claim. My father—your lord—gave me in treaty." She paused and looked at Hernando, and her voice dropped to a low warning. "If you kill this green-eyed god, we will be at war with the Spanish."

"This is no god," Eztli spat, flinging an arm toward Hernando. "It is my right to demand satisfaction, as you were to be mine."

"Then take an offer of payment!"

"No. I demand the same rights as any cuckolded lover," he insisted.

Laocan stamped her foot. "We were never lovers!" she shouted.

Hernando came to her side, yelling, "Juan! Juan!" Juan came running up and the pair conversed in agitated Spanish, but she barely noticed. She continued her argument with Eztli.

Belatedly realizing why Juan had been summoned, Laocan turned to Juan. "Do not tell Hernando what has been said."

Juan looked squeamish. "I already have, my princess," he said, and retreated a step.

* * * *

"What is going on? What are they shouting about?" Hernando had demanded as soon as Juan arrived.

Juan listened for a few minutes as the argument raged on, then reported, "The warrior Eztli demands satisfaction. He believes you stole his intended wife and his destiny to lead his people, and robbed him of his chance to fulfill the prophecy against the Aztec."

Hernando realized that the embarrassment of being left behind hadn't helped the situation. At that moment, Laocan turned to Juan and barked what was clearly an order. Juan replied sheepishly and took a step back. Hernando spoke before Laocan could immerse herself back into her argument with the warrior priest.

"By what method is he asking for satisfaction? Ask her," he instructed Juan. "Does he mean to challenge me to a duel?"

Juan answered without consulting Laocan. "It is our custom that certain classes can ask for satisfaction when wronged by a member of the same class. Eztli believes you and he are of the same class, as you both serve a great chief."

Hernando frowned, perplexed, and gestured at the warrior's weapon. "Does he mean to fight me with that great axe?"

"A challenge would be settled with traditional weapons." Juan still looked sheepish.

"My traditional weapon is the musket." Hernando laughed at his own joke, but the warrior priest took this to be Hernando mocking him and became belligerent. "What did he say?" Hernando asked Juan as Eztli shouted angrily at him, then stalked off into the darkness.

"He will come for you at dawn," Juan translated reluctantly. "Your men may shoot him down like a Beltec, but he will come just the same."

Silence fell on the small group. Then Wells' voice drawled from somewhere just out of the light, "Looks like a bit of trouble, Commander." He stepped into the light, musket in hand, slow match smoldering.

Hernando turned to Juan. "So?"

"He comes for you at dawn. My advice to you is to kill him in his sleep. He will not expect that and will be off guard," Juan said dismissively.

"Will the warriors attack if I kill him?" Juan shook his head. "Will they attack if he kills me?"

"Maybe, but I think not."

Laocan spoke up in the middle of their conversation, then ran into his arms as Juan translated, "She says she is powerless to stop the priest now. She says, 'Tell Hernando that I love him and I don't want him to die.'"

She started to cry. He held her away and looked into her eyes. "Tell this pretty little princess that I'm not dead yet." His smile didn't seem to help, so he went on, "In fact, I will stay alive to prove my love for her."

With that, she sobbed harder and clung to his chest.

"Begging your pardon, sir," Wells interjected, "would ya like me to pay our priestly friend a visit tonight?" He grinned and pulled his sheathed dagger across his own throat to clarify his intent.

"No thank you, Wells. I'll have to deal with this myself. But put an extra guard on my door. I'm not as convinced of Toltec honour as everyone else seems to be."

"Yes, sir." Wells slipped back into the night.

Hernando calmed Laocan on the mats in his tent, stroking her shiny black hair and murmuring soothing words until they fell asleep in each other's arms.

Just before dawn, Hernando heard the cooks preparing breakfast. Sliding out of Laocan's embrace, he pulled on a clean white shirt and dark pants, buckled on his ancestor's sword, and made sure a small dagger was tucked into the back of his belt. He slipped out of the tent without waking her—or so he'd thought. He glimpsed black eyes watching him as the flap fell back into place, and suspected she had been awake for some time.

In the predawn light, Hernando saw that his extra guard included the sergeant. Wells caught his bemused look and answered his unspoken question. "I couldn't sleep." They grinned at each other like two schoolboys looking to play truant.

"I don't know if we are to have seconds," Hernando said of the coming duel, "but I would be happy if you would act as mine."

"Thought you'd never ask, sir!" Wells' serious expression belied his flip tone.

They moved into the little clearing just beside the firepit, where last night's confrontation had occurred. Hernando warmed up by slashing at the air with the Moorish sword. It sang as it tasted the morning dew.

"The lieutenant said your grandfather took that sword off a sultan," Wells said, making conversation to hide his nerves.

"Yes." Hernando paused to gaze admiringly at the blade. "He rode with El Cid when they pushed the Moors back into the sea. This sword has seen many battles, and I pray to God that today it is on the side of right once more."

They stopped talking as the warrior priest walked into the clearing, trailed by two of his men. One hand rested on a great battle axe he carried on his shoulder; in the other he carried the head of a man. As he got closer he threw it in their direction. When it stopped rolling, Hernando recognized the dead features of Laocan's male servant.

Juan and Laocan emerged from the bush and spoke to the two warriors who had accompanied the priest. They spoke for some time, and Hernando grew impatient. One of the two warriors, who bore a resemblance to Eztli, shook his head. When Laocan turned and retreated to the treeline to watch the coming fight, Juan came over to Hernando.

"What was that all about?" Hernando asked irritably.

"The princess warned Eztli that whatever happens today, she will hold his family responsible; she will take retribution for her servant when we return home. She asked his brother," Juan indicated the warrior they had been speaking to, "to convince him to give way and accept a tribute, but Eztli refused."

Juan turned away as the warrior priest spoke disdainfully from the middle of the clearing, his voice harsh. Juan looked to Hernando. "Eztli is ready." His voice fell, as if Eztli might understand his words if he overheard. "He will not give in until you are dead. Make no mistake, he intends to kill you."

"That's the only part I do understand," Hernando replied. He turned to José. "If I die, take the men to Cortez, and support him if he works for Spain and King Charles." He dropped a hand to the sword he'd slipped back into its scabbard while he'd been waiting. "Make sure this sword gets back to Spain and the house of Diaz. My two pistols are yours if I don't make it through this—you may have need of them."

José looked worried, but just nodded obliquely. Hernando knew it was crazy to risk everything on a duel with an adversary who didn't even know the rules, but the situation had grown out of his control. Turning, he drew his sword and walked toward the warrior.

Eztli let out a war cry and charged at Hernando with his great axe held two-handed above his head. He swung at the Spaniard before Hernando had brought the Saracen sword fully up, and Hernando just barely managed to guide the shining obsidian blade to one side. Parrying quickly, Hernando sliced through the buckler the warrior wore on his forearm. It came away cleanly, leaving a thin red line of blood on the warrior's arm.

The warrior responded with a kick that surprised Hernando, throwing him off balance. He staggered, but managed to stay on his feet. The great axe came around again, before Hernando had fully recovered, and sliced his side like the blade of a razor. Hernando felt the warmth of blood trickling down his side, but had no time to look. The warrior had spun in a complete circle and now brought the axe down; Hernando caught it on his blade with a clash of sparks.

Hernando pushed his arms straight above his head, driving both weapons upward until he and the warrior were eye to eye, their weapons poised above their heads. Hernando felt the massive strength in the warrior's body; the Toltec was stronger than him. On the heels of that thought, Hernando twisted his body sideways as the warrior drove his knee toward his groin, barely managing to turn the blow. As the warrior's knee glanced of his thigh, Hernando knew he was outmatched in a contest of strength. He would have to use his wits.

He felt his strength going and quickly formulated a plan that would be suicide if his opponent had a sword in his hand, but he was counting on the weight and awkwardness of the warrior's great axe in close fighting. As the priest raised his knee again, Hernando gave in to the pressure of the warrior's arms above his head, spun his body, and went down on one knee. At the same time, he brought the Saracen blade across his opponent's stomach, disembowelling him with one slash.

Dropping his axe, the warrior priest fell to his knees, his eyes wide in dazed surprise as he tried to gather up the slimy ropes of intestine spilling from his gaping belly. He looked at Hernando in disbelief, then fell on his face. His two brothers ran to his side. As they rolled him over, more innards spilled out.

Wells came to Hernando. "What do you call that move, sir?"

"Good fortune." He tried to laugh, but his side hurt too much.

"Good thing his axe wasn't two inches longer or it would be *your* innards on the ground looking to make sausage," Wells observed.

Laocan came to him and led him to the tent, where she and her maid fussed over Hernando's wound. Laocan said something quickly in her native tongue, and her servant giggled.

"What are you saying to her?" he asked in their pidgin language. "I hope you're not telling her our secrets."

Laocan smiled and ran a finger down his flank. "Skin ... not so pretty now." She smirked, and the servant giggled again.

Hernando smiled. "I think a day of rest is necessary," he agreed obliquely. "And the warriors will want a funeral pyre for their dead priest."

"Honouring Eztli will win you much loyalty," she suggested as she bent over him to kiss him deeply. The maid stifled another giggle as she cleaned up the bloodstained cloths.

That night, as the great moon appeared over the trees, Hernando made a presentation of feathers and blankets to the warrior priest's body, as Laocan had coached him. The two warriors who had accompanied him to the duel lit the funeral pyre, and Eztli's brother presented Hernando with his war axe. Hernando spoke a few words in Toltec to show respect, and the warriors cheered off their priest.

Chapter 10

The next day the Toltec guard was out in front. Laocan walked beside Hernando's great black stallion, bearing an uncomfortable Hernando. Two days later, they sighted the great golden city, built in the middle of a great swamp. The city was much larger than Hernando had expected, and grew larger as they approached.

Two light cavalry soldiers rode out along one of the causeways to meet them, shouting greetings from half a mile away. The Toltecs split to allow them passage as they rode forward to greet Hernando and his officers. Hernando eyed them as they pulled up their mounts before him. They were shabbily dressed and had already shown they had little discipline.

"Who commands your conquistadors?" one shouted above the commotion.

José answered, "We are soldiers of Charles V, King over Spain and New Spain. Hernando Diaz commands this regiment," he added when they seemed unimpressed with the king's credentials.

"We seek Cortez in the name of the Duke of Aragon," Hernando added. This seemed to generate a more favourable response.

"Yes, of course; follow us," said the one who had appointed himself spokesman. They turned their already lathered steeds and raced off along the causeway; Hernando and his officers touched heels to flanks and sent their horses trotting after them.

They entered the city, passing local women who had snatched up their children and scattered to the safety of their houses. The two soldiers had disappeared. As Hernando and his men stopped to allow those on foot to catch up, Hernando noted that a quiet oppression hung over the magnificent city.

The two soldiers reappeared with some companions. "You'll have to leave your Indians here in this courtyard," the spokesman said. "The inner city is off limits to Indians."

Hernando had Juan translate his orders to the Toltecs to stay put and stay out of trouble. Then he marched his men into the inner city, which was much more heavily guarded.

"Cortez waits for you and your officers in his palace," the spokesman told Hernando, twisting in his saddle to look back at him.

Hernando simply nodded, distracted. As they moved closer to the city centre, he marvelled at the architecture. Every building was an intricacy of colour and complex designs, rich with carvings and frescoes; it was too much to take in, and it was with a measure of relief that he focused on one of Cortez's men as he told Hernando that the regiment could take the quarters along the east wall of the inner city.

The assigned quarters were a luxury compared to the ground on which the men had been sleeping. Hernando stayed long enough to see his men settling in, then, accompanied by Laocan and José, he went on to the palace on foot, accompanied by the two young conquistadors who had first rode out to greet them.

When they entered the palace, Hernando was struck by its grandeur. Walls fifteen feet high were completely painted in frescoes illustrating great battles and coronations and fields of lush crops. The floors were tiled with what looked like green marble, and birds sang in antechambers.

A striking figure awaited them in a central courtyard. He strode toward them, hand outstretched. "I'm Hernando Cortez," he stated as he clasped Hernando's hand in a strong grip. "I hear you are looking for me!"

Hernando reached into his pocket and produced an oiled canvas package, sewn shut with sinew and sealed with red wax. "Here are my introduction papers from the Duke of Aragon," he said, handing the elegant package to Cortez.

Cortez gave it barely a glance. "Yes, yes ... but you've come at the perfect time; my men have been depleted and I'm in need of reinforcements. Come—I've arranged dinner for you." He whirled away and headed for the door, leading them into another room.

Hernando looked at José, who shrugged. They followed Cortez.

A long table ran the length of the room they entered, its surface covered with platters of roast pigs and stuffed ducks, and trenchers mounded high with vegetables and fruits. The aroma made Hernando's mouth water. Some of Cortez's men were already seated at the table, a few accompanied by Indian women. More diners were arriving through other doors.

"Sit and enjoy a meal fit for a king!" Cortez said, gesturing expansively. He pulled out a large carved chair and indicated that Hernando should take it. He leaned into Hernando's ear as he sat down. "I see you've taken an Indian girl," he said.

"She was a treaty gift from the chief of the Toltecs," Hernando stammered, thinking Cortez was judging him. He felt his face heat with embarrassment.

"Yes, my first one is also the daughter of the same chief," Cortez replied, his tone conversational. "But the Jesuits have turned her to Christianity, and the little mink wants me to marry her." He said the last part loud enough for his men to hear, and they howled with laughter. "Come—eat, and we will talk," Cortez urged as he took the seat next to Hernando.

A pretty young woman clad in white shirt and pants slipped into the seat next to Cortez. "Commander Diaz, this is Maria, the beautiful woman I was talking about only minutes ago," Cortez said.

She had a proud bearing and strong features. As Hernando stood to greet her formally, she inclined her head politely, but her eyes strayed past him to her sister, Laocan. They smiled at each other.

"Commander Diaz," Cortez said as he chewed on the knucklebone of some roasted animal, his lips shiny with grease, "I hear you force-marched your men from the sea. You must have been in a great hurry to meet me." Again his men laughed.

"My orders from the duke were to make all haste to reach you." Hernando hesitated. "There were some conflicting reports—"

"Ah, no doubt from that fat oaf in Havana," Cortez interjected. "If he would get off those little brown boys long enough to govern his territory, he would be sitting here instead of me!" Again a roar of laughter rose from his men. "What did these reports say? That I mutinied? That I burned his ships?"

"I really don't know." Hernando paused, holding Cortez's eye. "The king wants me to find the truth and make sure these new lands are being taken in his name."

"The truth!" Cortez swept his gaze along those gathered at the table, his tone exuberant. "The truth, my young commander—the truth is that this is a strange and wondrous land. A land rich in gold and silver beyond what any king could imagine, beyond anything you or any other could dream!" Cortez's gaze returned to Hernando, and his voice fell. "And I can assure you that everything I do here, I do for His Majesty, King Charles V." Cortez stood and raised his glass. "King Charles and Spain!"

With a loud scraping of chairs, his men rose and returned the toast: "King Charles and Spain!"

As they resumed their seats and their meals, Cortez leaned toward Hernando. "Eat, drink, Commander! There is plenty." He shrugged apologetically. "The wine is not good; we will have to import some vines and plant some vineyards in the hills around the city." Obviously Cortez was planning to stay put.

They both avoided the subject of the hostaged king and the ransom demand and stuck to trivialities for about an hour. Then curiosity got the better of Hernando. "How is it that you came to control such a large city?"

Cortez sighed, as if he'd hoped to put off an explanation. "My guide Maria told me of an ancient legend that said a god named Quetzalcoatl would return from the east and overthrow the Aztecs. This and my muskets helped me to exert my authority over the Indians." He turned away from the subject. "This land holds riches beyond anyone's dreams, more gold than in all the courts of Spain! Enough gold to fund the king's armies and destroy his enemies." Cortez's eyes seemed to glaze over as he spoke. "Whoever controls this city and this land controls the world."

Cortez paused, perhaps realizing he had said too much, because he quickly assured Hernando that he was still loyal to the king. "But there was profit to be made, and lots of it," he added.

Hernando wondered if Cortez was trying to convince him to join him in his venture. He had already learned that Cortez needed men, and he suspected that Cortez meant to have his, one way or another.

"Come." Cortez stood. "Let me show you something."

His men, taken off guard, scrambled for their helmets and cloaks and rose to accompany him. As Hernando and José followed Cortez, who was still rambling on about destiny and legends, Hernando leaned toward Laocan. "Talk to Maria," he whispered in their mixed tongue. "Find out what you can."

They entered a large, dim room. Cortez's men started lighting torches held in sconces at regular intervals around the room. As the light slowly grew, it illuminated a glorious mound of treasures, piled to the ceiling. The torchlight gleamed warmly on the myriad golden objects, the reflected torchlight dancing over Cortez's face as he spread his arms and turned to grin at Hernando. "There is enough gold here to fund the biggest army the world has ever seen."

Hernando could not speak; he had never seen so much gold. A large carved chair with golden legs, its back encrusted with jewels, sat in the middle of the treasures. A large golden disc leaned against the chair, its glow dazzling Hernando's eyes.

Cortez sat in the chair and put on a headdress of long green feathers and jewels. It glittered in the torchlight as he leaned forward. "What makes a king?" he asked. "Lineage? The support of the nobles? Religious support? Gold, Commander Diaz, gold!"

He's out of his mind, Hernando thought, although he had to admit that what the other man said made sense.

Cortez looked at Hernando and took the headdress off, as if he knew what the young commander was thinking. "Come, we'll see to your quarters," he said soberly. "Tomorrow we'll talk in earnest."

*   *   *   *

The room was empty when Hernando entered it. He settled on the bed and waited for Laocan, but when the palace fell silent and only the distant whirs and howls of the jungle's nighttime denizens could be heard, Hernando grew worried for her safety. He rose, paced the room, and had just decided to go and find her when the blanket covering the door was pulled aside by Laocan's maid.

The princess stepped into the room and immediately smiled when she saw Hernando. She rushed into his arms and they kissed and held each other for several moments, not saying a word. Then Laocan stepped back, impatient to tell Hernando what she had learned. She gestured to her maid, and in a short while the maid dragged a half awake and protesting Juan into the room. Laocan spoke quickly to him, then Juan looked at Hernando.

"The princess says that Cortez has imprisoned the great king Montezuma as a hostage, and demands that a great room be filled with gold as his ransom; Cortez has melted down the palace gold and stripped the temples of their religious tools." Laocan was still speaking rapidly; Juan translated as fast as he heard her words. "Her sister has told her that there is disagreement amongst his men, and some have left the city and are in the hills, doing the brown robe's work. She says to tell the green-eyed god—that is her name for you—" He stopped and waited as she paused to catch her breath. "She says her sister is having Cortez's baby and she longs to be queen at his side—"

"Wait, wait!" Hernando put his fingers over Laocan's small mouth to stop her from saying more. "What is this about his men and the priest—the brown robe?"

"The brown robe took almost half of Cortez's men into the hills to convert the Indians to the one god. He is with Montezuma's brother in his village now," she answered him through Juan, and quickly added, "I want to convert as my sister

Maria has. She says Cortez will be with her only, and no other woman, if he takes her as his wife. Is this true?"

Her question pulled his mind back from military speculation. He didn't want to disappoint Laocan, but he knew Cortez would never marry an Indian, even one as pretty as Laocan's sister. He did not have the heart to tell her the truth, how Cortez had laughed at the idea at dinner. "Maybe," he said, not looking at her.

Laocan sensed he was not telling the truth; her face fell and her voice was less enthusiastic. Hernando knew he had hurt her feelings. He changed the subject back to the Jesuit and Cortez's men, but Laocan admitted she hadn't asked any more questions about the brown robe. "I am sorry," she said through Juan, her manner reserved.

Hernando realized that she thought she had failed him. He gave her a gentle smile and dismissed the maid and Juan for the night.

Laocan undressed and joined Hernando under the brightly woven blanket. She slid her hand down his muscular body to his member, which instantly strained to make a tent out of the heavy woolen blanket. But Hernando knew her heart wasn't in it. He removed her hand, kissed her gently on the lips, and rolled her onto her side. Curling up behind her, he whispered in her ear, "I'm sorry I hurt your feelings." She could not understand the words, but he saw her smile at the soothing sound of his voice.

* * * *

Hernando awoke in the predawn, as the noises of the city coming to life filtered into the still-dark room. This was not what had awakened him, however. Laocan still lay wrapped in his arms, and it was her round buttocks wiggling against his groin that brought him alive. By the time he woke fully, she had enveloped him, and he found himself engulfed in pleasure.

Afterward, Hernando rose, dressed, and went in search of Cortez. He found him in the great room filled with gold, seated on the gilded chair like King Midas in his counting room, with treasure heaped around his feet. Dawn had brought a long parade of Indians carrying objects of gold and wooden boxes filled with raw gems and semiprecious stones. Beside him, his scribe scribbled madly, recording everything precisely as other men heaped up the treasures to make more room.

"Ah, Commander Diaz!" Cortez said expansively as Hernando entered the room. "I see you made it through the night. These native women can be very demanding, yes? I hope you have enough strength left to have breakfast with me." He laughed, but his accountant didn't even look up from his laborious task, or slow his quill.

"Yes; I would like a chance to talk to you," Hernando replied, fixed his gaze on the older man. "I hear some of your men have taken up missionary work."

Cortez's smile vanished. "Not here," he murmured, looking around the room as if expecting to see a spy hidden behind a pile of necklaces. He rose, and said in his normal voice, "Come, let's eat."

They entered a brightly coloured room, smaller than the banquet room of the night before, but no less exquisitely decorated. A large table carved with exotic beasts and mythical beings that danced around its edge bore platters of fresh fruit, all sliced and carved to resemble a battle scene between two warriors. Hernando picked up a piece of red melon and bit into it; the sweetness surprised him.

"I should have known, when women get together—especially sisters—all they can do is gossip," Cortez said as he watched Hernando munching on different pieces of fruit. "An Alpha Jesuit named Calsonia has taken some of my men into the mountains."

Hernando choked on his melon as he heard the name. "Ignatius Calsonia?" he blurted.

Cortez's eyebrows rose in surprise. "Yes; do you know him?"

"Yes, we attended the same monastery school, but he was a few years ahead of me," Hernando said, trying to recover his composure.

Cortez was looking at him intently. "This is a fine school you attended, to put out two young men who have risen so quickly to your respective positions."

Hernando sensed Cortez's uneasiness. "He and I never got along," Hernando added, wanting to ease Cortez's suspicions.

"This Jesuit has mutinied and taken my men with him," Cortez said.

"Surely a priest is not under your direct command. How could he mutiny?" Hernando asked.

"All right, he has caused my men to mutiny then!" Cortez snapped.

"Why don't you go after him?" Hernando's question just added to Cortez's anger. He was glowering now. "Because he has a stronger force than I do!" he admitted. "He has the support of Montezuma's brother."

"So it is true—you hold the Aztec king for ransom." Hernando picked up another piece of fruit to taste, glad that the topic had shifted from his relationship to Ignatius.

"Yes. This Jesuit has been trouble from the start," Cortez grumbled. "I think he means to kill me and take the gold for himself."

Hernando was stunned. He disliked his brother, but would he be capable of such a thing? Hernando shook his head. *Of course, he did have a hand in murdering his own father!* he thought, growing nearly as angry as Cortez.

The two Spaniards talked for another hour about what should be done, but Hernando had trouble focusing on the conversation. His mind raced back to his father's inquisition, and how his own brother had turned against his family. All the church's claims were unsubstantiated, until Ignatius came forward. His brother's testimony about their father's involvement in the Knights Templar was what had finally convicted him. His father had died, rather than give up his brothers in the temple.

The last thing Ignatius had ever said to Hernando was that their father could have saved his own life if he'd given up the others. "He shouldn't have been so stubborn," Ignatius said, shaking his head in disapproval. "He could have lived—it was his own choice."

Hernando had lunged for Ignatius, bent on making his brother pay for his treachery, but his mother had restrained him.

Cortez had paused in his ranting and was looking at Hernando. Hernando's mind came crashing back to the golden city as he realized Cortez was staring at him. "Ignatius Calsonia murdered my father," he blurted.

Cortez sat back in his chair. "What do you mean?"

Hernando hesitated, not knowing how to continue without revealing everything. "Ignatius testified against my father at an inquisition." He looked at Cortez, who seemed concerned. He went on. "My father was put to the rack because he would not name his friends as heretics to spare his own life. He died saying he was innocent of heresy and that he and Inquisitor Torquamata would meet on Judgement Day, and that he would ask forgiveness of Christ for Torquamata's dammed soul."

"Your father sounds like quite a man," Cortez said quietly. "You should be proud of him, Hernando." He leaned forward and rested his hand on Hernando's shoulder. "We'll have to teach this Jesuit a lesson in humanity, you and I."

Hernando felt as if a large rock had been lifted off his chest. He shook Cortez's hand and thanked him in a voice too small for his bulk.

Cortez raised his voice, clearly unaccustomed to so strong a show of emotion. "Eat, Diaz! You'll need your strength if you're going to persevere against this cobra who has taken your father from you."

After their meal, Hernando made plans to have supper with Cortez later, then excused himself and hurried to his men.

"Wells! Where are you?" he called, stomping along the roadway in front of the long, low building where his men were quartered. "When I don't need you you're underfoot," he grumbled, "and when I do—"

"Yes, sir?" Wells said from behind him.

Hernando jumped, then whirled to hide his reaction. "Stop doing that!" He paused to compose himself. "Wells, place a guard at all entrances to the city. It seems we may see a little action again very soon."

"Yes, sir!" A big, Cheshire cat smile spread over Wells' face.

Hernando nodded and turned away. Back in his rooms, he composed a list of questions he wanted Laocan to ask her sister. He felt elated at the prospect of dishing out justice to his brother after all the years of torment and hardship he had endured at Ignatius' hands, but more than that, he was going to exact revenge for his father's torture.

Laocan was affected by Hernando's mood. Mistaking it for happiness, she talked incessantly, until she realized he wasn't listening to her. She pinched his arm.

"Ow! What did you do that for?" She pouted. He chuckled, then kissed her again and again until she smiled.

"You are a strange one," she said in their pidgin language that was neither Spanish nor Toltec, but a combination with a dash of intuition. "You make love like a green-eyed god, but you ignore me like a man." She pouted again and Hernando kissed her.

Hernando told her about his father and his brother. When he said he would be meeting his brother again soon, her eyes narrowed with concern. "Don't worry," he said, then added solemnly, "But you must tell no one of this. You must promise to keep my secret, and in return … I promise that I will take no other woman."

She nodded, her expression one of uncertainty, but that was quickly replaced by a wave of excitement. "Wife? You mean wife?" she asked in broken Spanish.

What he had just done struck Hernando like a blow to the head with a mace. He had asked her to marry him! It hadn't been his plan, but that was how it had come out. He realized he was not unhappy with the prospect. He nodded and smiled at Laocan, who jumped into his arms and squealed like rope free-running through a set of blocks. Hernando covered her mouth with his so the guards didn't think he was sacrificing her to the gods. She continued to scream until their tongues began to fence.

* * * *

At supper, Hernando noticed that Laocan seemed more reserved in her conversation with Maria, and wondered why she was not more animated, with such good news to share. *Of course,* he realized. *She does not want to hurt her feelings. Cortez has not asked Maria to be his wife.*

He and Cortez spent much of the meal leaning together in resolute discussion about the strength of Ignatius' army and his probable plans.

"Does he know my men are in the city?" Hernando wondered.

Cortez thought for a second. "We try to control the movements of the Aztecs as much as possible, and the gold procession this morning would not have seen your men where I have garrisoned them. But the Aztecs seem to have an elaborate spy system; they would have seen the Toltecs outside the fortified inner city. Hah! That must have been a bit disconcerting, to see all those former allies in full warrior garb."

"What does he say he wants?" Hernando interjected.

"He said I've lost God's work, and that I only care for the gold, not about the souls of the heathens."

Hernando felt suddenly uneasy. Had he let his hatred of Ignatius overwhelm his emotions and cloud his judgement? Was Ignatius just doing God's work? Hernando had also seen the greed in Cortez's eyes. Was it Cortez who was the renegade, straying from the king's work? Laocan touched his arm, aware that something was troubling him. Hernando turned to her and saw her reassuring smile.

"I think Laocan is prettier than Maria," Cortez spoke up, sensing an awkward moment, "but Maria would cut out the heart of my enemy for me." He looked at his own princess with affection.

This Cortez is crude but honest, and I think he's trustworthy, Hernando thought as he searched Cortez's face for the truth. *How can I tell who is right in all this mess, or if indeed either is wrong?*

They focused on the meal for a while, a feast of roast pig and a fowl that resembled chicken, but was much larger. Then Hernando put aside his thoughts and paused in his eating to continue the discussion with Cortez. "His greatest strength seems to be in his Indian allies. We need to send our own spies into the mountains to gather some reliable information."

Cortez was stealing a piece of fruit from Maria's plate, but he was listening intently. "I agree," he said, eyes still on Maria. He had been flirting openly with her all evening, and she had been enjoying the attention. Now she caught his hand and pulled him away from the table while his men laughed at Cortez's plight. "We will talk in the morning Hernando," he called back as they left the room.

Laocan looked at Hernando, then a slight frown puckered her fine eyebrows when she saw his pensive expression. Hernando was not feeling the same need to retire early. He tried to explain his reservations about which side he should be on, but her frown deepened when she couldn't understand his words. She did pull him from the table though, and cooed and hummed as she rubbed him down with some musky-smelling oils in their room. Hernando relaxed as her little hands chased away the tension in his muscles, and her rocking motion as she straddled his waist lulled him to sleep.

Ignatius stood across a rushing river that boomed down into a deep canyon. At the bottom, the frothing whitewater reflected the sun like twinkling stars. Ignatius bore a bronze serpent staff and his brown robes fluttered in the wind. He looked like a young Moses addressing the children of Israel. Hernando waved to his brother and Ignatius answered by raising his staff. Lightning flashed from its tip, and thunder rolled.

Hernando jerked awake so hard that Laocan was tossed like a matador that had been gored by an enraged bull. She scrambled back to him. "Shh," she whispered, wiping beads of sweat from his face.

Hernando stared at her blankly, then smiled and lay back down on the blankets. Laocan again straddled him and continued to rub his chest. Her undulating hips brought him back to life, and she rode him long into the night.

Chapter 11

Hernando was watching the daily gold procession the next morning when Cortez took him aside.

"Every day, less and less gold arrives," Cortez said. "I believe that Montezuma's brother means to stop payment; he wants me to kill the king so he can have the throne."

"May I talk to Montezuma?" Hernando asked.

He was testing Cortez, but the older man surprised him. "Yes, of course—follow me," he said.

Hernando motioned Laocan and Wells to follow. Cortez took them to a small room guarded by two Spanish soldiers. Inside they found a frail, slight man, not the mighty warrior Hernando had imagined. He studied the man as Cortez made introductions. Montezuma looked defeated, a prisoner resigned to the fact that there would be no release.

Laocan asked Hernando's question of the once great king: "Do you know who we are?"

"You are the servants of the sun," he said dully. "You have come to destroy the Aztecs forever."

Hernando paused, thinking how to phrase the next question. "Do you trust your brother?"

A glimmer of life sparked in Montezuma's eyes. "Does the bird trust the tree boa with her eggs?"

Hernando smiled. Once again he was impressed with the honesty of these people. The once great chief stood erect and smiled back. "I believe your brother means to overthrow you," Hernando said, looking into his eyes, which now shone with excitement.

"I would do the same for him, if we traded places." Montezuma now stood tall, his fists on his hips.

"Would you help lay a trap for your brother?" Hernando queried.

Montezuma smiled broadly at the thought of one last battle. Hernando thought the king looked a lot like Wells, just before a big fight. They talked at length and laid some plans, with Laocan interpreting and Cortez nodding his approval.

* * * *

The next morning, as Cortez had expected, the gold stopped coming. He sent out Aztec emissaries that had already been prepared by the Spanish with the aid of Montezuma. They made their way quickly to the village where Montezuma's brother presided and were brought before Cuitalhuac, bowing and crawling on the dry earth as they approached. Their faces still in the dirt, they reported, "Your brother, the great chief Montezuma, is to be killed in two days and his head displayed to the people on a pole, if the Spaniard Cortez's demands are not met."

Cuitalhuac rose quickly, kicking at the two Aztec emissaries as they tried to back away on their knees. "Tell your Spanish masters that they do not have the courage to take the life of the great chief Montezuma, for if they do, the rain god Chaka will bring down such destruction on their heads that their names will be forgotten for all time." He kicked the messengers so severely that one of them passed out. The other, bleeding from the nose and ear, turned and ran down the mountain as fast as his freshly bruised limbs would carry him.

Cortez and Hernando questioned him in front of Montezuma, who told the young messenger to leave nothing out. They asked about warrior strength, and if there were any Spanish in the village, and numerous other tactical questions.

Hernando, who had remained silent throughout most of the questioning, spoke up. "Did you see the brown robe?"

"Yes. He stood beside Cuitalhuac," the young emissary replied, at last regaining much of his voice. Hernando and Cortez looked at each other.

After they had exhausted all of their questions, they dismissed him. The young warrior hesitated, and Montezuma asked him if there was a problem. The man mumbled about not wanting to leave anything out. Irritated, Montezuma raised his voice. "What is it?"

"In the town were men and women on trees," the messenger said.

"What do you mean?" Cortez asked.

"Like this." The young Aztec stretched out his arms in the shape of a cross.

"My God! They're crucifying people? Why?" Hernando exclaimed. The young man shrugged.

"Our spies will be back tomorrow," Cortez told him. "We will ask them."

Disturbed, Hernando told Cortez that he needed to know exactly what was going on out there, and that he would lead a small party to find out.

"That's foolhardy," Cortez protested.

"I must go," Hernando countered.

"You will not make it to the village alive," Cortez insisted, but Hernando was adamant, and Cortez acquiesced.

Hernando knew why. If he returned, he would bring very useful information; if he did not, Cortez would have his soldiers.

Laocan was twice as upset with Hernando. When she grabbed his arm and shook her head vehemently, he snapped, annoyed with her protests, "Ask your two warrior priests to accompany me and Wells, then."

* * * *

That evening, she brought the two warrior priests to Hernando, who was waiting with Wells near the gate blocking access to the inner city. "Explain to them that we must get to Montezuma's brother's village without being seen," he said, and turned to talk to Wells as she explained the plan to the warriors.

Laocan spoke to them at length, and when they both nodded their understanding, she touched Hernando's arm. "I have told them that if you do not return, then they should not bother coming back, either."

Hernando and Wells were busy rubbing soot from the lamps on their white faces as camouflage. Hernando smiled at her, then looked past her to the two warriors, who were copying the paler men. Hernando didn't stop them. It was good to have them on his side for a change.

Smiling, Wells observed, "They must think it's a pre-war ritual."

The moon was not up yet, and it was slow going, even though they encountered no pickets or guards set by the enemy as they drew close to Cuitalhuac's village. *I could have led my whole army right into their encampment while they sleep,* Hernando mused.

The moon was full and high in the sky by the time they reached the crosses with their human remains. Some victims still clung to life; others had already succumbed to a painful death.

"Why is he doing this?" Hernando whispered to Wells. He stood silently in the whitewash of moonlight, lost in thought.

Wells touched his arm. "Sir?"

Hernando turned and without a word, headed back the way they'd come. The others followed, glad to be away from the eerie sight.

They made better time on their way back to the city, and surprised the guards when their small group stepped into the light of a small fire. "We could have killed you both," Wells growled, angry that his men were more interested in dreams of whores than seeing to their duty.

"Yes, sir!" The two startled men struggled to stand up. "Sorry, sir," they added, more to Wells than Hernando.

"Stay alert!" barked Hernando as he passed.

Hernando seemed to take his own words to heart. He crept into bed next to Laocan, but when dawn came, he hadn't slept a minute. He'd lain awake for the balance of the night, pondering what kind of evil mind would crucify people. But he knew the evil mind that had committed such atrocities.

When Cortez's spies came back, Hernando questioned them at length, and what he heard sickened him.

"The brown robe does this to convert them to the one god," one of them told him.

Another reported, "Some people close to Cuitalhuac say he has converted but doesn't really believe; he only uses the brown robe to take the golden city."

Hernando thought the political maneuverings rivalled any story he'd heard about the Caesars of ancient Rome.

That afternoon, he called his troops together. "José, be careful," was his first comment to his senior officer, for he was unsure if the plan they'd come up with would work.

He was taking a chance that Cuitalhuac's spies did not know exactly how many men he had brought with him. Half his force would go outside the walls and make the Aztecs think that the two white men had parted ways, and that only Cortez's men were left inside the walls. They were hoping Ignatius, seeing a contingent leaving, would move quickly to take advantage of the poorly manned garrison, using Montezuma's death as the pretext for rebellion. He would be counting on the city's inhabitants joining in the slaughter of the Spanish. But since Montezuma would not really be dead, he would order the city residents to defend the city alongside Cortez.

Hernando's mind came back to the matters at hand. "Take the men for a walk, Lieutenant, but be at the river crossing below Cuitalhuac's village. You have the map we drew?"

"Yes, sir. Don't worry, we will be in position to cut off any escape."

Hernando looked at the soldier sitting uncomfortably on the big black stallion in Hernando's armour. "Don't put any holes in that armour, soldier!"

"No, sir! I'll look after it, sir," the young Spaniard said as he tried to steady the restive stallion.

"Take them out, José, and God protect you."

Hernando watched them go, then shouted, "Wells!"

"Yes, sir," the sergeant replied, once again at his elbow.

He gave Hernando a start, but he ignored the sergeant's disconcerting proximity and said, "Set up a crossfire behind the second set of gates. We will let them come that far unopposed."

Cortez joined them as Hernando was pointing out placement. "I wish you weren't sending away the cannon," Cortez said, staring after the departing weapon.

"If they saw it come in, they must see it go out!" Hernando replied.

"Yes, but the noise from the big gun always makes the natives' knees wobbly," Cortez said.

Hernando put the Toltec warriors with his men to protect them from counterattack while they reloaded. He explained through Juan exactly what they were to do.

Wells mumbled, "How long will they hold their line before they get so excited by the sight of blood that they charge right out into the line of fire?"

Hernando answered, "Are you talking about the Toltecs, or yourself?" He and Wells grinned at each other.

A runner came through the inner gate. Juan translated as the excited man blurted his message without stopping, running right past Cortez and Hernando. "Cuitalhuac's warriors are on the move."

Cortez held out his hand to Hernando. "God protect us this day."

"Amen," Hernando replied.

He had placed the two warrior priests with Laocan and Maria for their protection. They had chafed at the thought of not being in the fight, and Laocan, too, wanted to be closer to the action, but Hernando feared for the women's safety. He told the warriors through Juan that if the battle went against them, they were to take the princesses back to their home village. Hernando didn't realize that this would be seen as a disgrace, and the Toltecs would rather die than retreat, but they nodded at Hernando's instructions. Satisfied, Hernando returned to his men.

Hernando thought about Laocan as they awaited the arrival of the enemy. He was in love, he realized. The joy she had brought him in these few short months had replaced the oppressive weight of his father's death.

Turning his mind to the upcoming battle, Hernando looked around at his men. Both Spaniards and Toltecs were standing together, ready. They seemed confident. "Wells, tell your men not to fire until I drop my sword, as before," he said to his sergeant. "Tell them to wait for the smoke to clear before they fire their second musket." He had traded pikes for the muskets of most of the men who had left, hoping the extra firepower would turn the odds in their favour.

"Yes, sir," Wells said crisply.

They could now hear the Aztecs' marching chant. It was used to instill fear in their opponents and indeed, it was sending a chill up Hernando's spine. "Get ready, Wells. They'll be here soon." Hernando's and Cortez's men were arranged in a semicircle facing the main gate. The courtyard would become a death trap, with virtually no way for a round of musketfire to miss a body.

Suddenly the chant stopped. All was quiet, except for the occasional rattle of armour as the soldiers shuffled uneasily. Hernando drew his curved Saracen blade. It hissed like a desert cobra as it slid from the golden scabbard. He raised it into the bright sunlight above his head. Tension gripped the courtyard. A bead of sweat trickled down Hernando's cheek. Seconds seemed like hours.

Then a bloodcurdling scream rose up from the Aztec warriors on the other side of the wall. The gates were thrown wide, and a herd of stampeding warriors boiled through the opening. The courtyard filled to overflowing.

Hernando dropped his arm. A great volley of shot tore through the mass, some balls hitting two or three victims before becoming lodged in an abdomen or appendage. The smoke hung within the walls, a blue haze smelling of sulfur and blood.

Before the smoke cleared, a second screaming mass boiled through the narrow gates at the rear of Hernando's company—Montezuma's brother had split his forces and was leading them against Hernando's back. The musketeers turned their ponderous weapons on them to fire, but the Toltec warriors were in the way and most could not fire; the volley was sporadic, at best.

A great heap of Aztec bodies lay at the main gate, and now a second wave clamoured over them, waving war clubs and screaming. It was obvious that a mind familiar with musket warfare had planned this attack. *A Spanish mind!* Hernando thought.

He unleashed the Toltecs, who charged into the Aztecs, their war axes severing body parts as they went. Hernando too was slashing at the invaders, who had pressed the Spaniards into a great knot in the middle of the courtyard. Spaniards and Toltecs fought back to back. The battle had quickly turned against them. The Aztecs, sensing they had the upper hand, pressed hard.

Hernando was in close on an Aztec, his sword stuck in his opponent's war club, when he looked past the warrior to a figure yelling orders at the great gates. "Ignatius!" he yelled over the noise of battle, and somehow the name carried to the robed figure, who looked at Hernando in disbelief. The priest shouted orders that were lost to Hernando's ear in the uproar, but two Spaniards made for Hernando.

Hernando wrenched free his blade and severed an artery just below the warrior's ear, then passed by him before he had fallen to the ground, eyeing the advancing Spaniards. They struck in unison, and it was all he could do to parry their thrusts. Then another sword entered the mix of steel. Cortez had taken one of his mutinied men's thrusts on his sword. The young soldier hesitated, apparently reluctant to fight his ex-commander, which led to his quick demise.

Hernando concentrated on the other attacker. Staring coldly into his eyes, he watched for the opening that would first appear there. Then it came—his opponent glanced right. Hernando stepped left and let him thrust past him, turning to drive the Saracen sword into the man's metal breastplate, which separated for the finely crafted Damascus blade as if made of cotton.

He looked about. Cortez had disarmed his attacker by severing the sinews of his right hand. The man was on his knees, asking for quarter, his arms held high in surrender. The right hand bobbed limply in the breeze.

Two Aztecs quickly replaced Hernando's attacker, driving him back into the surging crowd of fighting men. His men were nearing exhaustion, but none gave an inch—they knew what the Indians did with their prisoners. They fought on, even though the battle looked hopeless.

Then another battle cry rose over the sounds of steel on steel and stone. The two warrior priests who had been charged with protecting Laocan appeared at the head of the eighty Toltec warriors who had been sent out with José to fool the Aztecs. These fresh troops joined the fray, squeezing the Aztecs between them and the rejuvenated troops around Hernando and Cortez. With the Toltecs hacking at the Aztecs' backs, the Spanish swords, more maneuverable at close quarters than the Indian axes, soon became deadly, and the tide turned in their favour. Hernando found Laocan at his side, a small dagger in her hand, her face splattered with Aztec blood.

Cortez had led a group of men forward, and cornered Montezuma's brother against a wall. Seeing this, the Aztecs around the Jesuit, as well as a few of his Spaniards, broke and ran.

Wells, who had been fighting at Hernando's side, yelled, "The priest is getting away!"

Hernando quickly looked about. "Gather some men to me," he shouted, and Wells responded by grabbing some men and pulling them toward the gate.

Hernando didn't wait. Followed by Laocan and the two warrior priests, he ran after the renegades. He turned at the gate and saw that Cortez and the Toltecs were mopping up what was left of the Aztecs. He checked to see that Wells was following, then took off after his brother, Ignatius. Laocan and the warriors kept pace.

Hernando knew he had to stop his brother before he ran into the trap at the river. José was under orders not to let anyone return to Cuitalhuac's mountain stronghold.

They caught up to Ignatius and his men in the forest at the edge of the river. "Ignatius! Give yourself up," Hernando called.

Ignatius turned. In his hand he clutched a staff with a golden cross on top. "You're the Devil's spawn, come to tempt my faith!" he yelled over the rumble of water cascading through the valley. "You will not dissuade me from my God-given duty, and hiding in my brother's husk will not let you stop me from vanquishing my god's foes!"

Hernando realized that his brother was completely mad, that reality had left him. Gone was the hatred he'd felt for his brother, replaced by pity.

"Kill them, kill them all!" Ignatius screamed, pointing at them with his staff.

His men turned on Hernando, who pulled Laocan close, realizing too late the mistake he'd made by leaving himself outnumbered. The Aztecs fell on them, but some had dropped their weapons when they had fled the city and now hesitated, looking for something to use against sword and axe. Others were slowed by exhaustion.

The two Toltec warriors, still fresh, dropped the Aztecs as they charged Hernando's small group. Hernando, almost too tired to lift his sword arm, sliced and hacked his way through the mob. The remaining Aztecs turned and ran when they saw Wells and his men coming through the forest.

Swaying with exhaustion, Hernando placed his boot on the chest of the warrior he'd just run through to dislodge his sword. Suddenly Laocan leapt forward. Startled, Hernando whirled in time to see Ignatius behind him, his gold-tipped staff sweeping down toward Hernando's back. Laocan dove into the path of the gleaming cross. It split her breasts and sank deep into her chest. Hernando could only catch her as Ignatius withdrew the cross. He heard the air rushing from her lungs, saw the bright red blood bubbling up, and then she slumped in his arms. Hernando stared in numb horror.

"Your brown whore has been smitten by the hand of God, Hernando, son of Satan!" Ignatius crowed, then he turned and ran as Wells approached them.

Ignatius jumped from rock to rock across the rushing river. On the far shore, he held his cross-tipped staff high and waved his other hand like a lunatic as he shouted above the rush of water, "God has spoken this day, my brother!"

Hernando looked up from Laocan as lightning flashed and thunder rolled, and Ignatius' body was torn apart by grapeshot. He watched little bits of brown robe floating back to earth long after Ignatius' body had dropped onto the boulders. Then he looked down at Laocan.

Blood gurgled in her chest as she spoke. "I love you, Hernando. I am sorry I cannot stay with you, but I will wait for you in the sky."

Hernando shushed her. "I love you too," he murmured, but her eyes already looked for the sky god.

Rocking back and forth, Hernando cradled her small, lifeless body in his blood-soaked arms as tears streamed down his cheeks. "God, how could you let this happen?" he whispered. Wells, his expression bleak, moved a respectable distance away. José and the others followed.

Hernando held her until darkness came, then he carried her limp body down to the golden city. Cortez and Laocan's sister came to him, but he would not release her to them. He held her tight until dawn, when he placed her on the funeral pyre, wrapped in the woven blanket the two had shared. All the warriors were being honoured according to their custom. Laocan had certainly proven herself worthy of a warrior's trip to the sky.

The fire was slow to start, then took off, roaring like some great beast from the gates of hell. He watched the fire take his lovely princess from him, carrying her into the sky where she said she would await his arrival. Hernando wept, his heart split open like a ripe pomegranate left in the sun.

Chapter 12

Cortez had called Hernando to supper, where he talked incessantly about the victory, but Hernando was too sick with grief for his Laocan to listen. Maria touched Cortez's arm and he fell silent, realizing the torment his guest was in. "You have eat," he said. "Keep up your strength, at least."

Hernando nibbled here and there, but the food lacked taste without his princess by his side.

For a week, Hernando moped around his room, then Wells stuck his head in. "I've been saving this small bottle of brandy for a special occasion, but I can't seem to find one." He placed a large black bottle and two cups on the table, paused, then lifted the bottle, pulled the cork off with his back teeth, and poured two cupfuls.

Hernando stared at the cups for a moment, then reached out and retrieved one. The liquid burned its way past his lips, tongue, and throat, all the way down to his stomach. He felt his face and ears flush with the liquor. He finished the cup and Wells filled the cup again, a small smile on his face. Hernando threw back the second and it burned less this time. Each cup went down easier, and the pain lessened.

At last Hernando broke his silence. "Thank you, Wells. I really thought I was going to spend the rest of my life with her."

Wells thought for a second. "We never know what the Good Lord has in store for us. My oldest sister, God rest her soul, said there is a reason for everything that happens to us, that God has a plan for us." Hernando wondered aloud how Laocan's death could fit into God's plan. "That we'll just have to wait and see," Wells murmured.

In the morning Hernando had a big head, but his heart didn't ache as much as it had the day before. And with each coming day, he found that his heart ached just a little less, while the memories of the good times with her grew stronger.

Cortez had executed Montezuma for his treachery in not bringing the Aztecs of the golden city to their aid, and he installed his brother, Cuitalhuac, as a puppet king for the time being. He was making plans to move his treasure back to the coast. Hernando was restless. The country seemed empty without Laocan. He offered to lead the gold party back to the coast and await the supply ships.

The night before he was scheduled to leave, Cortez held a great feast. Hernando partook of the evening's fare, for he knew that the hard march ahead would be without such luxuries.

"I'm glad to see you are your old self again," Cortez said to him.

"I will never be my old self again, but thank you," Hernando replied, and shook Cortez's hand.

"I'm glad you avenged your father. Now you can put that into the past with your brother," Cortez said.

Hernando gaped at him, mentally scrambling for a response. "Did Maria tell you he was my brother?" he finally asked.

"No," Cortez countered. "I think I always knew, from the time you mentioned his name. Only someone close would say his first name the way you did."

Hernando smiled at Cortez. "You are a wise man. Lead this land to greatness if you can." They embraced, and the soldiers cheered, raising their cups of wine.

*   *   *   *

Hernando led his men out of the golden city just after dawn awakened the land. With the Indians heavily laden with treasure destined for the court of King Charles V, it took twice as long to return to the sea, but the trip was uneventful. Only once did they encounter trouble, with the local tribes stealing supplies in the night. A few musket shots took care of them, but Hernando noted that it hadn't taken long for the Indians to grow accustomed to gunfire. They were no longer gods in the Indians' eyes—only men to be feared.

They arrived at the small group of huts known as the Villa Rica de la Vera Cruz, now fortified with a stockade, to find that Luis had set up fields and even raised some of the fowl that Hernando had eaten, but had never seen with their feathers intact. The Toltecs had been helpful with the crops, he reported, and there was a good water supply. José playfully teased his brother about being a farmer rather than a soldier, but Luis was proud of what he had accomplished and his chest stood out when his brother complimented him.

As the two brothers excitedly traded stories, Hernando walked down to where the surf rolled onto the beach. He missed Laocan. After his men were settled and the treasures secured, he would go and speak to her father, tell him what had happened and how bravely she had died.

He sat down in the sand, his grandfather's sword across his lap, his fingers tracing the jewels in the pommel as he stared out to sea. Somewhere out there, his mother, his only remaining family, was waiting for him to return. Their fortunes had changed. Surely the king would honour him with some title, and his portion of the treasure would make him very wealthy.

The fortunes of Spain were also turning with this enormous wealth. She could force an end to the endless wars. Hernando felt that he and his country were on the verge of a great new beginning.

* * * *

When two small merchant ships arrived in the bay from Hispaniola, before their sails were completely furled, Hernando had himself rowed out to one of them. He was piped aboard as if he was the admiral.

"Governor's compliments," a squat, grey haired gentleman said as he saluted Hernando. "Commander Diaz, I presume?"

"Yes, and who do I have the pleasure of addressing?" Hernando queried.

"Captain Rodriguez." He clicked his heels in the Dutch fashion. "The governor bade me call on you for news, although he would not say of what." The captain smiled.

Hernando deftly changed the subject. "I see you are armed, Captain."

"Yes—wouldn't do to ply these waters without a cannon or two to back you up! The English privateers are especially bold these days, taking ships right out of Havana harbour." The captain paused, waiting for a response from Hernando. When none came, he went on. "I too carry the papers of the privateer, but my two little ships are no match for those English sharks, so we give them a wide berth."

"Would you and your officers do me the honour of dining with me tonight?" he asked. When Hernando hesitated he added, "Commander, I can assure you of the finest delicacies out of Port Royal. I'm sure your fare has been quite bland of late."

Hernando wondered why Captain Rodriguez had called in at Port Royal, but agreed that he and his officers would dine aboard that evening.

* * * *

When José and Luis joined him on the beach later that afternoon, they wore their dress uniforms, which had been packed away until their return to Santo Domingo. Hernando greeted them absently, but continued looking at the two ships, narrowing his eyes against the light breeze. He was bothered by something.

He turned suddenly as Wells came up behind him. "What? Did you say something, Wells?"

"No, sir, I didn't. Are you all right?"

"I thought I heard Laocan's voice," Hernando said in astonishment. He shook it off. "Wells, ride to the Toltec village and bring back at least one hundred warriors." He turned back to look at the ships. "Be back before nightfall. I don't trust this Captain Rodriguez."

"What shall I do with them, sir?"

"Place them close to Cortez's treasure, just in case our new friend has any ideas. And double the watch. Get the men out of their quarters and into the forest for the night, full battle gear."

"Don't worry, Commander, there couldn't be a hundred men in both those little ships," Wells said as he started up the beach, on his way to the stable.

"Wells!" Hernando hollered after him. "Don't fall off that beast, now!" Wells grinned and threw up his arm in a wave.

Hernando returned to his hut and dressed for dinner, then loaded his two duelling pistols and stuck them in his belt under his jacket.

They rowed out to the ketch he was on earlier that day. Hernando gave the boatswain specific instructions, then followed his lieutenants up the rope ladder to the entry port. Captain Rodriguez met them and escorted them to the galley where his officers awaited them. After introductions, the meal began.

Rodriguez's men were in high spirits, and asked them many questions about their adventures. Hernando had instructed his lieutenants to say nothing about the treasure that lay on the beach. As dinner passed, the wine was exchanged for rum, and then the captain spoke above the merriment.

"We have heard that Cortez has found a great treasure in gold and silver."

His men fell silent and waited for Hernando to respond.

"It is true that Cortez found some extraordinary things, but our mission here was to secure this land in the name of the king of Spain. That being done, we await transport back to Hispaniola," Hernando replied smoothly. "How is the governor, by the way?"

"He's fine," the captain replied tersely, clearly irritated with the change of subject.

"How's his leg?" Hernando asked.

"His leg?" Rodriguez frowned in confusion.

"Yes. The last time I saw him, he had fallen from his mount and broken his leg."

Rodriguez recovered and nodded slowly. "Oh yes. The governor is still limping about, but he says it's much better."

Hernando smiled and looked pleased with the news, but he had caught the captain in a lie. Now he knew what had bothered him. If the governor had asked Rodriguez to look in on them, he would have sent a sealed letter of introduction; he had not. Hernando's mind raced. What were their plans? Did they think they could take the treasure? Surely they knew they were outnumbered.

The captain nodded imperceptibly to one of the mates, who rose with, "Excuse me, gentlemen, I must see to the watch," and left the cabin.

Hernando heard movement on deck, the sounds reverberating through the wooden hull. Captain Rodriguez spoke louder to cover the noise.

"What kind of extraordinary things did Cortez find, Commander Diaz?"

Hernando felt the small craft cant slightly, then slowly turn on its mooring line, as if a sail had been put to the light breeze to bring her around to lie parallel to the beach. Keeping his expression bland, Hernando spoke of the great cities, pyramids, and aqueducts, but his mind was on the captain's other motives for asking.

When he heard the unmistakable sound of the ship's cannon being run out, Hernando started to stand, but the captain placed a hand on Hernando's arm and a pistol at his chest. The first mate burst in with two others, all armed with pistols. José and Luis both stood, but the first mate put a cutlass to José's throat.

"Gentlemen, let's be civilized about this," the captain began. "We mean to have your gold and hold you for ransom. I'm sure your rich families back in Spain would pay dearly for your hides. Now, if you give me your word as gentlemen that you will not try escape, then we will treat you as such and afford you every comfort our little ship can provide."

Hernando's hand was on his pistol under his jacket but he could not draw it, cock it, and fire before Rodriguez discharged his own—it was pointed squarely at the middle of his chest.

"Now, if you give me that fancy sword of yours," the captain continued, "we'll go topside to see the fireworks."

Hernando and his lieutenants drew their swords slowly and dropped them on the table. Rodriguez shifted his pistol to his left hand and took the curved Saracen sword in his right hand. Noting Rodriguez's fascination with the sword, Hernando looked for an opening, but the mate's pistol was still pointed in his direction.

"This is a fancy piece of cutlery," Rodriguez murmured. "Toledo steel, but of Arabian design ... this should bring about ten gold pieces back in Port Royal."

Hernando was incensed at being captured, but angrier at the thought that this oaf would sell such a great sword to anyone with money to pay.

The captain gestured at his men. "Take them on deck," he ordered.

They emerged to find the ship rigged for night battle. Hernando glanced toward the shore. The two little ketches had indeed been pulled parallel to Hernando's encampment. Moonlight gleamed dully on the guns sticking out of the ship's flank. The bright flare of a red Chinese rocket lit up the sky farther down the beach, and Hernando realized Rodriguez had a shore party on land, ready to go in and mop up after the broadside he was planning for Hernando's sleeping men.

"Mr. Gunther, make sure your gunners don't hit the stores," Rodriguez ordered, leaving Hernando and his two men standing at the rail. "Only the encampment."

"Aye, sir," a barrel-chested sailor replied and turned and shouted orders in a language Hernando couldn't understand.

"All right, Mr. Gunther, let them have it."

Gunther barked and the cannons erupted. Their thunder struck Hernando's ears like a blow. The ship recoiled under his feet.

The first blast tore into the huts, turning them into geysers of splinters and flying palm fronds. Both ships spewed out destruction, with most of the fire focused on the encampment. Hernando was relieved he had taken the precaution of moving his men.

The roar continued for some time. Then Rodriguez called a halt to the carnage. One or two cannons still fired, but finally silence fell, and the deck stopped jerking under Hernando's feet. His ears rang and his nose was filled with the stench of sulphur and saltpeter. His feet and legs vibrated on the still deck.

"Send up a rocket, Mr. Gunther," Captain Rodriguez said.

The rocket fizzed into the sky. Moments later, Hernando could hear the shouts and clatter of the men streaming through the huts, looking for wounded.

"Let the men go ashore, Mr. Gunther, and get a longboat ready for us," Rodriguez said calmly.

"Aye, sir."

Gunther's men lowered the longboats and headed for shore. Soon musketfire and Toltec war cries told Hernando that his men were countering the attack. He shared a grim smile with José and Luis.

* * * *

On shore, Wells had kept his men well out of the cannon fire and not a man sustained injury. When more than a hundred ruffians charged up the beach in the moonlight, Wells ordered the musketeers to cut them down. The Toltecs didn't wait for the second volley; unable to restrain themselves, they ignored orders and ran into battle, screaming their war cries. The bewildered roughnecks, told they were going to clean up wounded, not fight a full-fledged battle, broke and ran at the sight of the fearsome warriors swinging their great stone axes, cleaving limbs from the slower ones.

* * * *

Rodriguez's brows drew down in a puzzled frown as he peered toward the shore. "Those roughnecks must have found the rum supplies already—listen to them screaming." Watching him, Hernando could tell Rodriguez had sensed something wasn't right. The captain hesitated, then turned to his first mate. "Call back the crew."

As the first mate hurried off to launch another rocket, Hernando drew his pistols and fired one into the chest of one of the mates. The man crumpled like an accordion. He poked the other into the captain's chest as he whirled to see what was happening. "Don't move, Captain, for I would gladly free your black heart from your chest." Rodriguez froze.

Hernando took his sword and José took the pistol from his other hand. Luis had already stooped to pick up the pistol and the cutlass from the dead sailor. As the skeleton crew left onboard recovered their wits and rushed forward, Hernando yanked the captain between him and them. José and Luis stood ready beside him. "Tell your men to stand to," he growled, pressing the pistol's muzzle against the captain's temple. Rodriguez licked his lips. The filigree on the pistol glinted in the moonlight, flashing in time with the captain's laboured breathing. "Tell them!"

The captain shouted the order and the men stopped advancing, but stood poised, waiting for an opening. Behind them, Hernando saw the first of the small boarding party that had been waiting in the shadow of the small ketch scrambling aboard through the entry port. He had wished to see them sooner, but the odds were even now; he'd soon have the upper hand. "Drop your swords," he shouted to the crew. "Your captain is as good as dead and my men are behind you!"

They turned to meet the soldiers coming aboard but held their ground, their swords levelled at the Spanish soldiers who were quickly peppering the deck thicker than barnacles on a ship's bottom. Hernando hammered the captain across the back of his head with the butt of his pistol and as the captain headed unconscious toward the deck, he fired into the closest sailor. His lieutenants followed with their own blasts. As the three sailors fell to the deck, Hernando's men attacked, slicing their way through the startled sailors.

Hernando grabbed his boatswain's shoulder, shouting, "Which one is the gunner?"

The boatswain's head swivelled like a barn owl's. He pointed. "There, sir."

"Take him below and check the cannon to see if they're loaded," Hernando ordered.

"Yes, sir!" The boatswain waded toward the gunner, slicing a sailor's shoulder as he passed.

The few sailors left standing threw down their weapons and lifted their arms in surrender. Hernando's men rounded them up. "Tie that bunch of scum securely, José!" he shouted. He saw his other lieutenant supporting himself against the rail. "Luis! Are you all right?"

"Just a scratch, sir," Luis managed. Hernando scowled. It was far more than a scratch; the man had taken a nasty cut to the chest. His dress jacket hung open, and Hernando could see a thick fold of red flesh hanging within its lapels; it reminded Hernando of a slab of beef hanging in the Seville market.

Kneeling, Hernando cut a strip of cloth from the jacket on the still unconscious Rodriguez, then rose and pressed it to Luis' chest. "José!" he called over his shoulder as Luis slid down to sit on the deck. His other lieutenant was supervising the trussing of the captured sailors. "Come here—let the others tend to that!"

More musketfire erupted on the beach as he was handing the makeshift bandage to José. Hernando stood and squinted toward the beach, trying to make out the state of the battle. Instead he saw the returning longboats materializing out of the darkness. "The longboats ..." He whirled. "Where's the gunner?" he called.

The boatswain trotted back on deck. "The guns are empty except the ones facing the sea—those are run out and ready."

"Tell the gunner to fire at will when I bring the ship to bear on the other ketch," he said, his voice urgent. "And take a couple of men to help you down there!" he called after the boatswain as the man acknowledged the order and hurried toward the hatch that would take him belowdecks.

Hernando turned on the captured sailors. "How do I turn this ship broadside to the other?" Silence. "Do you want to live?" he growled into the silence.

One young sailor, no more than fourteen, spoke up. "Cut the tie down on the mizzen mast."

Hernando immediately strode toward him. He cowered back, frightened. "Show me," Hernando blurted, pulling the boy to his feet.

He stumbled up the deck, hands still tied behind his back, then motioned with his head to where a thick manila rope was tied off. Hernando severed it with one stoke of his sword. The breeze spilled out of the single sail and the ship turned slowly on the anchor rope, swinging around broadside to the other ketch. Moments later, the air exploded as the gunner opened up each gun, firing in succession along the length of the ship. The grapeshot ripped the other ketch apart and caught the crewmen who had been standing at the railing, watching the sister ship come about.

"Man those small cannons!" Hernando shouted above the roar from below.

Bearing slow matches, his men moved to aim the semiportable cannons—really oversized muskets filled with shot for the purpose of repelling a boarding party or strafing the decks of an enemy's ship. As the longboats, already battered by musketfire, came into range, Hernando's men let loose with the small cannons. Their aim was not good, but still the spread of the shot wreaked havoc on the sailors. The few long boats that managed to veer before coming into range rowed off into the darkness, their wakes pocked with shot from the small cannons.

"Send the boarding party to the other ship to make sure it's secure," Hernando shouted. "And tell the gunner to stop firing before he sinks her!" He suspected the boarding party would find little resistance on the other ship. Hernando could see only bloody corpses and wounded sailors sprawled on its deck.

Hernando turned to Luis and José, who was still holding the cloth to his brother's chest. "How does it look?" he asked, concern lowering his voice.

"I don't know," José admitted in a trembling voice. "There's lots of blood, but it's not too deep—just peeled back the skin, looks like."

Hernando knelt and looked at the wound. "Get a bottle of bandy from the captain's quarters—and a sewing kit." He took over the cloth from José, who quickly disappeared below.

Beside him, Captain Rodriguez moaned and rolled over, then sat up, one hand tenderly probing the back of his head. Hernando lifted his Saracen sword and put its tip under the man's chin. A tiny red bead of blood grew to a dangling drip. Rodriguez stared at Hernando in disbelief.

"You missed the fireworks, Captain," Hernando told him. "It seems your ships are now mine—and you'll be dancing at the end of a rope for your troubles."

He did not answer, just favoured Hernando with a shark's stare—no blink of the eye, just dark, cold, and menacing.

With the ships secure, the prisoners locked in the hold, and José holding his brother, Hernando threaded the needle—not the delicate, curved needle of a surgeon, but the thick, blunt instrument of the sailmaker.

"This is going to hurt, little brother," José said, then poured the pungent brown liquid liberally over the gaping wound. Luis screamed, and his body went rigid with pain. Then he slumped, unconscious.

Hernando began to sew. "This is going to leave a nasty scar," he muttered as he worked, "but he'll be able to show his grandchildren what he brought back from the New World!" He knew he was rambling, but it seemed to help steady his hand as he did his best to close up the raw flesh.

Chapter 13

▼

Hernando returned to the beach in the cutter as dawn peeked over the horizon. As the boat pulled away from them, he turned to look at the two little ships, one of which was torn and pockmarked from the barrage his gunner had rained down upon it. He shook his head and looked to the beach, where his men were stacking bodies in a great pile

Wells waited on the wet sand to catch the boat as it surfed in on a foaming wave. "I'm glad to see you safe and sound, Commander!" Wells offered in greeting, along with his infectious grin.

"And I'm glad that you're still here to see me safe and sound, Sergeant," Hernando replied, grinning back. He turned his gaze back to the beach as he stepped into the warm surf. "How did we fare, Sergeant?" he asked as they waded ashore. "What were our casualties?"

"Ours were a lot lighter than theirs," Wells answered, pointing to a group of about twenty-five men who sat or squatted in the sand. Some were clearly wounded; others just looked forlorn. "Twelve dead, three on their way to meet their maker, and seven wounded who will live to fight another day," Wells reported as he and Hernando trod up the soft sand to the prisoners.

"Toltecs?" Hernando asked.

"They took light losses; they don't seem to have any wounded." Hernando glanced at him. Wells knew as well as he that the Toltecs dispatched their own wounded—better to die a hero on the battlefield than be a burden on the Toltec society.

"There is a slight problem," Wells added. "The Toltecs want the prisoners. I've been holding them off until you came ashore."

Hernando looked at the small band of ruffians. They looked half starved, and there did not seem to be a proper soldier among them. "Do any of you speak Spanish?" he asked them.

"Some of us are Spanish, sir," a slight man in the front said. Hernando realized he had been listening to Wells and Hernando's conversation. "You can't give us to those heathens," the skinny fellow added. "Some of us is Christians."

His appeal to Hernando's sense of religion didn't work. "Then you should have remembered you were Christians before you took up the Devil's work!" Hernando rebuked him, anger raising his voice. He waved a hand at the others. "Who are these men? Be honest with me, or I'll pluck out your heart and eat it myself!"

"Just a group who were promised riches for a little dirty work, sir," the man whined. "Mostly crewmen from various nations who for various reasons were stranded in Port Royal."

Wells chuckled. "You mean got drunk and could not make it back to their ships!"

The sailor glared at Wells, then directed his answer at Hernando. "Yes, sir, something like that. Captain Rodriguez ferried us over here weeks ago and kept us holed up in a camp a couple miles down the beach. He said we'd be rich."

Hernando thought about the troubles Spain would have in transporting this new wealth back to its treasury. He turned to Wells. "I'll be by the cargo. Bring me the Toltec leaders. And get these men out of the sun or they'll be broiled by lunch."

Hernando checked the treasure, which seemed to be intact, save for the occasional hole or splinter from stray musketfire. The two warrior priests, accompanied by Juan, joined him a few minutes later. Through Juan, Hernando thanked them and gave them gifts of blankets and metal knifes. Then he told them, "It is against our customs to allow you to sacrifice these prisoners."

The priests began talking rapidly to Juan, gesticulating angrily. Juan began to interpret before they'd finished speaking, but Hernando held up his hand. "It's all right, Juan. I get the meaning of their words. Tell them that at least two boatloads of sailors escaped last night and rowed south; my guess is that they were heading for the camp two miles down the beach." He pointed as he talked. "I would not know if something happened to them, and it would not concern me if the brave Toltecs went to visit them."

As Juan translated, understanding dawned in the eyes of the warriors. They smiled at each other, then held their hands out for a Spanish handshake—a gesture foreign to them, and their way of showing respect to Hernando. They left grinning.

Hernando turned to Wells. "I swear I don't know who enjoys the action more, you or the Toltecs." Wells grinned. "Now let's talk to the prisoners again."

"You've probably heard stories of the Indians' brutality to prisoners," Hernando told the prisoners when they once again stood before them. "Stories of sacrifices, of men being skinned alive. Well, it's very true, and our allies the Toltecs demand your worthless hides for their temple walls!" Hernando paused for effect. The motley group stirred restlessly and muttered. "But I appealed on your behalf because you are Christians, to spare you a gruesome torture and instead execute you with a quick beheading."

The men, frightened now, looked about for the Toltecs.

"But a thought has occurred to me," Hernando continued. "I don't know if you'd be interested, but I need a crew for that ship out there." He turned and pointed at one of the ships in the bay, winking at a puzzled Wells. "What do you think, Sergeant?" he asked.

"Let the Indians cut the blighters' heads off!" Wells growled, then added in an undertone, "They'll never agree to it, sir."

Hernando turned back to the small group. Some of the men had risen and were pleading vigorously for their lives. He frowned thoughtfully at them. "I don't think I could trust you, even if I could buy your freedom from the Toltecs."

The skinny man who had become spokesman tried to calm some of the others before looking at Hernando. "Sir, each man here would owe you his life—that would make him very loyal."

"Believe me when I tell you I have no doubt where your loyalties lie," Hernando told him, "but I will go to the Toltec village tonight and ask if I can buy your heads ... along with your bodies ... from the warrior priests. I do this against the good advice of my sergeant," he added ominously, then looked at Wells and jerked his head to indicate that he follow.

The two walked around the pile of treasure, out of sight of the prisoners, who had dropped back onto the sand in despair.

"Why the wait, Commander?" Wells asked.

"Let them have a sleepless night worrying about their hides," Hernando said. "It will make them all the more grateful in the morning." They smiled at each other. "Now let's tend to putting Luis' town and fort back together."

There was very little left of the settlement. The cannon fire had obliterated the huts, and even the palisade around them was a shambles. Hernando scratched his head, wondering where to start. "Use the wood to burn the bodies of the dead," he said at last. "We will start over."

The fire burned long into the night, the air heavy with the reek of charred human flesh. In the morning a huge pile of embers and some blackened bones were all that was left.

"How fragile life is, Wells," Hernando said.

"Indeed, sir," Wells answered. They stared at all that remained with bleary eyes, for neither had slept the night before.

"I fear this is only the beginning of the carnage that this treasure will bring," Hernando said bleakly.

"Yes, sir," Wells said again, and they were both silent as the sun god rose from his slumber in the east.

Hernando marched over to the small huddle of prisoners and looked somberly at the riffraff. The men gazed back, concern etched on their faces, fearful that he was unable to secure their freedom from the Toltecs. "Gentlemen—if I may use that term in addressing you—I was able to convince the Toltecs to spare your lives."

A cheer went up: "God bless the commander!" The men quickly fell silent when Hernando's expression remained stern.

"Unfortunately for you," he said, "that means you'll be wards of the master sergeant, who was against your reprieve. He will be looking for any excuse to have you dangling from a tree."

The men cast nervous glances at Wells, who returned their stares with the meanest look he could muster. Hernando suspected some of it was genuine; he had not let his sergeant in on this little speech.

"Sergeant!"

"Yessir!" Wells snapped to attention.

"Feed and water your new men."

"Yes, sir!" Wells executed a salute, then turned to look at the rabble. "Corporal!" he barked.

"Yes, sir!" A young man sprang to Wells' side.

"Feed and water the livestock."

The young man saluted as Wells turned and followed Hernando into the shade of an ancient tree overhanging the beach.

"Very well acted, Sergeant," Hernando observed as Wells dropped down beside him.

"Thank you, sir, but you could have told me my lines before the curtain went up."

They laughed and made themselves comfortable in the soft leaves. The breaking waves and buzzing cicadas lulled them to sleep.

Hunger awoke Hernando in the late morning. Wells was sitting quietly at his side. "It feels good to just relax a little, doesn't it," Hernando said.

"Yes it does."

Hernando sighed. "Maybe we'll just stay here and forget about the world and all its troubles."

Wells thought for a moment. "I think I'd miss the action."

José was coming ashore. Hernando reluctantly rose and went to meet him.

He had news of his brother. "Luis us much better. The fever has broken and he has an appetite."

"That's good news indeed," Hernando exclaimed. "He'll be in the hands of a good doctor in Santo Domingo before too long. I think we'll sail as soon as we can refit the twin that took the pounding." Hernando nodded out to the two little ships.

"Commander, my brother and I have been talking …" José hesitated, then plunged on. "If his injuries heal, my brother has requested that he be allowed to stay and rebuild Villa Rica de la Cruz."

Hernando looked at him. "Well, if that's what he wants, he is welcome to it. I'll go aboard and speak to him. What about you? What are your plans?"

"I'll return to Spain and petition the king for land grants and trading concessions. It is a large land, and Cortez shouldn't have all of it!" he joked, although he looked a bit guilty, as if he felt he was letting Hernando down. He continued. "Of course, your name would be on all documents. If it weren't for your confidence in us, we would not be standing here on this beach with such an enormous opportunity ahead of us." As an afterthought, José added, "We would resign our commissions if you wish, sir."

Hernando thought for a minute. "No, I'll say I commanded you to set up a fortified town and look after our interests. I believe there will be many who will try to take our newfound riches."

José smiled, for Hernando had just handed him and his brother great wealth and a political future that a successful military career could assure later in life.

* * * *

The next morning, as part of the treasure was being loaded, Hernando told Luis, who really did look a lot better, what he had told his brother. "If this land develops, as I believe it will," he added, "there will be a great fortune for your family. Remember, the Toltecs have dealt fairly with us and deserve respect in your treatment of them."

"Yes, sir," Luis began, but Hernando cut in.

"I asked your brother to call me Hernando and I now ask you, for soon you'll be a great man of power and I would like to address you as a friend, Luis."

Luis smiled shyly. "I would like that very much, Commander—I mean, Hernando." Luis stumbled over his own tongue.

Silence settled over them as both remembered the times they had spent together. Then Hernando checked his sewing job and transferred Luis to the longboat to be taken ashore.

Hernando stood on the deck, watching it depart. He was not a sailor, but he enjoyed the gentle movement beneath his feet. His eyes scanned the land, so green and lush; it seemed to call to him. He knew he would return, but for now he had to make a call to the governor of Hispaniola.

He went below to the captain's quarters to check that his few belongings were there. He opened the arched lid of his trunk and immediately spied the turtle shell comb Laocan had used on her shiny black hair, lying on top of his folded clothes. It was all he had to remember her by. He lifted it out, feeling guilty that he hadn't thought much about her in the commotion of the last few days. Lying back on the bunk, which was much too short for his frame, he drifted off to sleep, the comb clutched to his heart.

In his dream, he gazed on her pretty brown face as she told him she would go to the east with him to visit the great sun god. He longed to lie next to her, but she was busy talking, as she'd so often done. Her face grew grim. *There is one in the house of the great sun god who wishes you not to have your name,* she said in his mind. *You will know him by the fire around his neck.*

Her face faded and Hernando reached out for her. He wanted to sweep her up in his arms and smother her talk with his lips, but she slipped away.

He awoke to the sound of Wells yelling at his livestock: "You pieces of cow dung make me sick! You're lazy! You complain every time I politely ask you to lend a helping hand. Now, get that stuff stored below before I feed you to the sharks." Hernando grinned.

"How goes the battle?" Hernando asked his sergeant when he came on deck.

"If it was a battle, I'd have it mastered," Wells grumbled. "This shipping business is a little out of my field of expertise, sir."

Hernando nodded. "Bring Captain Rodriguez to the helm and leave the chains on him, Sergeant."

Wells brightened. "Aye, sir!" He turned and barked an order.

Several minutes later, Rodriguez was dragged onto the deck in chains, like some dangerous dog.

"Captain, I hope my men aren't treating you too badly," Hernando said.

"Your men *are* treating me badly, Commander!"

Hernando cut him off. "That's too bad, considering you tried to murder them all—or had you forgotten, Rodriguez?"

The captain clamped his mouth shut.

"Better. Now, Captain, I need to sail this ship to Hispaniola and I need your navigational skills to get there."

The captain smiled for the first time, realizing he had the advantage now. "So you take my ship and sail me to my own execution—what are the chances of that happening?"

"Well, we can wait right here until my own supply ships arrive, in which case I'll execute you in a half-hour for piracy, or you can stand trial in Hispaniola with my plea for leniency. You have one half-hour to decide." He turned his back on the captain. "Take this scum away, Sergeant Wells."

Wells pulled on his neck chain so hard that the captain almost toppled over. "No, no!" Rodriguez blurted. "Commander, I don't have to think about it—I'll sail your ketch to Hispaniola for ya."

Hernando turned a stern gaze on the man. "Take him below, Wells!"

"Yes, sir." Wells dragged the captain away by his chains.

* * * *

On the morning tide, the little ketch spun on her keel and made for open sea. Hernando stood on deck, waving at Luis and watching until he became nothing but a speck on the shore. He kept watching until the land slipped below the horizon. Still Hernando stared from the stern, longing for Laocan.

"Commander." Wells touched Hernando's arm to bring him out of his stupor.

"Ah, Sergeant," Hernando said, turning to Wells. "How are your livestock enjoying the voyage?"

"They're happy to be away from the Toltecs, sir." He grinned. "And that Captain Rodriguez, I can't figure him out. He's going to certain death and yet he sails his ketch fast and true."

"Yes," Hernando drawled. "Keep your eye on that one, Sergeant. He'll try something before we make port." He thought a moment. "Put a guard beside him to make sure he doesn't incite a mutiny."

"It would be a short mutiny, since we have all the weapons." Wells grinned at the thought of sticking the captain with a sword or blowing a large hole through his head.

They had no trouble from Captain Rodriguez or his men, and made Santo Domingo faster than expected. Hernando wondered if Rodriguez was counting on his good word at trial to save him, or if he was just savouring his last time with the planking humming underfoot when the ship's masts were trimmed to the maximum, and the ship jumped out of the water and cut the waves like a flying fish avoiding a barracuda.

As they furled the sails and set the anchor, Hernando noted the ships in port. The *Alva Cordova* was among them. Although he didn't relish having to socialize with Captain Colius Menindez, he knew that it would take the protection of great ships like his to ensure England and France didn't take away this new treasure. This small flotilla was his supply ships, but they were quiet and no supplies waited on the docks.

"José, take this letter to the governor. You might as well practice your politics where you can. It just requests a meeting as soon as possible. You may want to hint at the treasure we are carrying."

José smiled at the opportunity and went ashore immediately to seek out the governor. Within two hours the governor's son had come aboard the little ketch. Hernando greeted him as an old friend.

The ensign tried to salute him. "I have been gone too long," Hernando said, "if you do not remember we are comrades in battle." The young man looked puzzled, until Hernando breached protocol and held out his hand.

Averra eagerly took it. "It's good to have you back, Commander Diaz!"

"It's good to be back." A slight lie on his part; Hernando had come to realize that he was more at ease in the company of fighting men than with the pompous group who'd soon be clamouring for details about the treasure. "I have a special prisoner that I would like to entrust to your care." The young man's chest swelled with the honour of being asked to oversee this special assignment. "I'll send three of my men with you, and don't take his chains off—they make it harder to run," Hernando added with dry humour.

Ensign Averra was all questions and Hernando gave him some details, but he hesitated to say much; he only wanted to tell the incredible story once, preferably to a large crowd so he would not have to recount it over and over.

"My father is throwing a dinner in your honour tonight," Averra said as if sensing his reluctance. "I hope you're not otherwise engaged?" He paused for Hernando to except.

"Well, I did want to go to that nice pub you showed me the last time I was here, but I guess that I can wait for another time," Hernando teased, then added quickly as Averra reddened, "I accept." The ensign grinned shyly at Hernando's joke. "I will recount the entire story tonight for your father and his guests."

As the ensign took his charge to the city's jail, Hernando went below and prepared some of the nicer golden objects to take to the governor's ball. He pondered over different approaches, finally deciding that there was no way to keep the treasure a secret, so why try.

"Wells!"

"Yes, sir!" The sergeant was instantly at his elbow.

"For the love of God, stop doing that!"

Wells smirked. "It's my only pleasure aboard ship, sir."

Hernando humphed. "Well, how about dinner tonight with the governor?"

"Me, sir? You've got to be kidding! What would a rough master sergeant do at a fancy party like that?" His bantering tone turned thoughtful. "Will there be women, sir?"

Hernando grinned. He was warming to the idea. "Yes, the prettiest you've seen in a year," he jested. "And as for that, Master Sergeant, I *could* raise you in rank."

Wells snorted. "You could put more polish on the uniform, but I'm afraid it wouldn't take the roughness out of the man. Besides, I'd be afraid to get the new uniform dirty in a hard battle. No sir, a master sergeant is what I am and I thank you kindly for the suggestion."

"Good try, Wells. You're still accompanying me to the party, if only to get an eyeful of pretty Spanish ladies. You can look after these as your excuse for being there." He waved a hand at the golden samples he'd selected.

"Yes, sir—I'll be happy to look after your trinkets!" Wells saluted and smiled before he left the cabin.

Hernando looked at his dress uniform. It was frayed and tattered. *I guess they'll understand,* he thought as he polished his great sword's sheath, then his buckles and the brass on his uniform. He could have someone perform this task, but he found it soothing and his mind drifted off to the land of the Aztecs, and to Laocan.

That evening, Ensign Averra delivered Hernando, José, and Wells to the dinner and the three stood in the reception line and greeted the guests as they arrived. The only thing that made Hernando smile was that Wells was more uncomfortable than him. He watched the man squirm in his dress uniform, marvelling at how good Wells' uniform looked. *He must have been all afternoon, fussing over the polish,* Hernando thought.

Another introduction by the doorman brought him back to the party: "The Count and Countess of Durraldo." The servant motioned for them to enter with a flourish.

"The count is a very important man," the governor whispered, leaning toward Hernando.

But Hernando's attention was on the young lady who followed them into the room. As he shook hands with the count and exchanged pleasantries, his eyes strayed past them to the face of the young lady.

The count, aware of his stare, added, "This is my niece, Isabella Castro Morelas."

She curtsied and her eyes met his for the first time. They were large, as blue as the sea around Villa Rica de la Vera Cruz.

"Delighted," was all Hernando could manage to say. He kissed her gloved hand. They passed by, but as the count reached the end of the line, Isabella looked back and met Hernando's eye.

In the middle of dinner, the governor urged Hernando to recount his story. He stood and began the tales, mesmerising Hispaniola's elite. Only Hernando's strong voice could be heard in the room; no one spoke, or ate, or even moved, so rapt were they on his words. When Hernando reached the part where Cortez had filled a room full of gold and silver, he motioned to Wells, who opened the box he'd been clutching all night and extracted the precious objects. A golden bracelet encrusted with jade and jasper and a matching necklace that made the women gasp with desire was followed by golden idols of various deities, one with an especially large male member proudly sticking out, which drew chuckles from the ladies. One boldly asked if all the Aztecs were that well endowed.

"I do not know," Hernando answered, "but they fought like they did!" Laughter rippled around the table.

Hernando took the opportunity afforded by this pause in his speech to look at Isabella, whose big blue eyes had not left him since he began speaking. Suddenly nervous, his hands fell to the tabletop and fidgeted with the idols. Her gaze fell to his hands and she smiled shyly, then her cheeks flushed red and she dropped her head. Hernando looked down and realized he was fiddling with the god with the large penis. He cleared his throat and continued his story.

He concluded with a warning that it would take a great ship and a great captain to transport this incredible treasure to the king of Spain. He inclined his head toward Captain Menindez, who smiled at the compliment.

Later, when the sweets were being brought in, José leaned toward Hernando. "I'm glad I'll have you to relax the king, with that manner of yours."

"Don't worry, José, you'll be all right," Hernando assured him, though his eyes slid past José to Isabella, who was speaking with the older woman seated next to her. The light shimmered in her light brown hair as her head moved in time with her animated conversation. *It's streaked with gold,* Hernando noted, gazing at the long locks lying against her back. Her bare shoulders were as white as pearls.

She turned toward Hernando as she picked up her wine glass, and her generous red lips curved in another smile when she saw him looking her way. Hernando melted into them, until he was drawn back into conversation with the governor.

After dinner the men retired to a large drawing room, and the questions became more intense. The discussion ran on until music drifted from the great room, and the men slowly slipped out to join the women for dancing. Most everyone had left, save the governor and Captain Menindez, who turned to Hernando and asked, "Exactly how much gold is there?"

Hernando paused for a second, calculating. "Enough gold to fill all the holds of the *Alva Cordova* twice over."

The governor blew a gust of air through his fleshy lips. "Every pirate from here to Spain will be looking to take that prize," he said, lowering his head to his scalp under his curly wig. He looked solemnly at Hernando and Menindez. "This gold must reach King Charles so we can build more ships like the *Alva Cordova*."

The captain nodded. "Superiority on the sea is the only way to ensure the arrival of this fortune from the New World."

Hernando only half listened. His thoughts were on Isabella and her golden hair. Finally, the conversation exhausted, they too joined the dance. Hernando paused just inside the entrance and looked about the room, then jumped when Wells said behind him, "She's over by the big windows, sir."

Hernando turned. Wells was still clutching the wooden box. He had a big grin on his face. "Who is?" Hernando asked with exaggerated nonchalance.

"The little one you've been eyeballing all night," Wells said.

"You're imagining things, Sergeant," Hernando said curtly, then walked away when he felt his face heat. He turned with his back to the wall a few paces away and watched the dancing, examining his guilty reaction to Wells' good-natured ribbing. He realized that he was strongly attracted to the pretty young Isabella, and felt a new surge of guilt for betraying the memory of Laocan.

He looked in the direction Wells had so helpfully indicated and saw a small crowd of young men around her. He thought she looked at him through the crowd, but he couldn't be sure. He stood frozen next to the wall, watching as Isabella danced with one young man and then another. Hernando sighed. *I'll be leaving soon anyway,* he rationalized. *No sense even talking to her.*

Hernando was looking over a silver tray of sweetmeats and thinking about the exotic fruits he had eaten with Cortez when a soft, musical voice said behind him, "Your story was very exciting at dinner."

Hernando turned. Isabella stood close to him. She looked up into his eyes and for a moment, Hernando had no words, for her beauty had knocked the wind out of him. "Thank you," he said lamely.

"I was wondering why the Indian chief's daughter saved your life by throwing herself in front of the Jesuit's spear," Isabella said.

Hernando felt his cheeks flush. Had she sensed that Laocan was more than just the interpreter he'd called her, or did his story not make sense at that point? He tried to think.

"Was she very pretty?" Isabella pushed.

"Yes!" Hernando answered obediently, as if he couldn't control his own thoughts.

"I'm sorry she died," Isabella continued.

Hernando's thoughts ran wildly in different directions, like the waves in front of a gale. Should he tell her everything? He wanted to, but why? He didn't even know her.

"I'm sorry, this is none of my business," she said suddenly. "Forgive me, Commander Diaz."

"Please, call me Hernando," he urged, regaining some of his composure.

She smiled and inclined her head. "I'd like that. And you can call me Isabella." She paused, as if deliberately shifting to a less sensitive topic. "That's a famous family name you have. The governor told us your grandfather rode beside El Cid."

"Yes, it's going to be hard living up to the name." Hernando was relieved that he had stopped stammering. He felt some of his confidence returning. She had an amazing effect on him, reducing him to a boy with her presence.

"It sounds to me that you have already made a good start on your own fame." He noticed the dimple that appeared in her cheek as she smiled at him again. She held Hernando like a cobra, her gaze hypnotizing. Then, as if she'd used up all her excuses to talk to him, she blurted, "Don't you want to ask me to dance?"

"Yes, of course! Forgive me," Hernando almost babbled, feeling like a schoolboy at a dance with the nuns watching him. He held out his arm and said formally, "Would you like to dance?"

They waltzed around the room for two songs. Hernando was oblivious to anything but her sweeping form, his hand on her small waist, and her ample breasts pushing at the edge of her low-cut bodice. She thanked him and left him standing in the middle of the room at the end of the second song.

Hernando quickly recovered his senses and strode to a sideboard where a waiter was pouring wine. He accepted a glass and sipped at it, peering over the rim at Isabella, who had returned to the count's side.

"Quite a catch for some lucky man—if he can get past the count, that is," the governor said at his elbow, also holding a glass of wine. He turned to Hernando. "When do you plan to leave, Commander?"

"As soon as Captain Menindez is ready. Cortez will have the second load at Vera Cruz by the time we get there." Hernando felt an uncharacteristically wistful pang and realized he was reluctant to leave the beautiful young woman.

The count left the party after saying good night to the governor. Hernando was unable to say good night to Isabella before they left. His interest in the party instantly faded. *Where has Wells gotten to?* Hernando wondered. It wasn't like him to not be springing up underfoot.

He wandered about, then entered the gardens, where he found Wells and a serving girl sitting on the wooden box, locked in a kiss. "Does your girlfriend know what's in the box, Wells?" he asked.

Wells started, then jumped to his feet. The girl remained on the box, smoothing the front of her dress. "Mercy, Commander, you nearly gave me a burst heart!" he blustered. Behind him, his lady friend rose quietly and slipped into the shadows.

Hernando picked up the box. "I'm going back to the ship." Wells reached for the box. "No, you stay. Your girlfriend didn't run very far."

Wells turned to see the pretty young thing standing a short distance away, looking coy. "Thank you, sir." Wells feigned a salute.

Hernando smiled, sketched a response, and left.

* * * *

During the next week, the activity in the port reached a fever pitch, with supplies being loaded and the governor's own guard on the docks day and night. He wasn't taking any chances on the king's gold being spirited out of his harbour.

When the treasure had been transferred to the *Alva Cordova*, Hernando, with the help young Ensign Averra, leased his two little ketches to a local merchant who would, among other things, supply the Villa Rica de la Vera Cruz settlement and be paid from the governor's treasury. *A tidy arrangement,* Hernando thought, *supplying one's own village and being paid for it.*

His father would be pleased at what Hernando had accomplished in the New World—he had acquired a small shipping company, land, and interests in the Villa Rica de la Vera Cruz. But what he really desired was the return of his family estates, so his mother could live out the rest of her days in comfort and with pride. That would have to wait until he reached Spain.

Hernando wasn't looking forward to the crossing. He'd asked Sergeant Wells if he would prefer to wait at Vera Cruz for his return and the sergeant had commented that Hernando would get himself into trouble in Spain and would need him to rescue him. Hernando was thankful. At least he would have someone to spar with on the trip home.

He looked around his quarters. He would be spending much of his time here, writing reports for the Duke of Aragon. The cabin was smaller than the one he'd had on the ketch. He guessed he was still paying for past transgressions with Captain Menindez, for Hernando knew there were nicer quarters aboard this great fighting ship.

On the day before their departure, the cabin boy came to Hernando's quarters and conveyed the captain's wishes that he join them for supper that night. Hernando reluctantly accepted. At six bells, he donned his dress uniform and headed for the officer's galley to greet those he knew and be introduced to those he did not.

The galley door opened as he was about to be seated, and the Count of Durraldo and his wife entered the room, followed by Isabella. As introductions started again, Hernando smiled at Isabella, who acknowledged his smile with a slight nod, then looked away. Her cool response sent his eyes to the tabletop in embarrassment, and he regretted his obvious display of pleasure at seeing her. Why was she not pleased to see him? When the introductions reached Hernando, he politely greeted them and left it at that. He ate his supper in self-absorbed silence as the officers lavished attention on the count's niece.

At the end of the meal, the count abruptly left the table, followed by his two women. Hernando thought it strange behaviour, but no one commented on it, so neither did he.

Later he sought Wells in his quarters, which he shared with José. The cabin was smaller that Hernando's. "I would have been quite happy sleeping with the crew," Wells said, seeing Hernando scanning the small room. "The lieutenant snores like a banshee."

Hernando smiled, then settled on the end of the sergeant's bunk. "I want you to nose around a bit, find out what you can about the count."

Wells nodded, then offered, one eyebrow raised, "His niece is aboard."

"I know, I just had dinner with them."

"What'd ya eat?" Wells asked.

"Chicken. Cut it out—I'm serious. Something is strange about that count."

Wells held up his hands in surrender. "All right, all right, I'll ask around."

That night Hernando lay awake in his bunk, thinking of how beautiful Isabella was. He drifted off to sleep thinking that the crossing might not be as terrible as he had first thought.

Hernando was already on deck when the watch bell heralded the dawn. The light was strengthening when Isabella appeared on deck. Hernando hadn't heard her light footsteps until she was close behind him; he turned and she put her arms around his waist and pulled herself close. Stunned, Hernando stood with his arms hanging at his sides.

"I'm so glad you're aboard. I didn't expect you to be on the *Alva Cordova*." She rested her head against his chest.

He could smell her hair, its floral sweetness, with a hint of citrus. He placed his hands on her shoulders and he could feel her warmth through the silk. Before he could say anything, the morning watch came on deck and she turned and ran back down the stairway leading to the quarters in the stern. Hernando stared after her, wondering if he should follow her, wondering what had just happened. Then the captain came on deck and the first mate shouted orders, and Hernando turned his attention to the bustle of departure. Menindez nodded to Hernando and he took that as a good sign.

The big galleon lumbered out of port followed closely by her two escorts. Hernando wandered the deck all day, hoping for a glimpse of Isabella, but he didn't see her again until the evening meal, where she was again cool and aloof. Later he had a rum with José and Wells in their cabin, where there was hardly room to raise a toast to the king and Vera Cruz.

Finally the conversation got around to the count and his odd behaviour. "Seems your count gets jealous when too much attention is paid the young Senorita Morelas," Wells said.

"She is his ward. He is just being protective of her virtue," Hernando said, not wanting to seem all that interested.

"Very. The captain ordered his men to ignore her, under threat of severe penalty for violation," José added. "One of the young officers said he heard the count yelling at the captain in his quarters after dinner the first night."

The little party fell apart quickly. Hernando made for his room, a little groggy from the rum, and quickly fell into a deep sleep.

He awoke early and headed topside. On his way to the stairs he paused at the count's door, heard only silence inside, and continued on.

On deck, he stood at the same spot where he had encountered Isabella the morning before, one eye on the companionway, hoping she would come again. It was still more dark than light. *It's too early,* he thought. Then a small hand reached from the shadows and touched his arm, startling him. He turned, saw Isabella, and embraced her without hesitation. He felt her trembling.

"My uncle the count is a brutal and dangerous man," she explained when he drew back slightly and looked at her with concern. "He'd beat me if he found me here."

He wrapped his arms around her and they stood quietly in each other's arms. Hernando breathed deeply, wanting to memorize the scent of her. When light started brightening the deck, she said, "I must go." She reached up and lightly touched his cheek, then left him standing in the early morning chill.

This went on for days as they made for Villa Rica de la Vera Cruz. Each morning he would hold her in the safety of his arms. Several times Isabella looked at him uncertainly and opened her mouth as if to speak, then changed her mind and nestled against him. What did she want to tell him? Didn't she know he would understand?

Isabella did explain how she had come to be the ward of the Count of Durraldo. "My father died owing the count a lot of money, and the count visited my mother to get the payments. The pressure finally caused my mother to take her own life. All that my father owed was taken by the count as payment…" She dropped her eyes, as if ashamed. "Including me."

Hernando didn't understand why the count would want Isabella. He knew that debtors often became servants to repay family debt, but when he suggested he could pay off her debt, she only smiled. "How sweet," was all she said.

When they reached the sparkling beach at Vera Cruz, Hernando and his men went ashore to supervise the loading of Cortez's treasure. José and Luis caught up on gossip and made their plans for the future while Hernando inspected what Luis had accomplished in their absence. Luis didn't seem to be any worse for wear after almost being filleted by pirates.

Hernando reinforced the garrison and supervised the placement of a battery of cannon he'd had brought ashore. This would make future raids on the new village a lot more hazardous. Then he went to the Toltec village to pay his respects to Laocan's father.

In broken Toltec, which amused the old man greatly, Hernando again thanked Paynala and his people for their help and asked him to give the same support to Luis.

The old man thought for a while. "I will give the same support that I receive."

Hernando smiled, imagining this old politician back in the Spanish court. The old chief gave his hand to Hernando, which he gladly shook. He said his farewells and he and Wells made their way back to Vera Cruz.

Hernando sat half asleep in his stallion's saddle, lulled by the big beast's steady gait and the calming rustle of thousands of leaves in the jungle around them. Into that trancelike calm came Laocan's soft voice: "Don't be sad, my green-eyed god. Each one must make choices, and sometimes others have to live with those choices. What I did, I did because I had to—it was my destiny. Yours lies in another direction. It was that destiny I had to protect."

The words were so clear that Hernando swivelled in his saddle, looking for Laocan. Interpreting Hernando's sudden movement as a response to some danger, Wells drew his pistol and cocked it. "What is it, Commander?" he whispered, looking about for something to shoot.

For a moment Hernando considered telling Wells that Laocan had been talking to him. Then he shook the idea off. "Nothing," he said.

Chapter 14

Hernando watched as another load of gold ingots was ferried out to the *Alva Cordova*. Some of the artwork hadn't been melted down yet and Hernando ordered it to be saved so he could show the king and his court what it had looked like. He was more intrigued by the culture that created such marvels than with the gold itself. He had seen truly marvellous things here in this new land.

"Your ketch is just about ready for you to sail to Hispaniola, sir," a sawdust-covered man said as he approached Hernando. The *Alva Cordova*'s carpenter and his helper had just finished loading a longboat with freshly sawn lumber. They had been making repairs since their arrival.

"That's good," Hernando replied, pleased with the progress. "We will soon be finished loading ourselves."

The carpenter tapped his forehead, knocking some sawdust from his dark curls in the process, then turned to head for the rowboat. Hernando stared at the decks of the *Alva Cordova* as she gently twisted on her thick anchor rope, her sides catching the light breeze. She sat low in the water now, laden with the king's treasure. *A ripe target for any privateer with a spyglass and one good eye*, Hernando thought.

It was not the proud lines of the ship that interested Hernando today, but the pretty figure of Isabella. He scanned the ship's rail, longing to see her, and instantly brightened, spying two figures approaching the side of the ship, one with golden hair that danced in the breeze. Every day she walked with her aunt and uncle, but today the countess was missing; only the watchful count was by her side. The countess was probably not feeling well, he thought; she had been sick most of the journey.

Hernando watched Isabella and the count stop at a point on the deck where they were alone, and stand very close together at the rail. The count seemed to be upset with Isabella; he gestured forcefully with his hands and his mouth moved rapidly, as if spitting harsh words. Isabella listened with her head down, as if she was afraid to look at the count. The count reached out and touched Isabella's cheek; she pulled away. Hernando tensed, wanting to rush to her aid. The count stormed off, leaving her at the railing. Isabella looked after him, her expression twisted as if she was crying. Then she looked toward the shore and wiped her eyes.

"Sir."

Hernando dragged his eyes from the small figure on the *Alva Cordova* and turned reluctantly toward the two soldiers who stopped a few feet from him and saluted.

"The sergeant says we'll be loaded by nightfall and we can make the morning tide."

Hernando returned the salute. "Thank you." He looked back to the ship. Isabella had been rejoined by the count, and they were leaving the deck. Isabella glanced back over her shoulder and Hernando's heart leapt. When the count stopped and turned to see what she was looking at, Hernando whirled and walked up the beach to where Wells was doling out orders, fighting the urge to look back.

"Sergeant!" he called.

"Yes, sir?" Wells hurried over to Hernando.

Hernando stopped with his back to the ocean. "Who is on deck?"

The sergeant peered around him. "Sailors, sir."

"Anyone else?" he barked.

Wells looked again, taking the time to squint, in case this was some kind of test. He straightened. "No, sir."

Hernando turned to look for himself, starting to feel like a schoolboy with his hand caught in the cookie jar. "This is ridiculous," he scoffed, and stomped past Wells toward the soldiers who were packing the last of the treasure into crates.

"Do you want me to fetch your helmet, Commander?" Wells called after him.

Hernando stopped and looked blankly at Wells.

"I fear the hot sun might be playing tricks on you," Wells said solemnly, then smirked.

Hernando lightened up. "Maybe so, Sergeant, maybe so." He wiped the sweat from his brow.

*   *   *   *

That night at dinner aboard the *Alva Cordova*, the count made apologies for his wife's absence as he sat down beside his niece. Hernando tried not to look too long in Isabella's direction, but it was hard. More than once he felt the count's stare on him.

Captain Menindez was jubilant at the prospect of sailing with the morning tide. He brought out his best brandy after the meal and he and the count drank their fill. Hernando stole more glances at Isabella as the two older men toasted just about every thing under the sun, with voices that grew increasingly slurred.

Isabella raised her glass of wine to her lips to hide the smile she cast his way. Forgetting himself, Hernando smiled back. Seeing that, the count's mood changed so abruptly that even the captain noticed.

"Is something wrong?" the captain asked, trying to pour another drink.

The count put his hand over the glass to stop the pour. "I'm worried about the countess," he said. "We should get back. Excuse us, Captain; it's been an enjoyable evening." He rose, shook the captain's hand, and seemed to push Isabella out the door before him.

Later Hernando lay on his bunk with the lamp still burning. He closed his eyes in thought, trying to figure out the count's relationship with Isabella. He did act like a jealous husband, as the officers had said. *Like a man who knows his wife is so pretty that every man desires her,* Hernando mused, a*nd he's worried that he is not man enough to keep her.*

At some point Hernando slipped off to sleep, only to be awakened by a quiet knock on his door. Hernando thought he was dreaming, until the soft rap came again. He rose and opened the cabin door.

The flickering lamplight illuminated Isabella. Her eyes were red and puffy from crying and a nasty welt was reddening her cheek. She moved quickly into his arms. He closed the door and guided her over to his bunk to sit down. She leaned against his chest, sobbing quietly.

"My uncle beat me for looking at you," she said.

He hugged her, trying to offer comfort, and she jumped in pain. "Isabella, what has he done?"

She turned away from him as if ashamed, and through the gaping back of her nightgown he saw the angry red welts from a belt laid across her back and shoulders. "This is outrageous!" Hernando's anger forced him to his feet. "I'll show that old bastard what it is like to be whipped!"

He turned to make for the door, but Isabella grabbed him from behind. "No! Please, stay with me. My uncle has passed out from the brandy. This may be our only chance to be together."

Hernando sat back down beside her and she brought her warm lips to his. He was not ready for her advance, and pulled away. She started to cry again. "You don't want me now," she sobbed. "You think I'm bad for coming here."

"No, no ... I was just surprised, that's all. I'm glad you're here." Hernando held her close. He raised her chin with his fingers and placed a kiss on her lips. She did not open her mouth to him, and Hernando reminded himself that she was inexperienced. He caressed her neck and shoulders, soothing her with his hands.

A small moan escaped her lips and her eyes flew open, as if she were surprised at her reaction to his touch. Then she relaxed and lay back on his bunk, pulling him on top of her. He kissed her, lingering on her lips. She smelled of berries and citrus. Intoxicated by her overpowering scent, he nuzzled her golden hair, then slid his hand under her back, lifting her waist. She arched her back like a cat, and Hernando felt her heavy breasts against his chest. He probed her mouth with his tongue. She reacted by pushing her pelvis against him.

Slipping her nightgown up over her thighs, Hernando slipped his hand under her plump buttock and pulled her even closer. Then he rolled over, drawing her on top of him, and pulled the nightgown over her head and off. Her long hair hung like a curtain around his face. He could smell the sweet citrus of it and under that, the damp musk of her readiness. She kissed him deeply, then moved back to untie his breeches and pull them down his legs, freeing his stiff member. She cooed at the sight of it and gently held it in her hands, as if fearful she would break it if she were not careful.

Hernando struggled with his shirt and Isabella helped him with it. She rode up on his chest as she pulled the shirt over his head, and Hernando seized her buttocks and pulled her to his mouth. She sat full on his face and giggled at the first touch of his tongue. At first unsure of what to do, she soon relaxed with his silent coaxing, holding onto the bulkhead and rocking her hips, overwhelmed by sensation.

Hernando gently lifted her off and lay her on the bunk while he drew several deep breaths. She looked disappointed that he had stopped, and covered herself shyly with her hands as Hernando looked at her. But she spread her legs to Hernando's touch as he slid on top of her, kissing his way to her face, only pausing at her perky nipple.

She looked into his eyes. "I have never been with a man before," she said, inflaming Hernando even more.

He parted her as gently as possible. She made a deep sucking noise through her gritted teeth and Hernando paused, but she smiled and pulled him into her with her ankles on the firm flesh of his buttocks. He moved slowly and gently, and the night passed in that manner.

Hernando awoke to the sound of Laocan's voice.

"She is very pretty," Laocan observed from the side of the bed. "Prettier than me, I fear. Be careful, my green-eyed god; all is not what it seems."

When the watch bell next woke Hernando, both Laocan and Isabella were gone. He splashed water on his face and inhaled the faint scent of Isabella's perfume that still hung in the air. He smiled into the mirror as he shaved.

He joined everyone on deck to wave good-bye to shore, as was the custom. Isabella stared straight ahead, not looking his way, but he saw the flush in her cheeks. *The lack of a night's sleep has not hindered her beauty,* he thought. The countess, on the other hand, looked like one of the skeletons carved on all the Aztec temples. Her cheeks and eyes were sunken into her head and she looked pale, even through her abundant makeup.

The soldiers on shore fired a one-gun salute, and the captain ordered the *Alva Cordova* out to sea. Slowly she turned on the wind, following her two companions, both more maneuverable than the heavily laden galleon. Hernando watched Vera Cruz become smaller and smaller until only the crew remained on deck. Then he turned away from the rail, saddened by the thought of leaving this rich coast, but he knew he had to reinstate his father's good name, and that he could only do in Spain.

The next morning Hernando was back at the rail, waiting for Isabella. When she came they embraced, and he felt her body respond to his caresses. For many weeks they met like this, until she was again able to sneak away to his quarters to be with him. Each time was more intense than the last. Hernando was happy, and cared little that the voyage was lengthy. He forgot all his duties and neglected the men, focused only on how he could spend more time with Isabella.

"I'm going to ask your uncle for your hand in marriage," he blurted during one predawn rendezvous. His announcement met silence, and Hernando strained to see if she was smiling in the darkness. But she was not; in fact, she looked fearful. "The count would never agree to it, my dearest," she whispered in his ear as she threw her arms around his shoulders.

"Let me worry about the count," Hernando suggested, but Isabella became agitated.

"No, Hernando! If the count had any idea of our early morning trysts, he would become enraged and violent. He will never agree to marriage. Promise me you will not say anything to the count."

"But—"

Isabella cut him off. "Promise you won't say anything until we get to Spain—promise!"

Surprised by her response, Hernando put it down to fear of her uncle. He promised, and Isabella immediately showed relief that their secret would remain theirs. Changing the subject, Hernando asked how the countess was doing.

Again Isabella became upset, though she tried to hide it. "She is much better these days," she answered, but she seemed annoyed by his questions and pushed her lips against his when he made to speak again. Hernando gave in, his passion being stronger than his curiosity.

Hernando was surprised when the countess passed away a few days later.

Wells leaned in close during the ceremony preceding her burial at sea. "That little missy will have some trouble with that old goat now, I'll wager."

Hernando looked across the canvas-wrapped body to her surviving family. Isabella was obviously distraught, her tear-filled eyes fixed on the body of her aunt. The count, on the other hand, was stone-faced. Hernando looked into his eyes as the count passed his gaze over the officers, and saw no emotion whatsoever.

When Isabella did not appear for their early morning tryst the next day, Hernando was concerned; when she missed the next one, he approached her at dinner that night.

"Where have you been? I've missed you," he whispered to her.

"Are you crazy? The count will see you!" she hissed, looking over her shoulder at the count, who was taking his seat at the table.

"I don't care," Hernando retorted. "What's the matter? Come to me tonight. I need to see you."

"I can't, the count will find out!" she blurted.

"Isabella, please," Hernando begged.

"I'll try," she said, but she didn't sound sincere. Hernando suspected she was merely trying to put an end to the conversation.

She walked to her seat and Hernando to his, but the count had seen the exchange, as had most everyone. The count glared at Hernando all through dinner; Hernando hotly returned the looks with equal distaste. Immediately after the meal, the count and Isabella left the table without saying their good nights.

Captain Menindez turned to Hernando, who continued staring at the door long after they had left. "Be careful, Commander. You may have friends back at court, but they will be unable to save your career if the count takes a dislike to you."

"It's not my future that concerns me," Hernando replied. "It's the well-being of the young lady that worries me."

Menindez acknowledged the truth in Hernando's voice with a nod, and added, "If it came to it, I do not believe the count would meet you on the field of honour." He leaned closer to Hernando, as if the count would hear. "His style is more the hired ruffian placing a dirk between your shoulder blades."

Hernando was surprised by the captain's concern. "I will take what you say to heart," he said, then rose from the table and left.

He paused at the count's door, ready to go to Isabella's rescue if he heard a strap being laid across her tender young back, but all was quiet inside. Hernando moved on to his own quarters. He lay awake all night waiting for her, but she didn't come.

Bleary eyed, he went on deck to await the first kiss of morning light from the sun god. He thought of Laocan and asked her in his mind, *What should I do?* She did not answer. *She has abandoned me*, her thought bleakly.

Soon they would turn on the trade winds and be carried across the Atlantic and on to Spain. Hernando lingered all morning on deck, deep in thought. The sun was high in the sky when the count and his charge came on deck. Hernando made his way to them.

"Miss Morales; Count," he greeted them. Isabella's face was flushed with anxiety.

"Go for a little stroll, my dear," the count told her. "I would like to speak to the Commander alone." Isabella turned on his command and moved a small distance away to stand watching as the count turned back to Hernando. "Now, sir, I do not know what your game is, and I understand you may be attracted to her beauty, but I can assure you she has no interest in you. In fact, she is betrothed to another. I tell you this to save you from embarrassment, as your advances will be rejected."

"Thank you for your concern," Hernando said stiffly, "but there is no game and my feelings for your niece are genuine. I intend to ask for her hand in marriage when we reach Spain."

"Impossible," the count snapped. "I've already told you that she is spoken for!" He raised his voice. "I must ask you to have no further contact with my ward, or I will be forced to speak to the captain about your reprehensible behaviour."

Hernando's blood was also heating up. "Let me assure you that the captain has no say over my behaviour!"

"Sail ho!" the sailor in the crow's nest shouted, his voice carrying on the blustery wind and inadvertently breaking the tension between the two men.

Hernando looked up and the count hurried to gather up his charge and head for safety belowdecks.

"Sails portside!" the lookout continued, pointing and looking to the bridge.

The first mate called general quarters. The captain hurried to the helm. "What is it, Mr. Higuero?" he demanded.

"Three ships bearing down on us, sir!" The first mate handed the captain his brass telescope, adding, "Not showing their colours, sir."

"Rig for battle, Mr. Higuero; sound the alarm."

"We going to see some action, sir?" Wells asked, sidling up to Hernando's side. He squinted into the distance, trying to see the oncoming trouble.

Hernando didn't answer. He was looking to see if Isabella was still on deck. He glimpsed her disappearing down the stairs after the count and turned back toward the oncoming ships, instinctively feeling for his sword.

"Run out the colours, Mr. Higuero," the captain ordered.

"Aye, Captain!" As Higuero barked the order, the long white standard emblazoned with a large red cross was unfurled. Mr. Higuero lifted his telescope to his eye, then lowered it. "No reply, sir."

"Signal the escort ships," Menindez said. "Battle plan beta—we'll see if they have the stomach for sailing between two broadsides."

"Aye, Captain." Higuero shouted orders to a signalman, who waved small flags that resembled a butterfly caught in a strong wind, desperately trying to make headway. The two smaller ships stood off the sides of the *Alva Cordova*, just out of range of her big guns.

"Run out the cannon, Mr. Higuero; let's let them see what they're up against."

Hernando heard the gun carriages rumble as the guns poked their muzzles out into the daylight. He had donned his half-armour and loaded his pistols. Wells was by his side, grinning. He reminded Hernando of the Toltecs, which made him smile himself.

"That's the spirit, Commander," Wells joked as he took his helmet from under his arm and plunked it on his large head.

"They've run up their colours, sir," Higuero stated, as if everyone couldn't see the English flags unfurling as the ships bore down on them.

Hernando realized immediately that it wasn't the Royal Navy, for there was a golden lion emblazoned in the middle of the flag.

"Privateers, sir!" Higuero announced. "Must have been lying in wait for us to make our Atlantic crossing."

The three barques were a sleek black with freshly painted white trim. Their guns were run out. Mr. Higuero continued to state the obvious. "They mean to run the gauntlet, sir." He looked to the captain for orders.

"Steady as she goes, Mr. Higuero."

As the six ships headed on what seemed like a collision course, silence fell on the bridge. The enemy ships drew so close that Hernando could see the English sailors' faces. They were whooping and taunting, waving their cutlasses in the air or swinging grappling hooks over their heads. Hernando had never seen pirates, but they fit every description he had ever heard—wild and crazed with the idea of taking a big prize like the *Alva Cordova*.

At the last possible second, the three barques cut across the outside of the eastern escort ship, passing so close, Hernando thought they had collided. Their cannons blazed, levelling three full broadsides at the smaller ship. The balls and shot tore through the wooden vessel as if it were made of balsa wood. Splinters and smoke combined with the smoldering rigging to cover the deck in chaos. Unable to muster a second volley, the escort ship quickly fell behind the *Alva Cordova*.

"Bring her about, Mr. Higuero!" Menindez ordered.

The winds spilled out of the sails as the helmsman spun the wheel and the great rudder slowly turned the ponderous ship. The second escort ship had already returned to hover over its wounded sister, but the privateers had also turned and were descending on the two ships like vultures looking for supper.

The second escort ship had fired too soon and most of its shot fell short, bursting into huge geysers of foaming water, but with little effect on the barques. They returned fire and strafed the little ship's decks with grapeshot. It was obvious they wanted to take them for prizes, not sink them. As the *Alva Cordova* rounded on the barques, they cut behind the wounded ships, putting the crippled vessels between them and the *Alva Cordova*. Very few of the guns answered the three barques' fire as they passed by.

"Turn into the wind, Mr. Higuero!" Captain Menindez shouted, furious that he couldn't get a shot at the English privateers.

"Sir?"

"Turn into the wind, I said!"

Higuero called the order. The great ship lost its wind and slowed as it came about. It was now in a position to meet the oncoming barques, but it had no speed. The first barque was upon her, but misjudged the speed and size of the *Alva Cordova*. Most of the shot passed harmlessly over their heads, tearing a few holes in the sails but doing no major damage. The *Alva Cordova* returned fire with three guns to every one of the barque's, and they were loaded with ball, not shot, for maximum damage. The barrage tore a large hole just above the waterline, and as the barque turned, she took on water and listed quickly.

The captain had fired all of his cannons at the first barque with the intention of quickly taking her out of the fight, but now the *Alva Cordova* was unable to return fire on the next two barques. Hernando knew that the captain was gambling that their cannons were still loaded with grapeshot, and that they would not risk sinking the galleon with her great treasure aboard.

The pirates' greed kept the cannons strafing the deck of the *Alva Cordova*, but the thick Spanish oak planking took the shot with little damage, and the crew was ordered to lay flat on the deck as the shot warmed the air above their bodies.

The third barque nudged the *Alva Cordova* and sent grappling hooks over her rails. The pirates climbed the manila ropes like the monkeys Hernando had seen around the jungles of Vera Cruz, but they had seriously misjudged the amount of damage they had wrought on the crew of the big ship. As they scaled the ropes, the Spanish sailors stuck them with pike poles as if they were spearing sardines in a barrel.

The other barque had turned and was making to board the *Alva Cordova* from the stern, where she would be out of gun range as she closed. Captain Menindez watched his men repelling the boarders. "Full volley into the barque, Mr. Higuero."

A great roll of gunfire erupted into the ship snugged against the *Alva Cordova*, and huge chunks of ship turned into deadly flying splinters. What fire, heat, and shot didn't destroy, the splinters did. The barque canted slightly as she took on water. Hernando, moving forward to fend off the boarders, felt the galleon's deck tilt beneath his feet.

"Cut those ropes, Mr. Higuero, and bring her about!"

Axes fell on the taut lines holding the listing barque to the *Alva Cordova*, each blow sounding like a musket shot as it struck the straining ropes. Hernando's great sword slashed into the pirates scrambling aboard as the last of the grappling ropes were cut. He stumbled, but kept his feet as the galleon rocked to an even keel and her sails filled with wind. He was fortunate; most of the crew were knocked to the deck.

A musket ball grazed Hernando's helmet and careened off with a scream. Hernando whirled in the direction of the shot in time to see a telltale puff of smoke and the count, recovering from the jolt of the freed ship. *He tried to kill me!* Hernando realized, and his anger flared. Lifting the blade of his ancestors over his head, he charged forward.

"What are you doing? Are you mad?" the count screamed, eyeing the deadly length of steel glinting in the sunlight as he backed away quickly.

"You tried to kill me, you coward!" Hernando shouted, levelling his sword at the count's face.

"No, no, my pistol accidentally discharged—that's all! I'm sorry."

Hernando stopped his advance. *It could be true,* he admitted to himself, but he knew better.

Captain Menindez was shouting orders and the *Alva Cordova* was bringing her guns to bear on the last sleek barque. But the barque turned and cut close to the great ship's stern, firing her cannons. Grapeshot cut down those Spaniards and Englishmen still fighting hand to hand on the deck. Some of the barque's cannons had been reloaded with ball, and did some damage to the stern as she passed.

Hernando could see her captain, blonde hair trailing in the wind and his matching blonde beard tied in braids with red ribbon. He smiled and executed a mock salute to Hernando, standing at the *Alva Cordova*'s rail, as his snipers took aim from the barque's rigging. Seconds later, musketfire ripped the air, dropping men around Hernando, but he stood his ground as everyone around him dove for cover, eyes on the watching captain.

The barque leaned into the wind and made away from the *Alva Cordova*. The heavily laden galleon had no chance of catching the faster ship. "Take us back to the escort ships, Mr. Higuero!" the captain ordered.

Hernando watched as the distance grew between the two ships, and then realized that some of the damage in the stern would be in the cabins belowdecks. He rushed below to see if Isabella was all right.

The door was locked. Hernando kicked it open, then froze. Isabella lay on the bed, her bodice undone. The count lay on top of her, his hands on her heavy breasts.

The count jumped up, his face red with anger. "How dare you enter my private rooms!"

Isabella tried to cover her breasts, lowering her eyes in embarrassment. Hernando stood open-mouthed for several seconds, then found words. "You pig! Touching your own niece."

"She's not my niece—she's my lover!" the count blurted. "We will be married when we reach Spain."

Hernando looked to Isabella for a denial, but she lowered her head and began to cry, her sobs making her breasts bob in her arms as she tried to hide herself from him. Hernando backed out of the room, his heart torn from his chest. He went back on deck and wandered numbly amongst the dead and wounded. When he saw the ship's surgeon cleaning gashes and sewing them up, he offered to help.

One sailor was beyond repair, for he had taken grape through his stomach and was bleeding into his bowels; his lower stomach was distended and inflamed. Hernando mopped his brow as if giving comfort to another could somehow take away his own pain.

The *Alva Cordova* took aboard the crew of the sinking escort ship and sent men to help make repairs to the other. As the small ship took on more water she rolled to one side, her shattered rigging lying in the swell. The air escaped from belowdecks with a great hissing and gurgling. The crew stood solemnly at the rail. As they watched, two great leviathans of the deep surfaced near the groaning ship. They turned on their side to swivel one great eye at the men on the rail and breached high into the salt air. As the ship finally slipped below the surface, the two great grey beasts followed her down. Only bubbles marked the spot where she'd sunk. The other debris had already been scattered by the waves. The men were somber as they went about their duties for the rest of the day.

Hernando skipped supper that evening and lay awake in his bunk for most of the night. He did not go on deck before dawn, as was his custom. He followed this pattern for the following week, with Wells occasionally knocking on his door only to be shooed away like a bothersome fly. Wells started leaving dinner outside his door.

Hernando roused himself on the eighth day, moving stiffly in deference to a body that ached from inactivity. He found Wells and they sparred on the deck with the ship's cutlasses. No one paid much attention, except for the young Isabella, whose head turned his way as she walked the deck with the count.

Hernando was pressing an attack on Wells, working up a sweat on both of them. Wells countered gamely, but finally protested taking the brunt of Hernando's frustrations. "You know, Commander, if you cut me you'll have to sew me up," he said as he parried a thrust.

Hernando relaxed a little and even managed a smile. He looked past Wells to Isabella and was almost cleaved in two by Wells' sword. At the last possible second Wells pulled up his arm to prevent contact as Hernando ducked the slice.

"What are you doing, Wells? You could have killed me!" Hernando exclaimed, stumbling back a step.

"Usually in a duel, your opponent pays heed to what's happening." Wells turned and saw who Hernando was looking at. "Something that pretty can only be trouble, sir," Wells warned, turning back to his opponent. "I take it you're finished for the day."

Hernando twisted the cutlass loose from Wells' hand and flung it high into the air. Wells ducked; it stuck into the deck at his feet. "I think so," Hernando said, handing Wells the other sword hilt-first before walking to the stern of the ship. He stared at the water sliding past the ship's hull. The Atlantic was as still and dark as Hernando's mood.

The ship's boy approached. "A message, sir," he said timorously, and handed him a small scrap of paper, folded in half. He turned and scampered off.

Hernando unfolded the paper and saw *Please meet me at dawn*. Crumpling the scrap, he threw it into the wake of the *Alva Cordova*.

He lay awake late into the night. When he drifted off, he dreamt of Toltecs and sacrifices and of Laocan's sweet face. She did not speak to him, only placed a small kiss on his lips. He awoke as the first grey light of dawn appeared, and made his way on deck.

Isabella was waiting in the shadows. She tried to hug him, but he held her away from him. She leaned as close as she could and whispered, "I'm so sorry, Hernando."

"What's going on?" Hernando demanded. "Is what the count said true?" His ears longed to hear a denial, but it did not come.

She gazed at him with agonized eyes. "How can I possibly explain to you, to make you understand?"

"You said you'd never been with another man." Hernando shook his head slightly, as if trying to free some understanding from the dark corners of his mind.

Isabella pulled herself closer, so their bodies made contact. "That's true. But he made me do other things before his wife died, and then after, he wanted more. I tried to refuse, but ..."

Hernando felt her breast rubbing against him and pulled her close. "I don't care," he murmured. "I love you; you will move into my quarters. I will—"

"I can't!" she protested. "What will people say? What about my debt?"

"I am a rich man," he told her. "I will pay what your family owes."

She looked into his face for a moment, her expression uncertain. "You are sweet, but ... The count would make our lives very unpleasant. He is very powerful."

Hernando began to reassure her, but her expression shifted and she looked quickly away, as if to hide it. "My uncle has not tried anything since you broke in," she said, her voice strangely neutral. "He says he'll wait until we are married in Spain."

The sound of the word "uncle" made Hernando cringe. The thought of the count doing things to sweet Isabella made him cringe. But he was hopelessly in love and needed desperately to be with her, so he listened to his heart and not his mind.

In the last few weeks of the crossing, they resumed their early morning affair. Every day Hernando would think about the count and Isabella together and every day he would build up the nerve to tell her it was over. The next morning she would press her plump breasts into him and he would forget everything except the feel of her soft body, and another day would pass.

When the lookout sighted land just before noon one day, excitement lightened the atmosphere on deck as the crew's thoughts turned to home. Nevertheless, they were still in dangerous waters prowled by both English and French ships that would set upon the *Alva Cordova* like a pack of dogs worrying a cornered boar. The officers were tense, looking often to the crow's nest to see if the sailor perched in the canvas bag was awake and minding his duty as the eyes of the ship.

When the lookout cried, "Sail ho!" general quarters were sounded and the crew rushed to their positions as if they'd been awaiting the warning. Mr. Higuero was squinting thought the telescope when the captain asked what she was.

Higuero turned to the captain with a great sign of relief. "She's Spanish, sir."

Menindez studied the closing ship. "Run out the cannon, Mr. Higuero," he said.

The first mate looked puzzled and raised his telescope to peer at the oncoming ship with the crimson cross fluttering from the main mast.

"Mr. Higuero?" the captain prodded.

"Yes, sir." Higuero started shouting orders. The gun carriages rumbled forward and the gaping mouths of the 24-pounders poked from the gun ports.

Hernando came on deck in full armour. "What is it, Wells? English, French?"

"I'm not sure," Wells replied. "The ship is flying the cross, but the captain ran out the guns."

The sleek ship moved quickly through the water on a course that would intercept the much larger ship. With a start, Hernando recognized the little black barque with its white trim.

"Battle stations!" the captain yelled, also recognizing the pirate they had traded cannon fire with on the other side of the ocean.

The barque veered off without coming in range of the *Alva Cordova*'s cannons. As she cut through the waves, she raised the English flag with the golden lion and struck the red cross from her mast. The black barque's golden-haired captain stood at the railing, smiling at Hernando and Menindez. Hernando admired the boldness of the pirate and wished he was cutting away to the open sea with him, instead of heading for land and the task ahead of him.

"Stand down Mr. Higuero. A bold one, that one," the captain said as he left Hernando standing at the rail with his thoughts.

Wells, ever present, spoke up. "I'd like to cross swords with that man."

Hernando turned from the disappearing barque to look at Wells. "That pirate captain has the confidence that comes with being very skilled in the use of one's chosen weapon. Crossing swords with someone like that may not be a very good experience in life." He smiled at Wells and clapped his hand on his shoulder. "Come, I'd like to speak with you."

He led Wells to his little cabin below. Wells looked curiously at Hernando as he sat on the sea chest. Hernando also studied the man he'd come to think of more as a friend than someone merely under his command. He knew Wells would obey without question any order Hernando gave him, but more than that, he trusted this man who had proven his loyalty many times over on this journey. He had decided to share his secret with Wells, for he would need his help in the coming months.

They talked for hours. Most of the conversation focused on Hernando's life, with him explaining his father's demise and the confiscation of their lands. Wells listened intently, his face showing compassion at the telling of Juan Calsonia's torture and death.

When Hernando had finished he looked at Wells for a response. Wells, being more at home in the midst of a good brawl, undid his half-armour and reached inside his jacket. He drew out a little leather folder and a flask of whiskey and placed them on the small writing desk, the only other piece of furniture in the cabin. Hernando smiled and lifted two small pewter cups from the wall, where they'd been hanging on a nail.

Wells filled the cups with the golden liquid and lifted his. "To your father! May God give rest to his soul," he said solemnly.

Hernando lifted his cup, and they drank. Hernando grimaced at the harshness of the beverage, then watched as Wells opened up his leather folder. Inside were two small painted portraits. Wells took a moment to look fondly at the pictures, then passed them to Hernando.

"My father was killed in a duel with my mother's brother," he said. "My mother's family has disowned her for marrying my father. I would like to visit my mother when I get back on land."

Hernando looked at the portraits. The woman was a beautiful Spanish lady who exuded an air of nobility, unlike the man, who was quite obviously very common. "Your uncle killed your father in a duel?" Hernando questioned, looking up at Wells.

Wells was pouring another round of whiskey. "It's a long story," he sighed as he passed the pewter cup to Hernando. "My mother was a countess and her family was not happy at all about her marriage. It got worse over the years. I was eight when it happened."

Hernando felt sympathy for Wells, but he also felt that he was no longer alone, that Wells' history was so similar to his own that they were tied like brothers to their horrible pasts.

The acrid brown liquid seemed to go down easier. They finished it off together.

Chapter 15

The next morning the *Alva Cordova* made port. The piers were alive with activity. People pushed and crowded the gangways, loading and unloading ships of every description: merchantmen and man-of-wars and dhows from the African coast. Spain was cut off from the rest of the Christian world, and found her supplies wherever she could.

Hernando thought about the Arabs who unloaded supplies to further Spain's war efforts against the English and French. They were not allies as such, just opportunistic merchants filling orders for a besieged nation and an almost bankrupt court. Cortez's treasure was about to change all that.

Hernando sent a carefully worded letter to the Duke of Aragon. As he applied his family seal to the red wax, he thought about all that he had been through in the last couple of years, and he thought about his mother, who was at the duke's home in the country. His thoughts made him smile as he handed the message to the courier. "This letter must be placed in the hand of the duke alone!" he warned. "All speed."

"Yes, sir." The young man beamed as Hernando flipped a gold coin in his direction. It was more than the man could make in three months. "Yes, sir!" he exclaimed as he snatched it from the air.

* * * *

Rosa Diaz entered the drawing room as the duke was dismissing a messenger with a few small coins. Her brother smiled as she curtseyed to him.

"It seems we will soon have a guest at the estate," he said.

She queried who, not daring to hope that her youngest son had returned from the New World.

"Yes, Hernando has returned safe from the Indies," he assured her, and his smile broadened as her eyes welled with tears of joy. "We will go to the city in the morning and see if we can't get your son to expand on this letter of his." He passed the parchment to her.

She smiled as she recognized the handwriting. "It says Cortez has captured a rich country for the king and he needs an audience with you as soon as possible," she said, scanning the document. Her heart sank a bit at how formal the letter was, and that he made no mention of her. She placed a hand to her forehead and told herself to be practical. *This is a formal letter to Hernando's patron,* she thought. He had no way of knowing she would be reading it. But like all mothers, she looked for some mention of her name in the letter. Finally, satisfied that he had returned in one piece, she folded the letter and pressed it to her bosom.

Enrique was about to reach for the letter but withdrew his hand when he saw how tightly she had it pressed to her heart. "We should retire; we'll have to get an early start if we want to be the first to welcome Hernando back to Spain."

Rosa was full of questions, but she knew Enrique had no more news; she inclined her head, wished him a good night, and retired for the evening.

* * * *

The Duke of Aragon watched his sister leave, then called a servant to wake his secretary. He dictated letters to his friends in the court and an official letter to the king, requesting an audience and telling him it was an emergency and a matter of national security. He knew that if he came at the king from different angles, he was sure to get an audience.

"They must be delivered into the hands of the men to whom they are addressed, tonight!" he said as he placed his seal on the letters. "Wake whoever you must to get this done."

When the secretary left him alone by the smoldering fire, he sat back and raised his glass of port, saluting himself. He sensed that his life would never be the same. Just maybe, he thought, he would have a hand in changing Spain's destiny.

* * * *

As the servants bustled about the next morning, Rosa applied rouge and powder to hide her sleepless night. The duke's personal servant had come to hurry her along. She sensed great excitement in the estate, which had obviously filtered down from her and Enrique and infected the whole household.

They skipped a formal breakfast, but nibbled on cold meats and pastries as the carriage sped toward the city. Normally a large escort and a retinue of servants would be accompanying them, but they had left them behind to catch up as best they could.

"The letter was quite vague as to what Hernando has found in the New World," Rosa said.

"These are difficult times, my dear," Enrique reminded her. "Hernando knows better than to trust too many words to a letter."

The carriage lurched to one side as a wheel dropped into a pothole. Rosa caught herself on the padded side panel and waited for Enrique to say more, but he remained silent, though she sensed his cautious excitement. "What is it, my brother? Why are you so quiet on this journey?"

He looked at her but delayed his answer by removing his wide-brimmed hat. She sat looking at him, trying to decipher the expression on his face. He knew she was not a woman for whom the affairs of state were of no concern.

"It's funny," she observed. "You look exactly as you did so many years ago, on the night of your wedding to that much-too-young wife of yours; you look as if you are about to pick a ripe cherry." She felt her cheeks flush at what she had said, but it worked; Enrique stared at her for a second, then burst into laughter. She joined him. It had been so long since laughter had been part of their family.

* * * *

Hernando and Wells had breakfast together, and between bites Hernando laid out a plan of action for them to follow.

"We must get to the duke and explain what we have found. He will know best how to proceed. I want you to put your best men on the treasure. I don't want any of it to go astray."

"You have my word on that, sir," Wells assured him.

Hernando nodded, savouring a bite of fresh poached egg and fried pork. Wells stopped chewing long enough to comment on the hard, maggoty biscuits they'd eaten for months aboard ship.

"After you check on Cortez's treasure, I want you to find out where the count and his niece have disappeared to," Hernando continued.

"Sir, we really don't have time—" Wells began.

"Please, Wells, do this for me!" Hernando almost pleaded.

His tone seemed to unsettle Wells. "I'll find them for you, don't you worry about that, sir," he said quietly.

"Thanks, Wells. You look after that for me, and I'll attend to the Duke of Aragon."

* * * *

The commander will be famous when the king rewards him for bringing the gold back from the Indies, Wells thought as he trudged back to the pier, which was not very far from the pub where they had eaten. *He could have any woman he wants, but he pines after that whore.*

"What news, Master Sergeant?" One of the guards called as he approached.

Wells scanned the docks, scrutinizing every dark alley. He turned back to them in time to see the amused look they exchanged. "What?" The guards shifted uncomfortably. "Come on, out with it!" Wells snapped.

"Well ..." After a glance at his fellow, the first guard blurted, "You look as though you're expecting to be jumped by Aztecs at any moment, sir."

Wells allowed a smile. "Any action on the dock this morn?"

"Just the count and his niece," the vocal guard replied. "Won't be sorry to never cross paths with that one again!"

"They hailed a carriage from up the street," the other guard said, sensing Wells' interest. He jerked a thumb toward a hire stand, where several carriages were lined up along one side of the road.

Wells set extra guards and checked on his men, most of whom had big heads after a night of revelry. Then he walked up the street to talk to the carriage drivers. The driver who had carried the count had not returned yet, but he would; the count's luggage still awaited delivery. Wells nodded a curt thank you and went back to securing the docks, all the while muttering about Hernando's intentions for the count's niece.

An hour later, Wells followed the carriage carrying the count's luggage to two luxurious apartments in "the fancy part of town," as the driver of his cab called it.

He spent the balance of the morning and the early afternoon standing on a street corner, wondering why he was there at all. He'd only seen the count's niece throwing open the heavy brocade curtains in an upper window, and a group of nattily dressed men who had arrived and left again shortly afterward, about an hour ago. As the sun moved across the sky, his anger grew. "I'm leaving," he muttered. "This is no work for me!"

As he turned to leave, a cab came down the street, pulled up before the apartments, and waited. *Seems he's clomped onto the count's money chest,* Wells thought, recognizing the driver. He stepped back into the shadows of a doorway as the count and another gentleman exited the apartment and climbed into the carriage. It moved off at a brisk pace, and Wells decided he'd seen enough. He returned to the inn to give his report to Hernando.

* * * *

Time seemed to trickle by as Hernando waited for the duke to arrive at the inn he'd named as their meeting place. He looked about at the other patrons of the port-side pub. *Assorted lowlifes,* he thought, turning his gaze back to his cup of strong black coffee. But when he again absently scanned the pub, two of the uglier patrons were again eyeballing him. *Just paranoia,* he told himself, and finished his coffee.

When the Duke of Aragon strode into the room, Hernando smiled. The barrel-chested aristocrat's bearing commanded attention from the ragged crowd he passed through. *What a magnificent sight,* he thought with some relief as he rose to take his uncle's hand and incline his head respectfully. His smile widened as he straightened and his gaze shifted to the lovely woman who followed close on the older man's heels.

His mother's eyes welled up with tears and she pushed by the duke, almost knocking him down in her haste to throw her arms around Hernando's neck. As she buried her face in his chest, Hernando and the duke exchanged a helpless glance, both caught off guard by the depth of her emotion. Hernando hugged her tightly until she at last murmured an apology for her public display and released him.

The duke settled his sister into a chair, sat down next to her, and pointed to Hernando's chair. "Sit, my son. How are you?" he asked, but didn't give Hernando a chance to reply before urging, "Tell us of your adventures."

Hernando's mother leaned forward as if wanting to ask her own questions, but then sat back as the count asked, "Did you find Cortez?"

"Yes!" Hernando blurted before he was interrupted by any more questions. "Cortez ..." Hernando paused, not for effect, but to search for the right words. "Is loyal to the crown."

The duke blew out a relieved sigh and leaned back in his chair, a small smile creeping across his face. Then he leaned forward to whisper, "Is it true about the treasure?"

"More than anyone could possibly imagine," Hernando said with a slow smile.

The duke slapped his great hand on the tabletop. "I knew it!" he crowed. The other patrons looked in their direction.

Realizing that this wasn't the best place to go into details, Hernando rose and said, "Come, let's walk."

They left the pub. Wells, who must have arrived after the duke's carriage had rolled up to the inn, stepped up beside Hernando as they walked toward the docks. Hernando slowed so that the duke could take his mother's arm, and Wells whispered in his ear, "You're attracting attention." He nodded over his shoulder.

Hernando cast a surreptitious glance behind them and saw two men following, their eyes intent on the group. He instinctively reached for the hilt of his sword, but the duke caught the movement and said, "Actually, they are mine!"

Hernando blinked in disbelief, then smiled. His uncle had been watching over him since he'd learned of Hernando's arrival in port.

"Just a couple of ruffians I use from time to time," the duke said, waving a casual hand. "They are as loyal as the pay is good!" He laughed at his own joke, and Hernando joined in.

His mother again took his arm. "It is good to see you happy," she murmured.

"It's good to be home," Hernando replied, squeezing the hand resting on his arm.

When they were challenged at the *Alva Cordova*'s gangway, Wells stepped forward with an authoritative air and bellowed, "Get out of the way before I turn you on your ear!" but Hernando caught the smile he flashed at the guards as he passed by them and they offered a mock salute. Behind the duke, Hernando broke into a grin and almost chuckled as Wells gave them a two-finger salute of his own.

The ship's captain waited at the railing to welcome his patron, looking anxious. "Captain Menindez," the duke said smoothly, heartily shaking his hand, "I hear you had a great and successful voyage!"

The captain glanced at Hernando. "I just ferry the men and goods, sir. This young man is responsible for what bulges our holds."

He knows who is related to who, Hernando thought as he watched Menindez buttering up the duke. "The captain is being modest," Hernando said in his best diplomatic tone. "We would not be here if he hadn't outsmarted the hungry pirate who traded cannonballs with us." The captain smiled his appreciation.

"Pirates?" Hernando's mother squealed. "Oh merciful God, I'm glad you're safe."

"I'm looking forward to the whole story," the duke said, "but can we see what all this fuss is about as you're telling us? And don't leave anything out!"

As the captain led the way below, Hernando's mother listened quietly as he recounted his adventures, while the duke often stopped him to demand details. But when Hernando got to the death of her eldest son, tears welled up in her eyes, and she asked questions about Ignatius' death and about his burial. *She truly loved him, even with his troubled soul,* Hernando thought. *She would embrace him now if he were here, despite his treachery and betrayal of our family.* He did not have the heart to tell her that there had been so little of Ignatius' body recovered that it seemed pointless to hold a proper burial. He welcomed their arrival and the captain's flourish as he bade them examine his cargo; it ended her uncomfortable questions.

The Duke of Aragon strode slowly forward, his expression one of awe, and lifted several golden samples, turning each over and over in his hands without really looking at them. His eyes glazed over with the implications of the treasure, and he heard little of what Hernando and his sister were saying.

When Hernando finally finished his story with more praise for Captain Menindez in outmaneuvering the pirates to bring them safely to Spain, the duke seized his forearm. "Hernando, you have saved Spain from certain catastrophe! Spain is bankrupt and the court is in disarray; there are traitors on all sides of the king. But with this ... Spain can be free of her debtors, build new cities, ships, armies—she could become a real world power. You and I, my son, will save her from her enemies!"

The duke turned and sped up the stairs to the deck. Hernando stared after him in surprise, then looked at the captain, who shrugged and quickly followed the duke. Hernando turned to his mother.

"Go, my son," she said, waving toward the steep stairs, "destiny awaits you."

"I think destiny can wait until I make sure the water rats don't make a meal out of you!" Hernando countered, taking her arm to help her up the first few stairs.

Then she paused. "Thank you, my gallant prince," she said, and blew him a kiss. They laughed. "Go," she said again.

Hernando burst into the sunlight and found the duke standing facing the open water of the bay, one hand holding onto the thick manila down rigging. Seeing him deep in thought, Hernando waited for him to speak.

"I must go to the king and you must guard this treasure with your life," the duke finally said. He turned to Hernando. "You have exceeded all of my expectations, young man. The king will be very thankful; I imagine you could ask for just about any reward."

Hernando smiled. The duke knew of Hernando's desire to reinstate his father's good name. "I must thank you for this opportunity you have given me—"

"Enough, enough," the duke jumped in. "Let's get to work!"

Hernando whirled. "Wells!"

"Yes, sir!" the sergeant replied from just behind him.

"Sweet Jesus, Wells, will you stop that?"

"Yes, sir!" Wells smiled unapologetically.

"Check the guard and call the duke's carriage," Hernando said.

"Aye, sir."

Hernando handed his mother into the carriage when it arrived and watched as the carriage moved away, feeling dazed. Was he really about to restore his family's name and lands? "Wells," he called softly.

"Yes, sir," Wells replied just as quietly at his elbow, making Hernando jump.

"Aw, crap! I'll never get used to that!" His pensive mood dispelled, Hernando ordered briskly, "Secure the dock, then take me to the count's lodgings."

Wells made a face but didn't argue. As he turned to see to his duties, Hernando thought of Laocan and wondered what she must think of him whimpering after the count's charge.

* * * *

Enrique, Duke of Aragon, had set up rooms at the best inn in town. When he and his sister arrived, Rosa hummed to herself as she laid out their belongings and joked with the servants, who had finally caught up to them. Enrique immediately settled at the writing desk and wrote then sent a flurry of letters.

A short time later, the duke started receiving his guests in the antechamber. All spoke in low voices, but the air grew heavy with excitement. The duke had ordered the rest of his own standing army to march on the port; the troops would be there in the morning. Until then, it was political maneuvering.

* * * *

Hernando and Wells stood just down the cobbled street from the apartment where the count had sequestered his niece. Ignoring Wells' fidgeting, Hernando stood staring up at an open window, hoping for a glimpse if Isabella.

The metal scrape of a sword slipping from its scabbard jarred Hernando back to reality; he turned, but too slowly. Wells, his own sword already drawn, dashed aside a cutlass slash to his head, but the four ruffians were on Hernando before he could draw his Saracen sword. He ducked under a blow, then kicked the attacker in the groin as the man's sword lodged in the door frame behind him. The man crumpled, his body delaying the second attacker long enough for Hernando to draw his sword. As the man swung his weapon in a slicing arc, the great Saracen sword cleaved the ruffian's sword arm and carried on through his neck to the middle of his chest. The attacker stood dumbfounded for a moment, not realizing he was dead.

Hernando glanced around. Wells had obviously taken care of one of his two attackers—a man slumped against a wooden door, desperately trying to stem the gush of blood from the hole in his chest. Wells was smiling at the other, who backed away, then stopped when three more ruffians charged up to join him. Wells moved back to join Hernando.

"Well, you've got some action now, Wells," Hernando noted, eyes on the attackers.

"Aye, sir," Wells replied cheerfully, then jerked his chin at two more men who trotted up from another direction, with two more behind them. "I make that eight to two, sir—just about the right odds." He grinned.

Hernando spun to take the two new arrivals as Wells put his back to him, facing the other four. One of the ruffians pulled a pair of pistols from his leather doublet. Hernando froze as the man raised both pistols and fired. Two of Wells' attackers were blown off their feet; the others took to their heels and ran away.

Hernando lowered his sword, realizing that these were the duke's men, who were supposed to be protecting them. He grabbed Wells by the shoulder as he rounded on them. "Wells—Wells! They're on our side."

The other two had also caught up and drawn their pistols. They ran past in pursuit of the assassins. "Who were they?" Hernando asked one of the duke's men.

"Don't know, Cap! But this one will tell us something." He kicked the only attacker left alive and made some remarks about him puking all over himself from the pain of crushed gonads. "You better make yourself scarce, Cap," he said to Hernando. "The port guard will be here soon, with all the commotion."

Hernando thanked him, but they were already hauling away their prisoner. "Okay, Wells, you got your action, now let's get out of here," he said, then glanced up at the window. Had that been Isabella, stepping back into the darkness of the room? Wells cleared his throat. Hernando sheathed his sword and they turned and moved quickly down the street toward the port.

Chapter 16

The morning air was fresh with the smell of the sea. Hernando inhaled, thinking about the strange, spicy smell of the air in the New World. He thought of Laocan, and how she used to look at her "green-eyed god." He thought of the dense green jungle and the heat of the tropical sun.

Wells brought him back to reality as he joined him on the deck of the *Alva Cordova*. "Do you hear that, Commander?" he asked.

Hernando turned his head as if doing so would help his ears identify the sound. "Marching—it's men marching in the distance."

"Yes," Wells said, "and it's getting closer."

Hernando looked at Wells who was also tilting his head, his expression intent. "Assemble the men," he ordered.

Wells snapped alert. "Aye, sir!"

As Hernando's men boiled onto the deck, a large contingent of finely dressed Port Guardsmen rounded the corner. "How many do you think, Wells?" Hernando asked as his sergeant rejoined him.

Wells paused, then shook his head. "Lots, sir."

"Mm-hmm ... set musketeers—three lines."

The Port Guard formed up in line, six or seven deep, in the square at the top of the pier. Hernando and Wells stood to one side of their own ranks of men, standing ready on the *Alva Cordova*.

A tall young officer came forward and saluted. "Commander Diaz! We are to take charge of your cargo. Here are my orders." He strode up the gangplank and handed Hernando a neatly folded parchment.

Hernando looked at it for a moment. "I don't recognize your commander's name," he said, handing back the paper. "I'm sure our cargo is quite safe with us."

"My order is to secure the cargo by any means, sir," the officer said.

Wells nodded and the musketeers lit their slow matches.

"No thanks, Lieutenant," Hernando replied. "We'll deliver the cargo to its owner ourselves. Thank you very much for your concern."

The young officer looked flustered. "Sir, you are outmanned and outgunned. Relinquish your authority!"

"Lieutenant," Hernando replied, matching the officer's tone, "get off the ship!"

The lieutenant turned and strutted down the gangplank to his second in command. Some orders were shouted. The Port Guard aimed their muskets at the men on the ship.

With a rumble, the guns of the *Alva Cordova* were run out. The gaping mouths of the cannons were just yards from the lines of Port guardsmen. The guardsmen looked at each other and shuffled their feet. Their lieutenant tried to steady them.

Hernando hid a smile. The Guard had no way of knowing that the cannons were not loaded. An uneasy standoff ensued as the lieutenant mulled over his options.

Captain Menindez joined Hernando at the rail and addressed the officer in a voice loud enough for all his men to hear. "My cannons are loaded with grapeshot. Stand down your Port Guard, Lieutenant!"

An uneasy murmur rose from his men, then they slowly started backing up.

"Stand your ground, men!" the lieutenant shouted, drawing his sword to point it at those who had lowered their guns. "Take aim!" He spun around. "In the name of Commander Cervez and the Port Authority, I command you to lower your weapons and vacate the *Alva Cordova*!"

"That's not happening, young man, so let's get to the fighting!" Wells shouted out of turn, making some of his men laugh.

Hernando scowled at him. Wells humped up his shoulders in query. "What?"

At that moment another contingent of soldiers rounded the corner and took up position at the top of the court, behind the Port Guard. Hernando recognized the standard of his uncle, the Duke of Aragon, as did his men—a cheer went up. *They've found themselves a tense situation,* he thought.

"It looks as though you are now the one outmanned and outgunned," he called to the lieutenant, who strained to see what was happening behind his own men.

More disconcerted mutters rose from the Port guardsmen. They broke their lines to turn and face the new enemy. His lines in disarray, the lieutenant shouted orders, but his men turned aimlessly one way and then the other until half his men were facing the enemy in the back and half toward the ship.

"Lieutenant, you're not going to subject these fancy boys to a fight with my riffraff, are you? They've been cooped up in the ship for so many days, they're just spoiling for a fight."

The murmur rose in pitch as Hernando's men pushed toward the railing as if on cue, grinning and jeering. Panic slackened the faces of the Port Guard. The young lieutenant tried to steady them. A moment passed in deadly silence. Then the young officer sheathed his sword and turned to his sergeant, who bellowed a moment later, "Fall in!"

The lieutenant marched through his men and through the duke's men, who parted to allow him to quickly leave the docks, followed closely by his Guard. The duke's men closed behind them, sealing off the court.

"Just in time, Captain!" Hernando saluted a welcome and then shook the hand of the young soldier who came forward and clambered up the gangplank.

"Wells looks disappointed," Captain Menindez said at Hernando's shoulder.

"Thank you for your quick thinking with the cannons," Hernando told him. "It stopped the Port Guard in their tracks."

"Good thing the young man didn't call our bluff!" They laughed together and Menindez slapped Hernando on the shoulder.

The young soldier stopped them with before they turned away. "We have brought heavy wagons," he said. "The duke wants to transfer the cargo to the king's treasury as soon as possible."

"That's a good idea," Hernando said. He turned. "Wells, help this young gentleman load the wagons, then escort his lads to the treasury."

"Yes, sir—I'll be glad to see the end of it," Wells commented.

For days, the large wagons ferried their cargo to the treasury. Hernando watched anxiously, expecting an attack from some unknown force trying to take the gold away and spoiling his chances of reclaiming his father's lands. But there was none.

As he was watching the last of the Aztec gold trundle off with its escort, a letter arrived. Hernando expected it to be from the duke, but it was from Isabella; she wanted to see him. His heart leapt. *Any time, any place,* he thought, but her letter said she would arrange the time for them to meet. Over and over he read her words, how she'd missed him, and that he must keep the tryst a secret. As he was answering her letter, another, more official messenger arrived bearing an invitation to a function at the royal court, encrusted with an elaborate wax seal.

* * * *

Wells and Hernando fidgeted in their new dress uniforms. The tailors had worked all night on them, with Wells grumbling complaints during the entire fitting.

"I'm not cut out to be a peacock, sir," he said yet again. "I'll probably spill sauce down my front. And how am I supposed to turn my head, with the collar so tight?"

Hernando wasn't listening. He was thinking about restoring his family name, and thoughts of Isabella kept creeping in, no matter how hard he tried to concentrate on the matters at hand. He knew Wells truly did not wish to accompany him, but the sergeant was honoured when Hernando told him he wanted him to guard the large chest of handpicked jewels and ornately crafted pieces of Aztec gold that he intended to present to the king.

Why hadn't Isabella returned his message, he wondered for the hundredth time. Had the count intercepted it?

"Commander. Commander?"

Wells' voice brought Hernando back to the present. "Oh yes, of course," Hernando answered, pretending he'd been listening all along.

"You think we should go to the party naked?" Wells grinned, having fun at Hernando's expense.

Hernando smiled sheepishly, then added, "We would be more comfortable—and look it." They both laughed at how ridiculous they looked in their fancy dress. But Hernando noted the female eyes they drew when they were presented alongside his mother and uncle, and realized they made a striking pair.

"The Duke of Aragon, the Countess Diaz, and Commander Diaz," the courtier shouted, and the room hushed as heads turned.

The duke and his sister were resplendent in their finest clothes, but it was their beaming faces that attracted attention. His uncle looked full of himself for funding the expedition, Hernando thought; that, and the knowledge that his position at court was about to change dramatically. His mother's proud smile fell most often on her son, and he suspected she was happy to be invited into society again, but he knew that she also had some inkling of how important this evening would be to their family.

Those present craned their heads to see the young man they had been hearing so much about. Not wanting to disappoint them, Hernando stood tall and threw back his shoulders. Like a pack of wolves, the crowd descended on them, the politically astute jockeying for position and the old ladies pushing forward unwed daughters. Hernando was taken aback and Wells almost broke and ran, but the duke and his sister revelled in it, portioning out their attention as if they were giving candy to children.

The duke had timed it perfectly; they were the last to arrive, just before the king's retinue. "His Majesty, King Charles V," the courtier announced, and every man knelt while the women curtsied deeply. Wells was almost left standing, but recovered quickly.

The king's advisors and hangers-on were introduced one by one, but the king came directly to the duke, who bowed again. "My trusted friend," he said, nodding to the duke but looking at Hernando, who was still on one knee, eyes on the tiled floor. "Stand, young man!"

The duke pulled Hernando off the floor with one hand. "This is my nephew Hernando Diaz, Your Majesty."

Hernando bowed again.

"Come along, young man. Stop grovelling!" the king exclaimed. "From what I hear, you've faced opponents who were a lot scarier than I." Those in the king's retinue forced laughter, but Hernando smiled sincerely. The king seemed to pick up on his honesty, for the smile he returned looked relieved.

After introducing Hernando to his entire entourage, the king pulled Hernando and the duke aside. "How much gold is there?" the king asked in a low voice, looking directly at Hernando.

He quickly snapped a look to the duke, who nodded his approval. Still, Hernando had to think about his answer. "More than enough to fill all the holds of the *Alva Cordova* five hundred times over."

The king's eyes grew huge. He turned to the duke. "We must talk, my friend. You will come to court as soon as possible."

Hernando spoke up, ignoring his uncle's startled look. "May I present the king with a small sample of his treasure?"

The king paused. "Yes, but let's entertain the court," he replied, sharing a knowing look with the duke.

After more talking, some dancing, and more talking, Hernando glimpsed Isabella and the count. They were talking earnestly with one of the king's advisors.

The man had been introduced to him, but Hernando could not remember his name. Hernando stared across the room so intently that his mother followed his gaze, then smiled when she saw the pretty young woman who had drawn his attention. Hernando had not told his mother of Isabella, let alone of how intimately he knew her.

Isabella did not look at Hernando, but the count did. Hernando held his stare until he turned back to his conversation with the king's advisor. The duke leaned toward Hernando. "Those men in the alleyway who tried to kill you and your man Wells were hired by the count. Is there something I should know about your relationship with him?"

Hernando hesitated, then told the duke everything except the most explicit sexual details. Hernando trusted his uncle as he had his own father, and looked to him for advice. But the duke only said, "Be very careful; this is a dangerous man. We will deal with him in good time." Later, Hernando noticed the duke staring at the count and wondered if he and the count had their own dealings.

As one of the courtiers called for a halt to the music and started praising the king in a lavish and poetic speech, the duke sidled up to Hernando and asked where Wells and the chest of gold were. Hernando's heart skipped a beat when he looked around and couldn't see the man.

A hasty search turned up Wells in the courtyard outside. Once again he was using the chest as a seat for himself and the serving maid nestled on his lap. They were entwined in a passionate kiss that ended as soon as Hernando cleared his throat. Wells stood abruptly, dumping the winsome lass onto the flagstones. A small squeak escaped her lips as she landed, but she quickly rose, brushed off her ample rump, and scurried off, casting a rosy-cheeked glance over her shoulder to wink at Wells. He hefted the chest and made for Hernando, but looked back at the maid with a sigh.

Hernando and the Duke of Aragon were formally announced to the king, now seated on a dais at one end of the opulent ballroom with his queen beside him and his advisors clustered behind. They approached and knelt, then rose as he waved at them and bade them stand. He nodded to the duke.

"Your Excellence; Your Majesty," the duke said to the king, then the queen. He inclined his head to the advisors, then turned to the rest of the room. "Honoured guests of His Royal Highness. Today, by the mercy and good grace of God, my nephew Hernando Diaz has returned from New Spain. Again the Diaz name has helped this great country. He carries good wishes and gifts from Cortez and the new subjects of King Charles V." He paused for applause and cheering.

Hernando looked from the king's stoic face to the faces of the advisors. They were not a happy lot. He looked back to his uncle as the duke confirmed, "Cortez and Hernando Diaz have claimed a great and rich land in the name of the king and the church!" He paused, waiting for the uproar to quiet down. "A land rich in natural resources, rich beyond any other in the known world. A land of spices, exotic animals, wild peoples, and gold." The guests fell silent. The duke turned back to the king. "We present to you, my most gracious lord, for your forethought and support in this venture, a small sample of what awaits you in your city treasury at this very moment."

He nodded to Hernando, who was relieved that all the hubbub was over. Hernando turned, received the chest from Wells, who stepped back into the crowd, then stepped forward and knelt at the feet of his king. He opened the wooden lid and the light caught the jewels and bounced off the golden idols.

An audible gasp came from the king's lips. The queen leaned forward, and the king's advisors pressed in as Hernando produced from the cask precious stones and gold figurines of gods and Aztec kings, arranging them on a red velvet cloth spread at the king's feet. He placed gold disks emblazoned with exotic flying birds in a small pile beside thick gold and jewel-encrusted bracelets, finely crafted necklaces, and heavy gold earrings fashioned after tree frogs. The king picked up pieces and handed them to his queen as Hernando explained what they were or what he knew of them.

When Hernando at last reached the bottom of the cask, he found what he thought was one of the best pieces; it still impressed him, even after all he'd seen. He lifted out a beautiful gold necklace studded with clear and red stones, each polished to a fiery luster. The stones tapered in size from either side of a gold pendant in the shape of the Aztec sun god; Hernando believed it had belonged to Montezuma himself, or someone of similar importance.

The queen reached for the necklace and Hernando handed it directly to her, head bowed. She held the necklace to her neck. A murmur of awe rippled around the room as the stones threw back the flickering lamplight as fiercely as if the sun itself shone from her chest.

And Hernando heard Laocan whisper in his ear, *Beware the one with fire around his neck.*

The hair stood up on the back of his neck. He turned, half expecting to see her behind him, then looked around and spotted Isabella staring at the necklace with greed in her eyes.

The duke's touch on his arm brought Hernando back to reality. He turned quickly and laid out the rest of the treasure, then rose and stood quietly. The king stood and thanked Hernando and the duke for their services, but Hernando could only think of Laocan, and that luscious green coastline with the waves throwing themselves on rocky outcrops between long stretches of white sand beaches. He longed for those distant shores.

When the king left with his chest of golden samples, most of the guests, who had attended for a chance to be noticed by the king, left. But they took with them the story of the treasure that would soon electrify the country.

Hernando's mother had finally got him alone, and they talked for most of an hour while the duke was off lining up allies and setting plans in motion. Wells had again vanished; Hernando suspected he had found a private place with the serving maid.

The duke finally joined Hernando and his mother. "It is late," he said. "Let's return to our lodgings so we can get an early start in the morning." He looked at Hernando. "You'll have to relate your stories to the king; I'm afraid he has invited you to court. The tide is changing. We must act fast and not get hung up on a reef."

The water was about to become more treacherous than either of them could possibly imagine.

Chapter 17

Hernando had moved into the duke's large and luxurious apartments to be close to his mother. When they returned he fell into a deep sleep and dreamed of Aztec treasure and new adventures. Deep in the night, though, his eyes flew open. He blinked, trying to clear his groggy mind of the cobwebs of sleep. Had he heard something?

His eyes searched the darkness for a reason to be awake. He lay still, listening, but heard nothing but his own breathing. Then the floorboards outside his door creaked, caused not by the stumbling footsteps of some sleep-drunk servant making early morning preparations, but the careful footfall of stealth.

Hernando's heart started pounding. He strained to hear the next movement. He lay listening for endless minutes then, just as he'd dismissed the sound as his mind playing tricks on him, he heard the faint metallic scrape as the door handle turned. That had not been his imagination!

Slipping silently from his bed, Hernando felt over the floor for his Saracen sword, but it wasn't where it should be. Where was it? He cast back in his memory, replaying the events of the evening, and remembered the servant who had removed his clothes from the room. Hernando had been so tired that he had paid little attention to the man. *Traitor!* he thought.

Hernando stood and backed against the wall. It would be from there that he would see an intruder, if there was one. The room was all but black; very little light found its way through the curtained window, just a thin splash across the floor between him and the bed. He could only assume that the door was ajar and the intruder had entered the room.

Time ticked by. Hernando started to feel a little silly, standing pressed against the wall in the darkness. He had heard no noise, and had strained his eyes without seeing anything. Was the stress of his recent adventures getting to him?

He was about to step toward the bed when a glimmer of reflected light stopped him in mid-stride—the unmistakable glint of a blade catching the moonlight. Hernando held his breath. *Is the knife in his right or left hand? Should I move now, or wait?* At that moment he saw the glint as the knife was raised, then again as it fell. It hit the bed with enough force that it would have been driven deep into his ribcage.

Throwing himself forward, Hernando hurled his full weight against the assassin, smashing him against the wall. Hernando groped for the hand with the knife, but found both of the attacker's hands empty; the weapon had been knocked free to skitter across the floor. As the man twisted around to flee, Hernando drove his fist into the back of his neck. With a grunt, the man collapsed to the floor, and Hernando went down with him, making certain he would not crawl away.

He heard a commotion of voices and footsteps in the hall, then the door burst open. Hernando rolled off the assassin's limp body. He landed on something hard and groped beneath his butt; his hand found the attacker's knife as his eyes registered the two men in the half-light of the doorway.

A shot rang out elsewhere in the apartments, and Hernando feared for his mother. The two men in the doorway turned to look back out. Hernando sprang toward them, and the trio tumbled out into the hallway. More shots echoed down the hall, along with the clang and scrape of swordplay. Concentrating on the two bodies writhing underneath him, Hernando swiped the blade under the chin of one of them and heard air escaping through the wound.

The other man had righted himself and was now coming at Hernando. He leapt to his feet to meet the attack. The man had blackened his face and wore the dark clothing of a professional assassin. A blade appeared in his right hand as if out of nowhere, and he stabbed it at Hernando's face. Hernando only just dodged the razor edge and managed a swipe with his own blade.

He's quick as a viper, Hernando thought. Every time Hernando slashed at his opponent, the man was no longer there. He had to get a hold on him, then he would have a better chance in this contest. Feinting a slash to the right, Hernando reached in with his other hand, but the quicker man turned out of Hernando's grip and slashed Hernando's forearm as he whirled away. The cut stung immediately, and Hernando knew it was deep.

The assassin pressed the attack. Hernando backed away, trying to parry each slash of the assassin's long knife. Then he tripped backward over the body of the man whose throat he'd severed. He went down hard and scrambled to get up as the attacker lunged for him. Hernando twisted desperately, fearing for his life.

A shot erupted behind Hernando, and a musket ball blew the assassin's cheek and jaw clean away, snapping his head sideways. He grabbed his face and turned to flee down the hallway. A second shot took him square between the shoulder blades, and he dropped.

Hernando looked up at Wells through the pale blue smoke wafting from his second pistol. Still breathless from the fight, he could only nod his thanks.

Wells helped Hernando up, then scowled at his arm. "That's a nasty cut, sir."

Ignoring the wound, Hernando dashed toward his mother's room. Pushing past the two men stationed outside her door, he flung it open. His mother ran into his arms, then pulled back in horror.

"Oh my God! You're hurt!" Snatching a silk scarf from a table beside the door, she fashioned a hasty bandage around his arm.

The duke came into the room, breathing heavily and covered in blood. He looked more like a butcher than an aristocrat. Hernando's mother gasped. "Don't worry," he assured her, "it's not mine. Thank God for your men, Hernando; they saved our lives. My guards lie dead where they slept. Thank God for yours."

Hernando looked at Wells, who had appeared in the doorway behind the duke, and nodded a thank you, but Wells, uncharacteristically serious, turned and left.

Servants were materializing from the woodwork. They began hauling away bodies and cleaning up as if it were an everyday occurrence. Hearing shouts and the sounds of a struggle farther along the hallway, Hernando rose from the chair where his mother had seated him to work on his cut. He found Wells wrestling down the assassin Hernando had smashed into the wall earlier. Dozy with a concussion, he was subdued easily.

"Don't kill him, Sergeant!" the duke said from behind Hernando. "We need to get some information out of him."

Wells and another soldier hauled the man to his feet and took him off to a private setting for a talk.

Suddenly dizzy, Hernando staggered. His mother caught his arm and led him back to her room and urged him to lie down on her bed. In moments he had drifted off to sleep. As if from a great distance, he sensed his mother shaking him to try to wake him, but he ignored her insistent prods. He was dreaming of a Toltec beach, where waves crashed and the lush trees swayed in the breeze.

He looked up and down the beach for Laocan, but could not find her. Instead an army of Aztec warriors materialized from the greenery, their faces and bodies painted with bright colours and their hands gripping war clubs. They walked above the sand without touching it. In front was the warrior priest he had killed, trailing his entrails like shiny ribbons in the sand. His face was a mask of pain and hatred. As he approached, his features faded rather than growing clearer, until it was Ignatius striding toward him, his body bloody and torn from cannon shot, carrying a golden cross with a spear point on the end that dripped with Laocan's blood ...

* * * *

Rosa Diaz mopped her son's brow, then glanced at Enrique, who nodded. Poison. Something on the blade that had slashed his arm, no doubt. She looked again at her brother, and saw that he was as worried as her.

"He is strong," Enrique said. "If anyone can survive ..."

* * * *

Hernando backed away from the horror in front of him, but behind them he saw a familiar figure waving to him. He could not hear her voice, but her mouth was open as she called to him, encouraging him to come to her. But how? He would have to pass through the mass of warriors.

He pushed forward. His skin crawled as gouges and cuts opened in their flesh, as their limbs fell off and maggots boiled out of the openings. He looked only at Laocan, walking toward her, trusting only her. The warriors screamed and spat on him and swung their clubs close to his head, but he only looked at Laocan. Her voice was so faint, nearly lost in the tumult of wind and surf and the screaming demons around him, but he knew she was calling to her green-eyed god.

As he got closer, she too faded, until all he heard was ...

"I love you, Hernando."

He opened his eyes. His mother cradled him in her arms. "I love you, Hernando," she said again, her eyes half closed and bright with tears.

"You're squeezing me too hard, Mother," he complained. "I can hardly breathe." He smiled as she opened her eyes and a rush of joy transformed her face. "Is it daytime already?" he asked.

"It's been two and a half days since the attack, Hernando."

"Two and a half days?" Hernando blurted. "How could that be?"

"You were poisoned, my son. On the blade," she added, gesturing toward his arm.

He looked at his forearm. The cut was red and angry, oozing yellow pus. It throbbed painfully. He tried to sit up, but he was too weak. So she propped him up on her finely embroidered cushions and finished changing his dressing.

Over the next few days, a procession of well-wishers came to visit. His mother allowed only a few a day. The ones that weren't politically important, she sent away.

"Where's Wells?" Hernando asked. "I need to see Wells." He was not taking his forced rest well and needed the company of a friend.

"Your uncle the duke sent him on an errand," his mother finally answered.

After a very long couple of weeks of bedrest, Hernando was declared fit enough to travel, and he, his mother, and the duke together with their servants packed up and moved to Seville, to the court of King Charles V. The king had personally signed a letter asking after Hernando's health. They were accompanied by a large bodyguard and security was very tight. The duke sent the rest of his army back to his estate.

Two days later, Wells showed up. "You decided to join us?" Hernando teased.

The duke entered the room. "Ah, Wells. How was your trip?"

"The count had already flown the coop when we arrived," Wells replied, clearly in a foul mood.

Hernando realized that Wells had been sent to kill the count.

"We will talk later tonight," the duke told them as he turned and headed for the door. "Stay alert! And don't look so concerned, you two—it is they who are in retreat, not us!"

"Wells, it looks as though you could use a wee nip." Hernando produced Wells' flask and reached for two glasses.

Wells smiled for the first time in a while. "I thought I'd lost that."

"It must have been uncomfortable in the pocket of such a ruffian," Hernando said as he poured the amber liquid into the first glass. He moved the silver flask to pour the second shot. "It seems I am constantly thanking you for saving my life. But this time, my mother and the duke—"

"I'm sorry, Commander," Wells broke in. "I should have been there. I was—well, I was."

All of a sudden Hernando realized what was bothering Wells. "Are you kidding me, Wells? If you hadn't been there, we'd all be pincushions right now." Wells looked at Hernando, who met his gaze with honest appreciation. "I mean my mother, my uncle—thank you, Wells. I mean it."

Wells smiled. "Must be the awful liquid you call whiskey talking."

They smiled at each other as Hernando poured two more shots.

The next few days were spent in endless meetings with court officials, setting up an appointment with the king. Each bureaucrat had to be appeased or bribed. Impatient with the whole process, Hernando longed to be marching into battle with a real enemy. "I don't understand," he finally exploded as they awaited yet another appointment. They had been waiting on a bench for two hours. "Doesn't the king want to see us? Surely he knows the significance of the new land."

The duke hushed him as another aide approached. "The king will see you now," he said officiously.

Hernando could not believe his ears. "And none too soon," he muttered as they rose to be trotted along with five others into a smaller room. This one was closer to the chambers where the king received his subjects and foreign dignitaries. They hadn't been there long when an elderly, splendidly dressed gentleman asked them who they were. The duke stood and gave the man his full official name, and the man beckoned them to follow him.

The man stopped before a pair of massive, carved oak doors and tapped his cane three times. The doors creaked open. The guards on either side didn't seem to take note of them, staring straight ahead and closing the doors after they were clear.

The trio stepped into a long, narrow room. At its end sat the king, leaning forward in a large golden chair on a low dais. He was talking to an advisor who stood beside him. The old man announced them in a voice so strong, it surprised Hernando. The king sat back and looked their way. He seemed pleased to see them.

Hernando and the duke made their bows and said their pleasantries, then the king again leaned forward, full of questions for Hernando. What was the land like? Its people? Were there spices—and what about the gold? Hernando responded with detailed answers to each question, and the time flew by. He enjoyed the memories the conversation conjured, of the Toltec people and of the battles fought. The king also seemed to enjoy himself, by turns expressing amazement and delight. He asked again about the gold.

"My boy, if there is one tenth the amount of gold you say there is, you have saved this great country from certain collapse. The wars with England and France and the Portuguese test my patience …" He trailed off in thought. "Tonight you will speak at the court dinner. Let's give the disbelieving nobles an earful." Then he leaned in a little and dropped his voice. "Cortez is loyal?"

"Yes, Your Majesty."

"The governor of Havana?"

"I don't know," Hernando admitted. "I know only what Cortez has told me. *They* will come to blows if put in the same room."

"And the governor of Hispaniola?"

"A fine man, and honest," Hernando replied immediately.

"Yes that's what Captain Menindez said," Charles said slowly, as if checking his notes in his head. Then he slapped the arms of his chair. "Well, Mr. Diaz, Spain owes you a lot. You have been tested time and time again and you've proven true to God and king. What price should I pay to keep your loyalty? Let's speak. And if it is mine to give, you shall have it."

"There is no price for my loyalty, for you have that already, and it will never waver." The duke smiled as Hernando remembered what his uncle had coached him to say. "I ask that my two lieutenants, Luis and José Hermosio, be granted trading rights in Vera Cruz, to establish a port and govern whichever territory that Your Majesty deems appropriate. I also ask that you consider Cortez's applications contained in this sealed letter to you." Hernando paused as an aide stepped forward with the packet. "And that Captain Menindez and my men be awarded something extra beyond their regular pay for their bravery in the face of an unknown enemy. And …"

Hernando paused again. This next was most important to him. "I wish to petition Your Majesty for the restoration of the lands and estates and the good name of my father."

"Who is your father?" The king looked confused. "Is your name not Diaz?"

"It is my mother's great name, and my uncle's. My ancestor was the general who served beside El Cid so many years ago."

"Yes, yes, I know. What is your name?"

"Hernando Calsonia. My father's name was Juan Gregory Calsonia. I took my mother's name, as is often customary, when my father died. He was unjustly persecuted by the Inquisition."

The duke leaned toward him. "Careful, Hernando," he murmured.

The king looked around the room, then waved another advisor toward them. Hernando had not even noticed the man in the shadows, and watched dumbfounded as the clergyman stepped forward. He wore long red robes and had a thick golden, bejewelled necklace around his neck that swung forward as he whispered to the king. There was no mistaking the origin of the fiery stones and golden links, but the Aztec god had been melted down into a Christian cross.

Hernando turned slightly toward his uncle. "The necklace he's wearing—the necklace," he whispered, but the duke was not paying attention. The hairs on the back of Hernando's neck rose as he remembered Laocan's warning.

The king looked back to Hernando. "This is what you ask for yourself?"

"No. I ask this for my mother and family, and for the sake of justice. For myself I ask nothing except the chance to serve you again in some small capacity, if you and God so wish it."

The duke nodded, pleased.

"Leave your petitions and we will speak again tonight at dinner," the king said.

Hernando placed his petitions on the small, ornate table at the base of the dais. As he and the duke bowed and backed away, the religious advisor leaned to whisper in the king's ear again. The king watched Hernando leave as he listened. Hernando opened his mouth to speak as they left the chamber, but the duke stopped him with a finger pressed to his lips.

Outside, Hernando could not contain himself. "How do you think it went? Who was that priest? Do you think the king will accept our petitions? Who—"

"Hold on, Hernando!" the duke protested mildly. "One question at a time. I think the king is well disposed toward you—he likes you. He wishes *he* could be a conquistador in a new and wild land. We have that in our favour. And he is truly grateful for the treasure and land and he would probably grant you anything you asked, but ..." He stopped before entering the carriage. Hernando looked at him. The duke sighed. "The church has tremendous power, and they hold title to your estates and properties."

"Who was the one in the red robes?" Hernando asked as they settled into the plush seats and the carriage lurched forward.

The duke's expression revealed that he knew the man very well. "He is our most dangerous opponent. He is the Bishop of Seville, Itolius Clementine, but that's the name he took when he became bishop. He is Rodrigues Alvira Diaz."

Implications quickly overcame Hernando's initial shock. "Then we have sway with him! His mother is my cousin."

Hernando sobered as the duke warned, "I'm afraid this doesn't help us. In fact, our previous history might make things difficult. He headed the Inquisition a few years back and, although he was not the Inquisitor, he was in charge when your father was tried. His title of bishop is a direct result of the amount and the wealth of the land that he brought to the church."

Hernando was quiet on the ride back.

Later that evening, they donned their finest clothes. Hernando decided not to wear his dress uniform, against the wishes of his uncle.

"It is important for the king to see that you are in his service," the duke insisted.

Hernando countered with, "I think it is important for him to see me as a man."

The duke thought for a moment. "Maybe you are right."

Hernando entered the banquet hall wearing a finely cut silk brocade coat with a brilliant white shirt. His mother was dressed to the teeth, and after all the introductions and pleasantries were dispensed with, she was beset by bachelors and widowers, some rather handsome, Hernando admitted. She didn't know what to make of it at first, but after a smile and a nod from Hernando, she let herself enjoy the attention. Hernando thought about how strongly she had loved his father, but it was nice to see her enjoying herself. If nothing else, at least she was having fun again.

As Hernando turned to be introduced to another political pilgrim, he spied Isabella gazing surreptitiously at him from across the room. Momentarily flustered, he lost track of what the politico had asked, and launched into one of his Aztec stories, to the delight of the small crowd around him. As he spoke, he looked past them to the beautiful Isabella.

As he finished another story, he saw Isabella break from her group and make her way to the tall, leaded glass doors the opened on a courtyard. She paused and looked back over her shoulder at him before stepping outside. He hastily excused himself and moved around the perimeter of the room toward the doors.

The king, seated with his queen on another dais, spied him from across the room and raised his glass to Hernando. Hernando bowed and smiled. Many heads followed the king's gesture to Hernando and he suddenly felt like the centre of attention. He slipped out into the dark quiet of the courtyard and looked around quickly.

Isabella emerged from the cool shadows and ran into his arms. "Oh Hernando, I missed you so much." She hugged him and nuzzled his neck before resting her head on his chest.

Hernando put his hands on her slim waist, about to push her back, but she looked up into his eyes and kissed his lips. She smelled so sweet. He surrendered, enveloping her mouth with his lips and playing his tongue around hers. She squeezed his buttocks and ground her pelvis into his. He felt his body responding with excitement. She slipped one hand down the front of his breeches, and his desire leapt with his manhood.

She stepped back. "Here is a letter. Meet me tomorrow at this address, and we will finish what we started." She nuzzled his ear and whispered, "I've missed you so." Then she fluttered past him and slipped back through the leaded glass doors.

He stood fully engorged, hot and ready, his breathing ragged. He opened his eyes in time to see her leaving. In his hand was an envelope. His breath trembled over his lips as he sighed and sank down on the corner of a marble table. He had missed her so much.

When he'd recovered his wits, he opened and quickly read the letter. In it she talked about how cruel the count was and how she needed to be with him, and asked him to come to her at 3:00 the following day, when she would talk about leaving with him. His heart soared.

The rest of the night, she shot him little looks, unnoticed by the count. He could barely tear his eyes from her.

Hernando's mother was in high spirits when they left. She chattered about the men she'd danced with and all the news she'd heard and the interesting people she'd met. But the duke was quiet, painfully aware that the king had not talked to them that evening. Hernando shrugged it off as preoccupation with revolts and the enormous task of running such a large kingdom, for Charles had inherited not only the kingdoms of Castile and Aragon and most of the Iberian Peninsula, but lands in France and the Netherlands as well. Soon the king would inherit the Hapsburg lands, a vast and unruly territory that stretched from Germany to Sicily—a daunting task for anyone. Hernando had learned that the king's purpose in visiting Seville was to put down a revolt by the nobles in the northern kingdoms. That, and to visit his sickly mother, who was still considered the rightful ruler of the two mighty kingdoms by some nobles.

Hernando's mind was on the beautiful Isabella. He fantasized about bringing her to the family estate after the king reinstated his rightful title. She would be the new mistress of the manor. He could see in his mind the servants greeting them.

"Hernando, are you listening?" his mother said, cajoling him out of his daydream.

"Yes, of course, Mother." He noticed his uncle's pensive mood. "Did it not go well for us tonight?" he asked.

The duke spoke of political alliances, patronage, and hegemony for the next half an hour as they made their way back to the apartments. All the while Hernando listened and fingered Isabella's letter in his pocket.

That night he fell into a deep sleep, with sweet thoughts of love pushing all reality from his mind.

Hernando stood staring at Isabella's door exactly at 3 o'clock, as she had instructed. He knocked on the heavy wooden door and it creaked open, revealing the sweet face of Laocan.

"What are you doing here?" Hernando blurted, feeling guilty.

"Be careful, Hernando. Nothing is as it seems. Danger is all around you!" she said as she reached for him.

Hernando bolted upright in bed. Sweat streamed from his face as he looked wildly around the room. *A dream,* he told himself. *A dream.*

Chapter 18

▼

Hernando woke at dawn to the soft sounds of stirring servants. He could hardly contain his joy at breakfast. He consumed a hearty meal and complimented his mother on how radiant she looked then, after chatting with his mother, he headed down to the stables on the outskirts of town, where his men and horses awaited Hernando's call.

He rode the big stallion hard in the arena, fantasizing that he was caught in some great misadventure that only his trusted steed could extract him from. When his groom came to take the stallion, sweaty and foaming at the mouth from the vigorous exercise, Hernando sent him away and rubbed down and curried the magnificent beast himself, believing that doing so bonded them—when Hernando needed that little bit extra, the black stallion would give it. His mind wandered with the repetitious brushing, and he remembered the dream in which Laocan had come to him. *She is just jealous,* he thought dismissively, then admonished himself. *She wants to protect me, as always.* He pushed the dream out of his head and finished up with his horse.

He arrived at his uncle's lodgings around noon and tried to eat, but restlessness stole his appetite. He paced and fidgeted absently with whatever came to hand, constantly marking the time. Finally he could wait no longer, and went to meet Isabella.

He arrived well before the appointed time and waited in the shadow of a doorway across the street. Even then, he quickly grew impatient. When he could no longer stand it, he crossed the cobbles and reached for the bell beside the door, then stopped. Best not to risk being seen by servants by showing up at the door ahead of the appointed time. He stepped back, studied the façade, then stepped toward a trellis fixed to the brick wall and began to climb. He paused only to pick a red rose and place it between his teeth. He would greet his love in the most romantic of fashions.

A narrow balcony, more a wrought iron railing running across the sill, fronted the window where he'd seen Isabella. He threw his leg over railing and cautiously pushed the window open. Her scent hung in the air of the room; he smelled his sweet Isabella as soon as he entered, although she was not present. He looked around, then moved to the neatly made bed, fingering a perfume bottle resting on the side table. Movement drew his eye. A moment of panic turned to amusement when he realized the full length mirror on the other side of the bed had captured his reflection; he strutted like a rooster and smiled at himself. *And well I should,* he thought; in a very short time, Isabella would be his.

Voices approached in the hall beyond the door. Glancing quickly about, Hernando slipped into a large wooden armoire and pulled the door closed, save for a small crack. A moment later the door flew open and Isabella and the count entered, chattering like children.

"Now, listen—everything is going to plan, but we must ensure that all the pieces fall into place. By tonight the king will be dead and before that, this very afternoon, Diaz will also meet his end," the count said with a trace of glee.

Hernando felt as if he'd been slammed with an Aztec war club. *What did he say? The king and me ... dead?* Hernando cocked his ear to the crack.

"You must make sure Diaz is totally involved with you, so he is unaware of my presence," the count continued.

"Yes, my love," Isabella cooed.

Hernando reeled back from the crack and sagged against the back of the armoire. He had been a fool to think Isabella wanted him!

They had fallen silent. Hernando leaned back to the crack in time to see the count pull her close and cup her buttocks beneath the layers of her dress. Leaning back, she slid her hand into his breeches and fondled him. Hernando watched with a masochistic fascination, unable to look away.

"Diaz must be on top, remember, so I can slit his throat when I emerge from your armoire." The count motioned to where Hernando was hiding.

Hernando instinctively moved farther back into the darkness of the large wooden cabinet, but the count had eyes only for Isabella. She had released her master's erect member from his breeches and now sank to the floor, her skirts billowing around her. She mewed as she engulfed him with her mouth.

His fingers were curled so tightly around something, his fingers throbbed. He looked down and realized he had unconsciously drawn his dirk. For one angry moment he considered killing them, but he remembered the count's words about killing the king tonight. Surely there were others involved. *If I kill them both now, the king still may not be safe.* Hernando moved closer to the crack.

As he came back to his senses, he felt a sharp pain in the palm of his other hand, and realized that the thorns of the rose had pierced his skin as he crushed the flower. Remembering his romantic intentions, Hernando was overcome with sadness. He was also still aware of the cool hilt of his knife in his other hand as he focused on the couple beyond the door. He listened intently, but the count was muttering unintelligibly as he pounded his hips into Isabella's face. It only took a few minutes for the count to finish. Then, spent, he fell back onto the bed. Hernando had to resist another urge to rush out and end their sorry lives.

Isabella wiped her pretty chin with a silk handkerchief. "Will we really end up with all of Hernando's lands?"

"That's what the bishop has promised." The count's breathing grew less laboured. Isabella tucked his penis back into his breeches and lovingly wiped a small spot off their front.

Hernando strained to hear every word, but their voices grew quieter and he could only catch bits and pieces. He did hear that the king's assassination was supposed to start a revolt.

Abruptly the count got up and left the room. Isabella straightened the bedclothes and spritzed the air with the perfume bottle beside the bed before leaving the room herself. *To await my arrival,* Hernando thought bitterly. He slipped out of the cabinet, crossed the room, and was out the window and down the trellis in minutes.

As soon as his foot hit the ground, a carriage pulled up. Wells opened the door. "Was it all that you expected, sir?" he blurted with a leering grin.

"Not what I expected at all!" Hernando retorted. He was already deep in thought. "We have big problems, Wells, big problems. Let's get to my uncle's."

Wells shouted orders, and the carriage leapt forward.

* * * *

Hernando barged into the dining room where the duke and his mother were having a late lunch. Both paused in their happy chatter to look curiously at Hernando.

"Uncle," Hernando gasped.

"What is it, Hernando?" his mother said, recognizing the tone first.

"The Count of Durraldo plans to kill the king!" Hernando answered, looking at his uncle.

"King Charles V?" he asked, as if trying to clarify what he had just heard. "How do you know this?"

Hernando hesitated. "I overheard the count talking to his niece."

The duke frowned. "You must have misunderstood. Why would the count say something like that in public? He is clever man. He would never tip his hand." He shook his head. "You must be mistaken."

Hernando fidgeted as he tried to word what he had to say with his mother in the room. "They weren't in public," he admitted, at a loss for any better way to say it. "They were in their bedroom."

His mother stood. "What do you mean, they were in their bedroom?" she asked sharply.

Hernando looked at the floor, feeling as if he were ten again. Then he sighed and related the whole story, from their time on the ship to the letter and his planned murder while in the arms of Isabella.

His mother looked sick to her stomach, though not angry, and he suspected she was more concerned with almost losing her son to such a woman. The duke sat silent as she questioned him. "It is obvious," she concluded. "This ... Isabella has played you like a lovesick harp, plucking your heartstrings for her own ends." She scowled, preparing to admonish him, but the duke spoke up.

"What exactly was said about the assassination of the king?"

"He said that it would happen tonight and that his death would start a rebellion."

The duke thought a moment. "Yes ... I know the cities of the north are restless, unhappy with the new king; they still support the queen, but she is unfit to reign. So who, then, is behind this assassination plot? Who has the means to put down all the usurpers if the land is thrown into civil war? Surely not the count." He looked intently at Hernando. "What else did he say? You must remember every detail."

As Hernando again went over all he'd heard, he felt his anger rising at Isabella's betrayal. Then a thought came to him. "Isabella said that if all went as planned, the bishop would give all my lands to them."

The duke leaned back in the large oak chair and blew air through his thick lips. "Of course! The bishop controls your lands. The bishop has the power and support to prevent the civil war. The bishop has the support of the pope. The pope is pulling the strings from Rome."

There was a long period of silence as the Duke of Aragon pondered their next move.

"We must save the king," Hernando blurted impatiently.

His uncle rested his elbows on the arms of his big chair and clasped his hands together under his chin, closing his eyes as if trying to discern the future. "Our family has long supported Queen Anne and before her, Queen Isabella," he said slowly. "And now the new King Charles. But we must do what is best for our family and secure our future and the future of Spain."

Hernando was unsure where the duke was going with his line of thought, but he held his tongue, waiting for the older man to continue.

The duke opened his eyes and looked at Hernando. "We may have an opportunity to change the course of our nation and place ourselves at the forefront of our emerging country's history. Or, if we make a mistake, we could help cause the downfall of the newly created Iberian kingdom—or worse yet, be blamed for it." He leaned back in his chair, still musing. "How to prove the king is in danger? Mere accusations will not be believed. The church is very powerful; it would exact revenge, probably put us to death by Inquisition. No, there's a lot to consider. But first we need all the available information."

The Duke shouted for his secretary. In the hour that followed, servants came and went. Riders left, pushing their horses immediately to a gallop. In no time, messengers were coming back and visitors were showing up. Some Hernando recognized as long-time friends of his father and uncle. Others were strangers to him. All gathered around the long dining room table with Hernando and the duke.

Hernando's uncle leaned over to him. "Get your man Wells in here. Do you trust him?" he added almost as an afterthought.

"With my life!" Hernando replied.

"Good, because that's what it is going to be—your life!"

Wells entered and stood listening behind his commander as the ten other men gathered at the table questioned Hernando and asked for his thoughts about the count's personality. There had been no time for proper introductions, and he answered the questions of many men he did not know.

He did recognize one name when he heard it—Fausto Morales, the man his father had told him to go to if he ever needed help, many years ago. He had forgotten that exchange with his father, but as the debate raged all around him, he saw again his father's face in his mind's eye. "Trust in this man above all else. He will be there in your greatest time of need," his father had said. The man noticed

Hernando looking at him and smiled and nodded a greeting, which brought Hernando back to matters at hand.

The duke rose and held up his hands for calm. "So what do we know?" he said when all eyes were on him. "The king is giving a surprise party tonight, no doubt suggested by the bishop. Many of us are invited, which normally might not be questioned, except that many of you might have grievances with the crown or church, or both. We have a full guest list here and the bishop is not on it. That is very strange indeed. I have never known the pompous ass to miss a chance to drink wine at someone else's expense." The others chuckled.

"We know the bishop has cancelled all leave for his private guard as of last week," he continued, "and most of the palace guard, including the sergeant at arms, has been replaced in the last few weeks." He paused and looked solemnly around the table. "Gentlemen, the bishop means to assassinate the king with us all there, arrest us as the culprits, and publicly try us all for treason, heresy, and anything else he can throw into the pot. He will seize most of the great estates of Castile and Aragon, eliminate the competition, and leave the pope in a position to appoint a new holy emperor. The pope means to stop Charles V before he inherits the Hapsburg lands and becomes too powerful to control. So, gentlemen—tonight we have a chance to change history. But in what way do we want to change it?"

His words generated a great debate. Everyone had something to say. Some wanted to do nothing and not attend. Others wanted to protect the king. Some said they must return to their estates and let the church and the king fight amongst themselves, while others said that Charles was the rightful king and it was their duty to protect him.

Then Morales stood and the muttering stopped. He had been quiet for most of the debate. "If we do nothing, the king may die or he may not. If we go back to our estates, we may keep them or we may not. If we do nothing, we may prosper or we may not. But if by some chance God wants us to intervene and we do not, we will surely burn in hell. If we intervene and are successful, we will live on our estates and prosper and we will see our king—our grateful king—become the ruler of the largest land mass since Caesar Augustus. Imagine our role in that state. Imagine God's justice in righting the wrong committed hundreds of years ago by the papacy. By God's right and the help of the knights, there will be an execution at the party tonight, but not the one the pope wants."

Suddenly the tone of the meeting changed. The men listening to Morales smiled, exuding confidence. Hernando had no idea what had just happened, but he felt as though a holy war had just been invoked. There was no more debate. Everything turned to planning.

After a fruitless examination of the guest list for a probable assassin, Hernando took a break from the discussions and sought out his mother. He wanted to apologize for his behaviour with Isabella. She set his mind at ease by joking that if he had not been a mouse listening from the cabinet, then he would never have known about the plot to kill the king. "God has a plan for everyone and we are not to question it," she told him.

He kissed his mother on the cheek and she hugged him tightly and whispered in his ear, "Never stop loving with all your heart, even if sometimes it bursts open like a pomegranate left in the hot sun."

He returned to the dining room. Maps of the palace were spread on the table and Wells was being shown where his handpicked men would be stationed. There was an air of great excitement that Hernando didn't yet comprehend—an air of revenge, of justice, of righting a great wrong. Without exception, the men worked as a team now.

*   *   *   *

Hernando and the duke arrived at the palace exactly at the appointed time. The palace guard was collecting sidearms which most guests gave up without a word. Hernando put the fancy dress sword he wore on the table before the guards, hoping the servants had tied their weapons to the undersides of the banquet tables as planned, or it would be a short fight. Most of the men who had attended the duke's meeting had left their wives at home and instead had brought stand-ins or concubines. They had made plans for their families to escape, should it all go terribly wrong.

The party began shortly after Hernando and his uncle were introduced and seated. The king had not yet arrived, as it was his custom to come late. Dinner would be first, then dancing. But most of the guests just milled about and talked in small groups. Hernando scanned the faces of the other men present, looking for any sign of nervousness or a clue to who the assassin was. Then the trumpets blared and the king and queen made their entrance. The crowd bowed deeply as the royal couple took their seats at the head table on its raised dais, and then the guests found their own seats.

A young man dressed in peacock finery read the news of the realm in a voice far deeper and older than he looked capable of producing. As court jesters came out to entertain after all announcements were made, the duke leaned toward

Hernando. "We forgot to check the entertainers. Nobody checked the entertainers."

Hernando's hand moved under the table to retrieve his sword, but the duke put his hand on his shoulder. "We must wait for the assassin to make his move," he murmured.

The night ticked by, minute by tense minute. Hernando was starting to think that they had the wrong night, or that the bishop had become aware of their information gathering and called off his plan. The entertainers came and went without incident. Then the king acknowledged Hernando and his uncle, who stood and bowed and then sat back down. The crowd hushed, looking expectantly at the king.

"Tonight we are glad to have the most important families of Castile, Aragon, and Seville here to share our table," the king said. He paused to pick a small sweetbread from a tray next to his throne and popped it in his mouth as if bidding his company to eat with him. He followed it with a mouthful of hardy Spanish wine. "I see our conquistador Hernando Calsonia is here tonight—champion of the New World, back from the golden city laden with treasure for his king."

The Duke leaned in to murmur in Hernando's ear, "He used your family name. He may have decided to reinstate your heritage." Hernando's hopes soared and his mind drifted from the task at hand.

"Hernando," the king continued, "please come and regale us with one of your stories; maybe the one about the great battle for the golden city."

As Hernando stood to light applause, he noticed movement in the wings. The palace guard, their numbers doubled or tripled, were pressing into the room. But all eyes were on Hernando. Guests at every table watched as he made his way to the centre of the room.

As Hernando turned to address the crowd, three men jumped up and pushed past him, shouting, "Death to the usurper! Long live Queen Anne!"

Hernando glimpsed the face of the sergeant at arms, accompanied by two nobles he did not recognize. Behind him, he heard the metallic hiss as the trio drew their swords. They had taken everyone off guard; for several long seconds, they moved unchallenged toward the king and queen. Then Hernando swung around and jumped onto the nearest man—the sergeant at arms, a large, burly man wearing half-armour and wielding a thin rapier.

One of the nobles was poised to attack the king, who had drawn his knife. Suddenly the man fell into the king's lap with a crossbow bolt protruding from his neck. Blood splattered the king, who sat stunned for a moment. The room erupted into violence. The palace guard boiled into the room, only to find the nobles were armed and fighting back.

A second bolt took the other assassin in the shoulder. Not Wells' best shot, but it served to spin the young man around and slow him down. Wells and his men entered and immediately made for the king, forming a ring around him facing the crowd. Behind their protective wall, the king, blood spotting his face, brandished his knife as he held his queen behind him.

The palace guard was quickly overwhelmed as more of Wells' men entered behind them, cutting off any chance of escape. Hernando's men sealed the room so no soldier could escape and report to the bishop.

Hernando still rolled around the floor with the sergeant at arms. Wells strode over and stood on his sword arm so he could not slash Hernando while the commander placed a few good blows to calm him down. The duke also joined them, and passed the Saracen sword to Hernando, who pressed the tip to the man's Adam's apple. It bobbed and quivered to avoid puncture.

"Don't kill him, Hernando!" the duke cautioned. "We'll need proof that will support our claims."

The king pushed through his new guard and looked at the sergeant under Hernando's knee. "My own guard?" the king gasped.

"Not your own guard, Your Majesty!" Hernando said. "The bishop's guard. He replaced this man and many others not more than two weeks ago."

"The bishop?" the king questioned.

"We must quickly move on the residences of the bishop before he escapes," the duke added.

The king hesitated. "I need positive proof before I can commit an act of war against the papacy. Will he talk?" He pointed at the sergeant at arms.

"Most certainly," Morales intoned as he joined them. "But it will take time. The bishop will soon realize his plan has failed. If our men rather than your own arrest him and hold him incommunicado, there will be time enough to gather proper evidence."

"Yes, and if things should turn out differently, I can hold you accountable," the king mused.

"Yes indeed, sir." Morales bowed.

"Do what you have to," the king said, waving his hand.

Morales nodded curtly. "Our forces are already in place, sir."

The king turned to Hernando. "I think you may want to lead the raid on the bishop's keep, for as I hear it, he was responsible for the confiscation of your rightful properties."

"Thank you, my lord." Hernando sketched a perfunctory bow. "But I will leave that to my uncle and his men. There are others who will need to be brought to justice."

"Make it so, gentlemen, and meet with me tomorrow, just after lunch."

"Yes, sir." Hernando and the duke bowed deeply, followed by the others.

Wells' men led the king away and the duke gathered a large contingent of men to approach the cathedral. Hernando made for the horses with a smaller group of men. He had his own traitors to round up.

Chapter 19

The great stallion blew froth all over the count's door as Hernando pulled back on the reins. Wells was already on the ground, kicking the door, pistol in one hand and sword in the other, grinning like a banshee.

The door burst open. A servant stepped in the way and was run through. He stood blank-eyed for a moment before Wells extricated his weapon and he crumpled. Shots rang out as they entered, and Hernando's men fell over themselves trying to get at the action. More shots; smoke filled the room. Two guards blocked Wells, halfway up the stairs, and he knocked away one man's sword with his pistol handle, which he was now using as a club against his attackers.

Hernando, close behind him, shot past Wells' ear, blowing apart the rib cage of the other guard. His fellow, now weaponless, turned to run. Wells slashed his calf and the man screamed in pain and went down. Hernando pushed past, bounded up the stairs and along the upper hall, then kicked in Isabella's bedroom door.

The count waited on the other side, with a pistol levelled at Hernando. Isabella stood in front of him. *Coward!* Hernando thought, *hiding behind a woman!*

Wells and two others entered the room behind him and circled the bed. The count tracked them with the muzzle of his pistol.

"Put down your weapon," Hernando ordered. "The king is safe, and by now the bishop is a prisoner."

The count swallowed hard but didn't lower his weapon. Hernando stepped toward him. "I'll take you with me!" the count shouted, waving the pistol around as Wells moved a little closer as well. He threw his arm around Isabella's neck, pulled her against him, and pressed the muzzle of the gun to her head. She said nothing, but a tiny whimper escaped her lips. "Stand back or I will blow off the head of your girlfriend."

Hernando felt a thrill of fear, for he knew the count was capable of anything. "You overestimate my feelings," he said with false calm. He paused, looking for an opening. "You will not escape justice."

The count and Isabella edged their way toward the door, but Hernando stepped directly in front of the doorway, barring their exit. Tension filled the air. The count's pale eyes stared malevolently at Hernando, and Hernando knew he was going to make his move.

Still, Hernando had not anticipated his next move. The count pushed Isabella toward the door and Hernando's raised sword. At the same time he fired the pistol at Hernando's head. The great sword was lost in the voluminous folds of Isabella's dress, but as she fell toward Hernando she twisted, and her flailing arms knocked the musket barrel toward the ceiling. The shot tore a hole in the plaster.

Hernando pushed his sword through her skirts and into the count. The count froze, a look of shock on his face as the blade slid deep into his fat belly. Isabella had fallen to one side. Her dress, still pinned between the count and Hernando, ripped away. The count grasped Hernando's hand, then slid off the blade to the floor.

Hernando knelt as if to pick up Isabella, but lifted a handful of her skirt and wiped the blood off his sword. He tossed it in her direction and said as he left the room, "Arrest everyone who is still alive." He heard Isabella call after him, but he did not stop.

* * * *

Hernando arrived at his uncle's apartment just as dawn was pushing its way through the darkness. The duke was already home and asleep upstairs, exhausted from the night's heroic events. Hernando sat in a wingback chair upholstered in dark velvet and attempted to pull off his boots, then gave up and sank back in the chair.

He awoke to Laocan sitting on the floor before him, tugging off his boots. "I'm so glad you made it through the night, my green-eyed god," she murmured. Her voice soothed him and he felt his eyelids sliding shut again. He hadn't realized how tired he was. "Shhh," Laocan whispered. "Sleep, my master. I will look after you while you rest."

"Hernando. Hernando!" His mother shook him gently. "My soldier—you're all right. You're safe. I waited up all night for you to come home." She pulled his head to her chest.

"It's all over now, Mother. Our land and our name will be returned to us."

"As long as you're safe, that's all that matters to me." She squeezed him so hard, he couldn't breathe. "Come, the duke is waiting on us at breakfast."

When she stepped back, Hernando saw his boots standing neatly beside the chair. He swept the room with his eyes, just in case Laocan was still there. Disappointment washed through him when he saw only an empty room.

After breakfast, they met with the king. Hernando noted that his men were still on guard and nodded a silent thank you to each of them. The king was in high spirits. To listen to him, it sounded as though he had single-handedly dispatched his would-be assassins, but in the end he was gracious in thanking and rewarding each of the men who came to his rescue. The nobles received land and political appointments that would become very significant as Spain's importance grew in the affairs of the rest of the continent. Fausto Morales spoke quietly and at length into the king's ear, then smiled and bowed deeply, pledging his allegiance to the King of Spain. Charles awarded the duke and Hernando land concessions in the New World, and gave them exclusive rights to build a new naval fleet that could protect Spain's growing interests abroad.

At last he called Hernando close to him. "Hernando Calsonia, I restore your rightful name, your ancestral lands, and all that is rightfully yours by birth."

Hernando's heart soared. He smiled broadly and bowed to his king.

Charles continued, "I would also like to talk to you about your future, young man, but that can wait. First you must rest and enjoy your homestead for a while; I will call upon you soon."

His business concluded, the king left the room. Silently the men bowed, but as they straightened, someone let out a cheer and they all shouted, "Long live the king! Long live the king!"

Hernando had let his men decide if they wanted to stay as the king's own guard or come back to the estate with him. Half of them returned with him for rest and relaxation; the others went on to Germany with the king, enjoying all the prestige that being part of the Royal Guard would bring.

The Bishop of Seville was defrocked and tortured until he gave evidence of papal involvement in the king's near assassination—testimony that would come in handy when Charles sought the pope's support to become the Holy Roman Emperor. Charles IV's father was on death's door, and he was about to inherit the Hapsburg lands, including parts of Italy, Germany, the Netherlands, and southern France. He would need strong generals, and he would call upon the men of Castile and Aragon who had saved his life to lead the Spanish armies against whatever new foe that should arise.

* * * *

Hernando rode onto his father's estate in full military dress uniform, his mother in a carriage at the head of the column behind him. The servants and staff waited in a line in the courtyard to greet them. As Hernando dismounted and helped his mother from the carriage, the staff bowed to their new mistress. It had been so long that none of the faces were familiar to Hernando, but then he spied the old cook, a bit more worn by the passage of time, but otherwise still spry. She smiled broadly and made for Hernando and his mother, but the overseer cleared his throat and she stopped abruptly, her smile fading. Then Hernando's mother held out her arms and she ran into them.

Hernando looked to the overseer, who cleared his throat again. "Juan Miguel, sir; overseer of this estate for His Excellence Pope Clements."

"Not anymore!" Hernando interrupted. "I will have a full accounting in one hour in my father's—in my study."

"Yes, as you wish." The priest nodded stiffly and stepped back.

Hernando wandered around the estate. Very little had changed. The stables were the same, the grounds were well kept, and the smells that greeted him as he pushed open the kitchen door brought back memories of his childhood. He could almost see Ignatius' pale and angry face. He pushed thoughts of his brother out of his mind as he again greeted the cook, who bear-hugged him in front of the astonished staff.

"You are so tall!" she exclaimed, stepping back but still holding his arms in her chubby hands. "You have grown into a proper gentleman." Then she chuckled and shook her head incredulously. "I can hardly believe you are real, that the family I cared for is back where they belong."

"It's good to be back, Beatriz." He kissed her plump cheek and then slipped out of her grasp to find his father's study.

* * * *

Seated behind his father's desk, Hernando studied the estate's ledger as the overseer stood before him under the watchful glower of Wells. The priest occasionally cast a wary glance his way, but otherwise had waited with his gaze intent on Hernando for the past twenty minutes.

The priest had been very thorough in the recording of profits and where they had gone. "So all the profits from sales were sent to the Bishop of Seville?" Hernando didn't look up from the big book.

"That's correct, sir—as ordered by the bishop himself," the priest added, as if to absolve himself of any responsibility.

Now Hernando looked up from the book. "That's fine; we should have no problem getting it back then, since the bishop has been replaced." The priest looked startled. *He had not heard,* Hernando thought, *being so far out in the country.*

Hernando sent the priest and his minions back to the city and settled in to deal with the estate for the rest of the day. Intent on his work, he didn't look up when Wells slipped back into the study. "Did you see the priest off?" he asked.

"Yes, but he loved your little farm so much I think he wanted to stay a bit longer." Wells had a grin on his face when Hernando looked up at him. "When Juan Miguel protested that he couldn't carry his belongings all the way back to the city, I helped him toward the gate." He paused. Hernando lifted a brow in query. "By firmly placing my boot against his buttocks, that is."

Hernando smiled. "I've set the men up in the workers' quarters," he said. "I want you to make sure they are comfortable."

Wells cocked his head. "I'd be a bit worried about your workers if I were you, especially the women, if you catch my drift."

"I have already moved them to the servants' rooms. It will be a bit tight for a while, but this will give us a chance to catch our breath."

"Right you are, sir." Wells turned toward the door, but turned back when Hernando spoke again.

"Could you give these letters to the rider on your way out?" He pointed his quill at a small stack of sealed letters on the corner of the desk. Wells nodded, picked up the letters, and left.

* * * *

Out in the hall, Wells handed the letters to the servant waiting there and instructed him to find the young man responsible for delivering them. Then he escaped from the manor and wandered across the courtyard toward the farm workers' quarters, pausing to banter with a scullery maid who was fetching water. Wells drew himself a drink as the maid mumbled about incurring the wrath of the cook for her tardiness and scurried off. He savoured the sweet, cold water, recalling the stale water they had drunk all those months aboard ship.

Something was niggling at the back of his mind. Not the uncanny sensation he felt whenever they were about to be attacked by Aztecs or some other foe, just a vague feeling that he'd missed something.

During the next couple of weeks, Wells grew increasingly restless in his role as Hernando's right-hand man. Men constantly came and went. There was endless talk of business, talk of land concessions in the New World and of shipyards here in Spain. Wells had always considered it his job to protect the commander from danger, but now it seemed that the greatest danger was that one of these squinting paper-pushers might bore Hernando to death.

He threw himself into training the men hard each morning, so mercilessly that some of them grumbled, though certainly not in his hearing. They had been outfitted with new gear, including swords of Toledo steel, which rang with a pure bell tone whenever two came together.

He was returning to the manor after one such session when he saw a carriage pull up to the front door. This was not unusual these days, so he gave it only passing attention—until a finely dressed woman stepped down from the carriage and moved to the entrance with the grace of royalty. Wells felt immediately uncomfortable, and hurried toward the house.

By the time he'd caught up, she had been taken to Hernando, who greeted her in the antechamber just off the great hall. Wells stood awkwardly in the doorway. Hernando was in the middle of introductions when he spied Wells.

"Come in, Thomas." Wells hesitated; he'd never before heard Hernando call him by his Christian name. "You know the Countess de Lorca, don't you? I believe she is your mother!"

As Hernando spoke, the regal lady turned toward Wells. "It has been so long," she said, holding out her arms. Wells rushed into them, wrapping his own around her in a tight embrace.

Chuckling, Hernando slipped out the door.

* * * *

Wells' mother the Countess de Lorca stayed for a few days. Hernando enjoyed watching mother and son interact. Gone was the burly soldier who revelled in the very hint of a fight, replaced by a gentle man who had obviously missed his mother and family deeply. There was talk of reconciliation. "Mostly," Wells said snidely, "because of our newfound wealth and fame!" Hernando knew he had no intention of forgiving his uncle for the death of his father.

Wells was silent as he and Hernando stood watching the countess's carriage turn out the gate and speed down the estate's long drive. Sensing Wells' tension as he groped for the words to express his gratitude, Hernando spoke first. "I would never have figured you to be from such good stock, Wells. Are you sure you weren't adopted?"

Wells returned his smile. "Thank you, Hernando." He held out his hand.

Hernando gladly took it, but pulled Wells close and threw his free arm around Wells' shoulder. "Come on, don't turn all pudding on me; I may be needing that other Wells—you know, that bloodthirsty, grinning banshee." He immediately caught Wells' attention.

"Why, what's up?"

"I'm not sure, but we have two distinguished guests arriving tomorrow: my father's friend, Fausto Morales, and an emissary from the king."

Chapter 20

Hernando slept fitfully that night. As dawn approached, so did Laocan. She walked toward him through a green mantle of jungle leaves, but stopped at the foot of his bed and came no closer. He tried to reach for her, but the distance between them only increased. He felt despair as she faded and he awoke.

As he dressed, he peered out the window. Wells was drilling the men, who moved through the light morning mist like wraiths. The sight pleased him, and he forgot his sadness over Laocan.

Hernando spent the morning preparing for his guests, who coincidentally arrived at about the same time. Hernando descended the broad front steps to greet his father's closest friend first, nodding his approval to Wells as he passed the line of soldiers arrayed in their new uniforms to impress the guests. "Mr. Morales," he said, extending his hand as the older gentleman's foot hit the ground.

"Hernando, you must call me Fausto," Morales insisted as he took Hernando's hand. "After all, we did save the king together!" He sobered. "We have important business to discuss, young man." But just as he piqued Hernando's curiosity, a second carriage rolled up and stopped behind Morales'. "The kings emissary!" Fausto exclaimed. "You are indeed an important man, Mr. Calsonia!"

Hernando hesitated, not sure what to do.

"Go, see to the fancy-pants getting out of that flashy carriage."

Hernando noted Morales' distaste for aristocracy in his voice. He turned, waved Wells forward, and said, "Mr. Wells, will you see to our distinguished guest?"

Wells looked discomfited at being asked to entertain guests. He jerked his head in a nervous nod that Fausto quickly picked up. "Come now," he said, "I can't be any scarier than a menacing horde of pagan Indians."

Wells grinned sheepishly, but seemed to relax. "I'm better at handling the horde, sir."

As Wells escorted the gentleman up the steps to the manor, Hernando moved to welcome the second visitor. "Hernando Calsonia at your service, sir," he said as the tall, splendidly dressed man moved away from his carriage.

"Good day to you, sir. I am Lord Villian. I have been sent by King Charles to seek your service."

"Please forgive me," Hernando said awkwardly, still new to the proper etiquette for receiving influential guests. "Come in and have some refreshments, and we can talk further."

Inside he introduced Lord Villian to his mother, who took over the reception, much to his relief. After several minutes of pleasant gossip about the court and talk of the king's dealings with his territories and protectorates, talk finally turned to why the courtier had come.

"King Charles has sent me to offer you a position on his staff," Lord Villian said, then paused as if trying to read Hernando's reaction.

Hernando was baffled. "Why would the king need me in his court?"

"Not *in* his court, exactly, although you would have great prestige and power," Villian replied. "You would be made commander of his army in Spain and as such, required to travel here and there to, shall we say, deal with rebellions and disputes of a military nature."

Hernando said nothing as he tried to grasp what he was being offered. The courtier went on as if he needed to sweeten the offer. "You would have control of the best trained and most well-equipped army that has ever existed. The king wants a man he can trust to command it." Again he paused before adding, "There may be trouble with the papacy."

Hernando sat back in his high-backed chair. "I don't know what to say. I will have to think it over."

He glanced at his mother, who looked mildly sick. He knew what she was thinking: you don't refuse an offer like this from someone as powerful as the king! When she spoke up, though, she was all gracious diplomacy.

"My son needs time to put his father's estate in order and see to some personal things," she said, allaying the lord's look of concern.

Lord Villian leaned forward and picked up a tasty treat from a plate on the low table before him. He popped it into his mouth and nodded, as if content that his task had been completed. A short time later, he left, and Hernando joined Fausto Morales in the study.

Morales turned from the window as Hernando entered. "The last time I was in this room, your father was still alive," he said.

Hernando's mind was still in the turmoil conjured by Lord Villian's offer. Morales' statement took him back to his boyhood, when he had hidden in the darkened corridor and peeked in on the two men. It seemed another lifetime ago.

"Your father was a good man, but very stubborn as well," Morales continued, moving to seat himself in the leather chair in front of the desk. "We asked him to deny the claims against him, but his honesty undid him. He would not call his son Ignatius a liar if it were not true."

Hernando spoke up as he settled into the other chair. "So it is true that my brother told the Inquisitor what he wanted to hear?"

"Yes, and more, I'm afraid. He gave sworn testimony at your father's Inquisition. Your father was beyond our reach at that point. I am told he would not betray his brothers and was very brave to the end. It would have been a long and painful death."

"Why do you tell me these things?" Hernando snapped, upset by the reminder. "Let the poor man rest!"

Fausto watched him, as if judging his character. "I do not mean to disturb by bring up the past, but you must know who you are dealing with when you are in the service of our king." Again he paused, watching Hernando's reaction.

Hernando was surprised that his father's friend was so well-informed, but he turned the conversation back to his father. "Certainly the king had nothing to do with my father's death."

Morales shrugged elaborately in concession. "Maybe not, but little happens in Castile without the persuasive hand of kings and popes. I want you to know who you'll be dealing with. These people would feed you to the lions if it furthered their own political ends, so trust them not!"

Hernando heard the disgust in Morales' voice; as if realizing he was not helping his argument, the older man softened his tone and said, "I'm sorry, my son. I get worked up when it comes to royalty and papacy and lunacy." He smiled at his own joke and as he did so he leaned forward; the chair's leather upholstery creaked. "Your father trusted too much," he said in a low voice.

The two looked at each other. Hernando saw warmth and concern for him in the other's eyes. After a short pause, Morales said simply, "We have a job for you before you run off to solve your king's problems."

Hernando was surprised. How had Morales heard so quickly about the king's offer? Sensing the intrigue in the older man's voice, he asked, "What do you mean, a job for me?"

Fausto caught his eye and held it. "Your father was a member of the Knights Templar, as you know. What you may not know is that I am Grand Master of the Knights Templar."

Hernando was not as surprised as he might have been. He remembered how the nobles had silenced and deferred to Morales at the meeting called by his uncle the duke before the assassination attempt on the king, and realized he'd sensed Morales' power even then.

"I am going to give you a brief history of the brotherhood that your father belonged to," Morales continued. "The order was founded on the principles of truth, honesty, and loyalty, as well as many other virtuous ideals. The Knights were loyal to only one king, the King of Peace, which became a problem for kings and popes over the years.

"Knights from France and Germany found themselves in the holy city of Jerusalem after being called to crusade by the pope and the Holy Roman emperor. They had been unable to stop or had participated in a great slaughter of the Muslim army as well as innocent citizens of the city. It is said that so many people were killed, the streets ran ankle deep in blood. The knights were sickened by their own behaviour and hastily made preparations to leave for their homes, ignoring the king's representatives, who pleaded with them to stay, for the common men of the army would unquestioningly follow the knights into battle but refuse orders from bureaucrats.

"Most of the knights left Jerusalem and retired to a castle in the north, at a place called Acre, a well-fortified city that had been taken earlier in the campaign. It was here that the pope's emissaries came to them and offered them lands and wages to protect the wild lands around Jerusalem so the pilgrims would not be harassed by robbers and killed by tribesmen of the desert.

"They became known as the Temple Knights because instead of razing the mosques and temples, they simply converted them to cathedrals. They were recognized for their zealous belief in Jesus, their titular king. They became well-known to the Muslims for both their bravery and their evenhandedness. They were learned men, and quickly realized that the Muslims had a great knowledge of medicine, astronomy, and architecture.

"When the Knights held the son of a sultan from the east for ransom, they learned of a secret order of builders that held ideals similar to their own. This guild used the tools of their trade as symbols to teach the new novices and to keep safe the secrets that allowed them to charge a king's ransom for their exclusive knowledge.

"The leader of the Knights, William de Comphry, was so impressed with the young man that he released him and returned home with him to learn more. In Egypt he saw marvels of engineering and gained knowledge of such ancient origin that at first he did not believe what he heard. Some time in the past, Christ had appeared to a pharaoh by the name of Akhenaten. As a result, the pharaoh changed the Egyptians' whole believe system, abolishing the old pantheon and installing only one god to be worshipped.

"The priests of the old system, having lost their power, rebelled. They murdered their king and obliterated all records of this period, along with any believers they encountered. So the believers went underground, but still taught about the one god through secrets and symbols. They possessed knowledge of great power, given to them by God and passed down secretly through the ages to keep it hidden from evil.

"While in this hot and humid land, de Comphry fell ill. His body was wracked with torturous fevers. While in the grip of this fever, Jesus came to him in a waking dream and told him that he would allow the angel of death to pass over him if de Comphry promised to keep all that he had learned secret, and not use it for evil works—for if he did, there would be swift and terrible retribution.

"De Comphry returned to the Holy Land a changed man; he toiled endlessly, almost without sleep, putting together a code of conduct and a system of teaching for passing on the his vast knowledge with the use of symbols and signs. He borrowed liberally from the builder's guild and Muslim knowledge and mixed it together with the new Christian beliefs.

"While de Comphry had been religious before his trip into the east, now he was a zealot and he affected all around him with the same fervour. The order grew strong and attracted hundreds of followers from all over Europe. The rich nobles brought their wealth and lands and gladly handed them over to the Knights, and the poor brought their brawn, which was quickly put to use fortifying a line of castles along the coast that in turn became rich trading ports.

"The pope had created the order, but the Knights believe they take orders from a higher authority, and that infuriated the Vatican. The pope became increasingly irritated with the order, which he had exempted from paying ecclesiastical tithes or papal taxes. They grew rich with land and gold.

"The pope created many orders over the years. Because of the increasing rift between the Templars and the pope and what he saw as their arrogance, he gave the task of ensuring safe passage of the pilgrims in the Holy Land to the Hospitalers, a sect whose original purpose was to provide safe hostels and medical care for the weary traveller. The Hospitalers had trouble controlling their members and many atrocities were committed against Muslims and Jews in the name of Christianity.

"A sultan named Saladin exploited the political unrest in Jerusalem and the infighting between the different orders after the king of Jerusalem's death and attacked, destroying the Christian armies. Saracens flooded into the Holy Land. Saladin and de Comphry met on a sandy knoll on the plain before Jerusalem. The Knights numbered eighteen hundred heavy cavalry and about four thousand sajants, or common soldiers. They were massively outnumbered by fifty thousand Saracens.

"Saladin rode out under a flag of truce to confer with de Comphry, whom he knew only by reputation. De Comphry brokered a deal to hand over the holy city in exchange for the lives and safe passage of the pilgrims and inhabitants within. Saladin knew of the Knights' formidable reputation and had no desire to see his men die in battle if it was unnecessary. Saladin, a just and honourable man, allowed the people to leave. The Templars retired to Acre. The pope was furious but could do little because he was fighting battles in his own backyard.

"The Templars and Muslims traded and learned from each other for many years. De Comphry never returned home but his descendants did, building castles and estates in the south of France, Germany, and here in Castile. The Vatican never forgave the order for giving up Jerusalem without a fight, even though the Muslims ruled fairly and permitted Christian pilgrims access to their shrines. This was mostly due to the quiet presence of the Templars, but also because they understood and were tolerant of other faiths.

"The order grew stronger and took no direction from the pope. In 1307, the pope outlawed the order and in a matter of days, our grand master and other leaders were arrested, tortured, and put to death. The most powerful members were tried for heresy and their lands confiscated by the papacy or King Philip of France, the pope's co-conspirator in this farce. Surviving members of the order were forced to hide the fact that they belonged to the brotherhood of God."

Hernando had been riveted to his seat, listening intently as Morales told the tale of the order to which his father had belonged. Now, for the first time, he had a partial understanding of why his father had died.

The two men sat back in their leather chairs, exhausted from their sprint through history.

"You said that you have a job for me," Hernando said, curious about Morales' earlier remark.

"Yes, we do indeed." The grand master's eyes shone. "But you will have to become a member of the brotherhood of Christ first."

Hernando sat up. "You mean become a Templar Knight? Of course I will!"

"Not so fast," Morales warned him. "This choice is not to be taken lightly. It is still an illegal organization and your membership could cost you your life, as it did your father."

"No, I will become a member of my father's brotherhood," Hernando said proudly.

They talked at great length, until they were called to supper.

As they took their places at the dining table, Hernando told his mother that he was going to Salamanca with Fausto to visit his estate. She looked uneasily at Morales, as if she knew the real reason for the pair's journey, and rubbed at the goosebumps that suddenly rose on the porcelain skin of her arms as if a cold wind had swept the room. "You must be careful, my son," she said softly, but she looked at Morales as she spoke. "You are all I have left."

Hernando turned to Wells, a frequent guest at the table. "Wells, make preparations for a trip. I think half the men should suffice."

Wells looked up from his plate, and was about to speak despite his full mouth when Morales interjected. "We travel at night and we travel alone."

Hernando was surprised at the cloak and dagger arrangements. "As you wish," he conceded. "You know best."

Wells, looking annoyed at being excluded, refocused his attention on his plate.

"The grooms have already been told to ready the horses. We leave in an hour," Morales announced.

Morales waited impatiently an hour later as Hernando said his good-byes to his mother and gave final instructions to Wells. Finally he mounted his black Andalusian stallion. They turned their horses, touched heels to flanks, and galloped for the gate.

* * * *

Wells gazed after them, not trying to hide his irritation at been left behind to mind the farm.

Beside him, the countess watched until her son and Morales were mere specks on the drive, then she turned to him. "What are you waiting for?"

Wells blinked dumbly at her, then past her as one of Hernando's men approached on horseback, leading Wells' saddled horse. A slow smile grew on his face.

"I expect my son's safe return, Mr. Wells!" the countess said sternly.

"Aye, ma'am," he said as he swung himself into the saddle. He spurred his horse to jump into a run and left the other man to follow as best he could.

Chapter 21

They drove their horses hard all night and arrived at the estate of a man who was a friend of Fausto Morales near dawn. The staff seemed prepared for their arrival and the master of the estate greeted them as if he'd been waiting for them all night. After introductions and a hearty breakfast, they were shown to bedrooms where the servants drew thick drapes across the windows to darken the room.

Hours later, Hernando woke from a solid rest and stretched his long legs before swinging them over the edge of the bed and sitting up. Laocan stepped out of the gloom, startling him.

She put her small brown hands on either side of his face. "My great green-eyed god is still sleepy," she cooed, and pulled his face into her breasts.

He put his arms around her tiny waist. "I've missed you so much," he started, but she shushed him and squeezed him tighter.

She climbed onto his lap and kissed him, slipping her tongue into his mouth. He felt her dark nipples hardening against his naked chest. Sliding his hands up her naked flanks, he fondled them. She reached down and pulled his hard member into her moist folds, then rocked on his lap, taking him deeply. She pumped hard and he seemed paralyzed, unable to move. He exploded into her and she finally came to rest, still impaled on him.

"Something evil is coming your way," she whispered in his ear.

A knock came at the door. Hernando woke and sat up, covered in sweat.

He found the grand master already up and seated at the dining room table, sealing the last of several letters he'd written with wax. The rider who had brought messages for him waited nearby. He handed the small bundle of letters to the rider and sent him off.

They ate another hearty meal and then again set off under the cover of darkness. Hernando thought about telling Fausto about his dream—at least the part about the ominous warning—but put it out of his mind, telling himself, *He would ask where I heard this, then think me mad.*

They picked up another rider at the next estate and three more before the journey was over. On the dawn of the sixth day, they came over a hill just outside Salamanca and gazed down at Fausto Morales' estate, nestled in a lush and misty dell.

Again the servants were awaiting their arrival. A breakfast lay ready for them, and as they ate, Hernando was introduced properly to the other men who had ridden in with them and to others who had been waiting for their arrival. Most were noblemen; a few he knew. When his uncle arrived later on in the day, Hernando let out an anxious sigh of relief. It had not occurred to him that this was the big event it was becoming.

At supper the duke gave Hernando a book bound in sheep's leather. "This was your father's copy. Guard it well, for it is the first secret that you will receive today."

Hernando opened the soft book. "It is a Bible." He looked up in surprise. His father had always read from the large hard-covered Bible in his study. He opened the cover and admired the beautifully written pages.

"This is your testament, written and handed down by the people closest to Christ," the duke continued as Hernando looked at the book. "You have been entrusted to protect two of the gospels originally written in Aramaic and translated to Greek at Alexandria after the crucifixion. There are fifteen books, each containing different gospels. Eventually you will get to see each."

"Thirty gospels?" Hernando hesitated. "I thought there were four."

"There will be more time for history later, but ..." The duke looked to the grand master, who nodded his approval. "The Holy Roman Catholic Church destroyed all the copies of the true gospels about three hundred years after Christ's death. They edited the writings down to four books—monks took out what they were told and added other things to support what the church believed it needed to keep control of the people. Some of the originals were hidden by the Templar Knights in Acre and spirited away to Alexandria for safekeeping."

"Why Alexandria?" Hernando wondered aloud, sensing that there was more to this story.

His uncle smiled. "Ah, now you've hit upon the real story of who we are! But first we eat and then we will continue."

As they dined, he heard stories of persecution and hardship, but also stories of great courage and loyalty. Hernando felt the anticipation in the air. He was to be the first inductee in many years, and the brotherhood of God was excited. After the meal, servants poured a strong coffee for each diner, a custom learned from the Arabs of the desert, his uncle told him. Hernando smiled politely. He had never been that fond of the taste.

"We wait for two more arrivals, then we can continue with the ceremony," the grand master said, then stood as they heard the servants heading to the door. He made his way to the entrance and the others automatically followed.

The large oak doors were pulled wide and in walked the king. Shock delayed Hernando's bow by a second or two; as he came to his senses and realized he was still standing, their eyes met and the king smiled broadly. Hernando bowed deeply.

The king had travelled with only two other men and no entourage. He declined an offer of food and proposed that they get right to it. Hernando was curious about the two men with him, who were dark-skinned and fine-featured, but he had no opportunity to ask about them.

Morales led them down a corridor, then stopped before a bronze statue of a veiled woman. He moved it aside, then leaned against a large section of dark oak panelling, which quietly swung away. They filed into a long hallway, pausing to light candles as they went. When they reached a solid wood and iron door, one of the others came forward from the back of the line.

"Who goes there!" he intoned. Hernando identified himself to the Tyler, as described by the duke during dinner.

The grand master answered for the group. "Keepers of the truth, masters of the truth, and novices."

The keeper of the door removed a large, ornate key from his breast pocket. "What do you seek?" the Tyler asked.

"We seek knowledge and enlightenment," the grand master responded.

"Enter the chamber of the brotherhood of God and receive the mysteries you seek." The Tyler turned from the door and placed the key between the stones of the archway. He turned it, and Hernando heard the scraping sound of stone on stone as a portion of wall moved away from the rest.

The party passed through into an antechamber with marble benches along two walls. The grand master turned toward Hernando. "As novices, you will wait here until we are ready inside."

Hernando only then realized that there were two novices—he and the king. They looked at each other as the other men were let through another door by the

Tyler, handing each man who passed a robe and saying, "Take nothing with you except your gospels."

Hernando and King Charles waited in the antechamber. He was about to say something to the king when the door to the other room opened and they were called inside. But first the Tyler blindfolded them and led them in. Hernando listened intently.

"Who goes there?" a voice asked.

"Travellers from the west." Hernando recognized his uncle's voice.

"What do they seek?"

"They seek the light."

"Come forward and prepare to receive the light. But step lightly, for you are about to be given a great burden, which you must carry secretly for the rest of your life. You may turn around now and walk away and nothing less will be thought of you."

It was quiet for a moment. Hernando took a step forward and came up against a sharp point of steel. Hernando stopped in mid-stride as it pressed against his chest.

"I again ask you to turn around, for if you betray what you learn here your heart will be run through with your own sword."

Hernando shivered at the thought of the point of his great Saracen sword only inches from his most vital organ.

"Come forward if you are faithful and pure of heart."

This time Hernando waited for the blade to be removed from his chest, but it was not. He knew how sharp his sword was but he moved forward anyway. The Damascus steel bit into his chest but he did not falter, and the blade was pulled away. Hernando felt a trickle of blood running down his chest. He also felt someone behind him, and a moment later a dagger was pulled up under his chin. He stopped abruptly.

"One last time, I ask you to reconsider your decision to stay. If you speak of what you are about to learn to anyone other than the brotherhood, your throat will be sliced from ear to ear and your tongue will be pulled through the opening for all to see." The speaker paused. "What is your choice, Hernando Calsonia?"

"I would like to know the mysteries of which you speak," Hernando said. He wasn't sure what it was proper to say, so he just spoke the truth.

"And what of you, Charles Bourbon?"

Hernando had almost forgotten that the king was there.

"I wish to become a member of the brotherhood and know its secrets," Charles responded.

The dagger had been removed from Hernando's throat, and now his blindfold was removed. Hernando looked around the immense room in amazement. Floors of black and white marble were polished to a brilliant shine that reflected the candlelight glowing within crystal containers. Three men were standing on a low dais at the end of the room: Grand Master Morales, the duke, and one of the dark-skinned men who had accompanied the King. All were dressed in white silk robes with a large red cross emblazoned across the left side, over the heart.

"Come forward and embrace the knowledge of the brotherhood," Morales told them.

As they made their way to the dais, Hernando looked around at the others who were seated along the walls. Many smiled at him, easing his tension.

"Kneel, novices," his uncle said.

Hernando glanced over to the king, who had gone down on his knees. *A king, bowing before the brotherhood!* he marvelled.

"You have freely accepted that you will become brothers of kings, princes, nobles, monks, merchants, peasants, pirates, and shepherds," Hernando's uncle said. "You must uphold the beliefs of the temple."

"That God can talk to you directly, that all the great mysteries of life are known to he who listens; a life conducted morally and truthfully will be rewarded," the dark-skinned man added.

Hernando found his mind wandering as he wondered about the origins of this man. *Palestine perhaps, or Egypt maybe.*

"Today you begin a journey to the east and although the sun will be bright at times, you must always look ahead," the grand master said. "Your travels will be clouded and dangerous at times, but you must trust in God and the brotherhood to see you through. Many years ago, a man was given an ancient secret which he has passed down to us, and we have guarded it with our lives. The secret lies buried in the east and must now be recovered."

"Aye!" the others shouted, startling Hernando from his wandering thoughts.

Fausto Morales turned and gathered up something wrapped in a fine oriental tapestry. He turned to the king. "Here is your dagger, returned to you stained with your own blood, the dagger you will use to take your own life, should you speak of what you have learned."

He turned again and picked up another bundle, then addressed Hernando. "Here is your sword, returned to you stained with your own blood—the sword of your ancestors with which you will take your own life, should you ever reveal the secrets of the brotherhood of Christ."

Hernando stood to receive the bundle, as the king had.

"You have begun the journey to enlightenment," the grand master told them. "The journey can take a lifetime or it can be quick; it is your choice. King Charles V, you now have the full support of the Templar Knights and their considerable wealth, as long as you hold dear the precepts of the order." The king inclined his head and took a step back.

Morales looked at Hernando. "For you, Hernando Calsonia, we have a special job—what the old knights would have called a quest." He paused and looked about the room, as if confirming the support of the others. "You will take our fleet to the New World and recover the Templar treasure that has been hidden there for nearly three hundred years."

A cheer went up from the gathered Templars.

*   *   *   *

Hernando set the bundle containing his sword down on a small writing desk in the room he'd been given by the grand master. He flopped onto the bed, his mind running over the events of that day. Then the journey to Morales' estate and the excitement of a new adventure overcame him and his eyelids sagged shut in exhaustion. Soon he had drifted into a deep sleep.

A noise woke him. He sat up on the bed.

"Oh, I did not mean to wake my green-eyed god," Laocan whispered "I was just looking at your new sword."

Hernando came up behind her and enveloped her slight frame in his arms. He kissed her neck and she giggled with delight. He undid her silken shirt and pulled it from her shoulders, then quickly undid his own. He could feel her soft back against his chest.

Laocan pushed her rump into his groin. "Is that all you ever think about?" Hernando murmured with a smile. He felt himself swelling.

So did Laocan. "Well I'm glad I still interest you, my lord..." She trailed off into a soft moan as he entered her. His breathing became laboured. Laocan gripped the small table where the sword rested for support, but their movement was pushing it across the floor.

Hernando fell spent on top of Laocan. Sweat dripped from his face onto the soft cheek beneath his. They lay still, panting, until the sweat cooled on their bodies. Then Hernando lifted her in his arms and took her to bed. They fell asleep in each other's arms.

Hernando awoke alone in the morning. "Another dream," he said softly to himself, and loneliness swept through him. He got dressed, then sat on the edge of the bed to pull on his boots. Then he froze. The small table holding his sword was pushed across the room, the rug rolled up against its legs. He smiled, then grinned. "What a dream!" he crowed as if to chase the loneliness away.

He stamped his booted feet against the floor and stood, still grinning, and strode over to the table. Freeing his sword from the cloth wrapped around it, he made to strap it around his waist, then paused. "*New* sword," Laocan had said. He drew the Saracen weapon from its sheath. It looked the same. He slashed the air with it—back and forth, back and forth. It felt the same. But something niggled at the back of his mind as he went down for breakfast.

The dining room was crowded with men when he entered, some already seated at the table, others standing and talking. Only the king was absent, gone on pressing business. Everyone greeted him warmly. "Come, sit beside me here," his uncle bellowed from across the room.

Noting that there were no servants, Hernando paused to pick up some food as he passed by a sideboard heaped with pork and wheat cakes, fresh bread and fresh fruit. He poured a large cup of Arabian coffee and then sat down beside the duke. He could feel the excitement in the air as the others took their places at the table.

Fausto Morelas suddenly exclaimed, "Hernando, you have no idea what you've just signed on for." He laughed as Hernando looked up from his slab of fried pork. "I envy you. To be given this quest is a great honour, but more than that, what you will be learning in the next few days will change your life and the lives of thousands!" He indicated the two dark-skinned men seated beside him. "These men are Joseph and Hamil Abiff, ancestors of Hiram Abiff, the architect and master builder of the temple of King Solomon. They will accompany you to the New World and help you retrieve the Templar treasure. They are the only ones who know exactly where it is, so guard them with your life."

Hernando spoke up for the first time. "This might seem presumptuous, but you may not fully understand the amount of gold that we captured from the Aztecs. Should we not spend our effort wisely and seek the surest source of gold?" Hernando was thinking of Laocan, not gold, if truth be told; he wanted to travel back to the land of the Toltecs to somehow be closer to her spirit.

The grand master looked puzzled for a moment, then broke into a broad grin. "Ah, to be young again!" Everyone laughed. "The treasure you seek will not fill up a cargo hold; it will not even fill this room. It is a box that can be opened only with the key that you now have in your possession."

The two Egyptians looked at each other with veiled concern. Hernando instinctively pulled out his sword and laid it on the table.

"Ha! I knew you were the one," Morales exclaimed. "How could you have known that the key is hidden in the pommel of your sword?"

"I do not believe it is even my sword," Hernando said slowly, not sure why he said it. He felt as if he were being prompted from the underworld.

"You are quite right, Mr. Calsonia. There are two swords—identical, except that one has a key to open the greatest treasure man has ever been given!"

Morales rose and strode over to a large oak cabinet and unlocked it. He returned immediately with the other sword. "You were to be instructed in all this at sea, but since you've opened the door, let's shine in some light. Tradition says that El Cid took the sword from the last Moorish sultan at the surrender of El Humbra and presented it to your ancestor for his tactical brilliance in the defeat of the Moors and the restoration of Christendom to the Iberian Peninsula. In our tradition, God gave these two identical swords to identical brothers—Boaz and Jacin—on the banks of the river Euphrates. The swords are never to be crossed or death will follow. Certain knowledge comes to the holder of the swords which, when applied to truth and honesty, brings enlightenment. When applied to evil, as has been done in the past, it brings only destruction."

Morales held the eyes of the newest Templar. "Hernando, you are charged with the safekeeping of Boaz and Jacin, the great swords of God. Wear one and conceal the other."

Hernando was suddenly uneasy. "Should we not hide both?"

"The best hiding spot is often in plain view," his uncle said, then added with a grin, "I wish I was going with you, young man."

Chapter 22

Wells looked through the spyglass as another rider left the estate.

"What if we have missed him and he is already on his way home?" the corporal complained.

Wells ignored him as he laid the brass telescope on his pack, then rolled over and sat up. They had been hidden at the top of this grassy knoll for days, watching men come and go, and now Wells was starting to second-guess himself. And his subordinate's constant complaining was getting to him. Tonight he would go down to the estate and see if Hernando's black Andalusian was still stabled, or if, as his corporal suggested, they had somehow missed their commander's departure.

The distant sound of shod hooves on cobblestone drew him back to the hill's crest. He lifted the spyglass in time to see Hernando's black stallion and another horse leaving the estate. He scrambled back down. "Let's go," he told the corporal.

They rode to a stand of dense bush, the first real cover on the road that left Morales' estate, and waited just out of sight on the far side for Hernando to pass by on the road. Moments later, Wells heard Hernando and the other rider coming up the road at a canter. *Good,* Wells thought; *they've entered the woods.*

But someone else was counting on the bush offering concealment from the eyes of the estate. Before Hernando and his companion reached Wells, a shot rang out, then riders crashed out of the tree line to fall on Hernando and the other rider. Wells and his man goaded their horses through the thick cover toward the sounds of fighting. They burst out onto the road right in the middle of the action.

Wells quickly scanned the melee. The duke had been unhorsed but had snatched his attacker's reins, trying to control the horse while hacking at the rider's legs with his sword. Hernando had already dispatched one assassin and had his horse locked against another. Wells saw Hernando glance his way, but there was no recognition in the look; he had to assume that Hernando would consider him and the corporal more attackers. He urged his horse forward, aiming to come at the assassin from the opposite side.

Before he reached the battling horsemen, the assassin's blade slid into Hernando's forearm and severed flesh, sinew, and tendon. Hernando dropped his sword to the ground. As his attacker raised his sword for the killing blow, Wells pushed his horse full on into the assassin's mare, throwing the rider. The man landed heavily on the ground. His horse, still stumbling to regain its footing, stepped squarely on the ruffian's chest. Blood burst from his mouth.

Wells spun his horse. The corporal was riding his horse straight toward a third rider who was reloading his pistol. The murderer fumbled to finish, then raised and cocked the pistol. The shot left the barrel just as the corporal slammed his horse into him. Horses and riders went down in a kicking, smoking heap. The corporal recovered first, pulling a dagger out of the back of his belt as he crawled over the writhing mass of horse and human. He pushed it slowly into the screaming man's neck.

Seeing another rider spurring his horse away, Wells urged his horse after him, running him down only fifty paces away and dispatching him with a brutal slash of his blade. Satisfied, he turned his horse back to the scene of the attack.

The duke had slashed the rider's legs and succeeded in unseating him; now he stood over him, his face flushed with rage.

"Don't kill him, Uncle!" Hernando called, then suddenly looked down at his arm. Blood was shooting from the gaping wound. Hernando dismounted and removed his belt to use as a tourniquet. He succeeded in staunching the flow.

Wells looked around for his corporal and saw the man stand up, stagger toward them, then fall to his knees. He wavered there for a moment as a large patch of blood grew across his shirt, then tumbled over into the dirt. Wells went over and knelt beside the man to seek a heartbeat. The fingers he pressed to the man's neck felt nothing.

Hernando picked up his sword in his left hand and came over to stand beside Wells. "This is one of mine," he said, then looked at Wells. "Although what he—and you—are doing here, I'm not sure."

The duke had regained his composure. "I'm just glad they were here," he said. "I shudder to think where we'd be if they had not shown up at the best possible time."

Hernando nodded. "Wells, it sure is good to see you!"

The duke spotted Hernando's wound. "Look at your arm. We'll have to sew that up right away."

"First we need some answers," Hernando said, moving back over to the man his uncle had subdued.

"Two got away," the duke said, looking around as he followed Hernando.

"Uh, one," Wells corrected him. "Unfortunately the other one didn't want to come back to talk to ya, commander." Actually it had not even occurred to Wells to try to capture the last assassin he had dispatched with speedy pleasure.

The ruffian's leg was bleeding where the duke had slashed it. Hernando stepped on the man's thigh. He winced in pain but did not cry out. "He's a tough one," Wells observed. "He may not give up any information."

"Who hired you?" Hernando said, adding to his threat by placing the tip of his sword against the man's throat.

To Wells' surprise, the man gave up the information with out hesitation. "A woman. In a pub." He elaborated when Hernando moved his sword: "She gave us your location and paid us in gold."

"A woman?" Hernando repeated, sounding surprised. "What was her name?"

"I don't know."

"What did she look like?"

"I don't know!" the man protested when Hernando again twitched the sword. "The veil from her hat covered her face. By her manner, she was a lady."

"What lady would have a person killed!" Hernando barked. He let off the pressure a bit. "Where is the pub?"

"In the port of Cadez," the man gasped. "It's called the Land's End."

"You should have waited there. We will be there in less than a fortnight." Hernando removed his foot from the man's bloody leg. "Here Wells, do something with this garbage."

Hernando moved unsteadily to sit on a boulder beside the road. Blood oozed from his wound. Nearby, his uncle was already unrolling a bundle containing his medical kit and some distilled alcohol.

"We should go back to the estate," the duke told Hernando as Wells hauled the ruffian to his feet.

Wells led the prisoner over to a tree and was about to tie him up when the man lunged at him. Wells tried to draw his sword, but the ruffian wrestled him to the ground. They flailed about, each trying to get the upper hand. The assassin's hand came up, clutching a fist-sized rock, and Wells abandoned his sword, instead sending one hand questing for his dagger while he gripped the man's wrist with his other hand. The man brought his other hand up to pry at Wells' fingers; Wells squeezed tighter and pushed harder, his arm trembling with the effort. His other hand found the hilt of his dagger; his fingers wrapped around it and tugged the weapon free. As the man ripped Wells' hand free of his wrist and reared back with a triumphant growl, Wells brought the dagger up and drove it home.

The man slumped over him and lay still. Wells also lay still for a moment, catching his breath. As the duke hurried over to him, Wells was already rolling the body off. It dropped to the ground with a thud, Wells' dagger protruding from the chest.

"I hope we didn't need to get any more information from this pond scum!" Wells gasped as he kicked the man's legs off of him and stood.

They took Hernando back to Morales' estate. Hernando was dropping in and out of consciousness as they arrived. Even Wells could tell that the loss of blood had been extensive.

* * * *

That night Laocan visited Hernando as he sweated through a fever. "Do not worry, my Hernando; you will wake in the morning, strong and beautiful. Ah, look what the witch has done to your alabaster skin! My best warrior priest could not scratch you, but this evil one has marked you forever." Hernando could hear her soft voice and knew she was near, but he could not open his eyes to gaze at her sweet face.

In the morning Hernando did awake as Laocan had promised. He felt well until he tried to sit up—then the wound burned as his uncle's crude stitches pulled at his skin. The previous day's scuffle rushed back to his mind. Who had perpetrated such a cowardly act? His enemies in the church? Hernando had a feeling gnawing at the back of his brain as he rose and dressed carefully.

"Good morning, young man," Morales greeted him when he joined the Grand Master and his uncle in the dining room. "We were a bit worried, but your man Wells said that it would take more than a little prodding from a toad-sticker to keep you down!" He chuckled.

"Good to see you awake, my boy," the duke added.

In a short week, Hernando was back at his estate making preparations for the recovery of the Templars' lost treasure. His mother, he knew, was not pleased about the adventure. Laocan visited Hernando almost every night. She giggled and buzzed with excitement. In another short week, he was in Cadez visiting his and his uncle's shipyards.

"It is amazing how far along the new ships are," Hernando commented as they strode through the shipyard, trying to pull his uncle out of his pensive mood. The duke muttered something about the king's wish and political will, but Hernando had already turned his attention to a tavern sign across the yard, on a small side street. "Land's End," he read aloud, and started toward the building.

The duke, unaware of Hernando's discovery, continued on for a few steps before realizing that Hernando was not only not listening, he wasn't even beside him anymore. "Hernando, where are you going?" he called.

"To get some answers!" Hernando called over his shoulder, noting that Wells had fallen in behind him, again his constant shadow. He grinned as he recalled his master sergeant apologizing to the countess for the puncturing of her son, and swearing that it would definitely never happen again.

Hernando stepped through the tavern door and paused to let his eyes adjust to the dimmer light. Only a few patrons were availing themselves of the tavern's services this early in the day; the rush would come later, as men left work and paused on their way home to their wives. The barkeep eyeballed Hernando's uniform then looked past him to Wells and puckered his lips as if sensing trouble.

Hernando leaned against the bar. "Port." He threw a silver coin onto the worn wood plank that served as the bar. The barkeep's eyes ballooned. He reached for the coin, but Hernando grabbed the grizzled man's hand. "Its all yours if you can answer a few questions," Hernando said when the keep turned his timeworn face up to him.

"Ask away, captain, and I'll try my best." He tried to pull the fist clenched around the coin away, but Hernando held tight.

"Two weeks past, in this bar, a lady hired some ruffians to murder someone." Hernando looked deep into the man's eyes. The keep squirmed a bit, and Hernando sensed he knew something.

The barkeep looked down at his hand and then past Hernando to the intimidating presence of Wells, behind him. "A lady sailed for the New World only yesterday, on the morning tide. I do not know her name; she was very private about her business. She stayed here for a couple of weeks, then left. That's all I know." The bartender waited for Hernando to release him. "She paid well for her privacy," he added when Hernando maintained his hold.

Hernando held his eye a moment, then loosened his hold. The barkeep scurried away to get a bottle of port.

"What do you think, Commander?" Wells asked, looking like he had his own suspicions.

Hernando turned and left without answering Wells. He too had a terrible feeling niggling at the back of his mind.

Chapter 23

It wasn't long before Hernando and his retinue were aboard the small fleet that had arrived from Malta. The four Templar ships were sleek merchants, heavily armed. Hernando was impressed with the speed at which they put to out sea.

Standing in the bow of the flagship, he enjoyed the feeling of Spanish oak humming underfoot as the bow split the waves. The wind was warm and his mind drifted off to that first voyage across the Atlantic. It seemed so long ago. He remembered the trepidation he'd felt on his first crossing, after the recent death of his father and the family upheaval. Now he had a sense of well-being in his gut and pride swelled his chest. He smiled and leaned into the breeze.

Hernando spent his days in meetings with the two Egyptians, learning how they would disable the many traps that guarded the Templar treasure. For the most part, though, Hernando was bored. He often sparred with Wells on the deck, but it was only half-hearted. Then one morning a familiar sent tickled his nose. He strode to the gunwale and peered ahead, looking for some sign of the New World.

"Any sign of land?" he yelled to the man in the crow's nest.

The man started from his heat-induced stupor and answered, "No, sir!" Then he looked about as if he'd missed something.

Hernando was sure he'd smelled the tropical land of Laocan, but another three days passed before someone bellowed, "Land ho!" Hernando felt himself getting excited as they sliced along under blue skies. They would put into Santo Domingo for provisions, and he was looking forward to visiting the governor and his son.

The small fleet made port just as the sun was about to set. The buildings around the port were awash in a red glow. Hernando saw a small delegation coming through the gathering crowd and recognized the young Averra pushing his way to the forefront. He waved widely when he recognized Hernando.

Hernando turned to Wells. "Did you bring your dress uniform?" Wells just grumbled and turned to see to the men.

The young officer came aboard and saluted Hernando. Hernando returned the salute out of courtesy. "I see you've been promoted since we last met," he added as he reached to shake the young man's hand.

"Yes, it pays to be the governor's son, I guess." He took Hernando's hand and shook it vigorously.

"I'm looking forward to visiting that pub we had so much fun in on our last visit," Hernando said, poker-faced, then paused when Averra looked suddenly ill. Hernando released a grin. "I'm kidding!"

Averra smiled at the joke but took a moment to put the memory from his mind. The young officer and Hernando talked for some time. Hernando was surprised to hear of the increased pirate activity in the waters around Hispaniola of late. Finally came the invitation to a party at the governor's palace. Hernando accepted graciously.

When he and his small retinue were announced at the entrance to the governor's palace, the governor immediately cornered Hernando. "Hernando! It is so good to see you, young man. We've heard about the assassination attempt on the king." He paused to shake his head with a disapproving frown. Then his expression brightened again. "Fame seems to follow you wherever you travel! Are you going to Vera Cruz? I hear that your man José has been busy fortifying his position there."

Knowing the governor would keep rambling, Hernando cut in before he forgot the first question. "Yes, we will stop in and see my good friend José and deliver some supplies. I imagine he's run out of good port by now." He smiled. "But it is good to see you again, Governor. How are you faring out here, so far from the action back at court?"

"Yes, it is difficult this far out. We get so little news." As the governor started to lament about his remote posting, a commotion erupted at the entrance to the ballroom. The peacock who had announced Hernando's arrival was now trying to prevent Wells and ten of his men from entering the party. Hernando likened the scene to a small bantam rooster confronting a large bull.

Excusing himself hastily, Hernando headed for the door, closely followed by the governor. "I'm sorry, Governor," Hernando said when he realized Governor Averra was beside him. "My gift for you is a little late."

Governor Averra waved off his guardsmen, who had also joined the fray. Wells' men carried cases of fine wine and port from Spain, Germany, and France into the room and deposited them at the governor's feet. There was a tear in the governor's eye as he realized Hernando had just brought him the most precious gift: a piece of home.

"Come, we shall dine and sample some of the treats the commander has brought us, here in this godforsaken land!" the governor called out, then swept away toward the dining room.

"You sure know how to make an entrance, Hernando," a sweet voice said behind him.

Hernando turned to identify the angelic voice and immediately froze, dumbfounded. Isabella stood before him in a flowing crimson gown. Her breasts jostled for position at the top of the bodice, which hugged her figure down to her narrow waist. Ringlets brushed innocently against the bare skin at her shoulders.

Feeling himself attracted to her, Hernando was immediately angry. "I-I thought you were—" he stammered.

"Dead?" Isabella offered. "Executed, burned at the stake, hung?" He could hear the venom in her voice. "I see you're as strong and healthy as ever."

A veiled reference to her trying to have him assassinated, he thought. Hernando could not have imagined he'd ever see her again. But here she was, beautiful and deadly, like a serpent coiling for a strike. He instinctively stepped back and she followed, pressing in close so others could not overhear.

"I'm not finished with you yet, Commander Diaz!" she whispered.

Unable to reply, Hernando whirled and walked away. Wells stepped in front of him and he came back to his senses. "Wells! It is nice to see a friendly face." Hernando forced a smile.

"Am I dreaming or is that not the count's niece?"

"No, my friend, I assure you we are wide awake." He turned to look back at Isabella with Wells at his side. The three glared at each other. The governor's guests were being shuffled into the dining room. Hernando wanted to make for the door and Wells, by the look of his scowl, wanted to slip his dagger up under her left breast.

Isabella was seated with an older gentleman at the end of Hernando's long table. He watched from the corner of his eye as Isabella giggled and openly flirted with the pot-bellied plantation owner who had brought her to the party. *She is up to her old tricks again,* Hernando thought.

The governor entertained his guests with stories of Hernando's exploits. Isabella did not look toward Hernando the rest of the evening. With dinner done and Wells chomping at the bit to get out of there, Hernando tried to make his excuses to the governor and leave, but the governor pulled Hernando aside.

"The pirates grow bold and raid our ships openly," Governor Averra said quietly. "You must appeal to the king for more galleons to defeat these mercenaries. We are losing so many ships to them, I fear the king will have my head soon."

Hernando smiled reassuringly. "My uncle and I have been charged with the task of transporting the riches of New Spain to the court. I can assure you, a large fleet of heavily armed ships is almost ready to sail as we speak." The governor seemed to relax a bit. "Who is that gentleman there?" Hernando nodded toward the portly man escorting Isabella.

"Where?" The governor followed Hernando's gaze. "Oh, that's the richest landowner in Hispaniola. His plantations far exceed my own." The governor sounded a bit jealous.

"Do you know the woman with him?" Hernando asked casually.

"No, but she is a welcome sight for weary eyes, is she not?" The governor smiled his appreciation.

"Do you remember the Count and Countess of Durraldo and their niece who travelled back to Spain with us on the *Alva Cordova*?" Hernando prompted.

"Yes," the governor answered uncertainly, as if searching his memory despite his assertion.

"That is his niece," Hernando said, "and what I'm about to tell you may shock you." He recounted the whole sordid story, from his romantic tryst aboard ship to the wife's mysterious death to the plot against the king to her murder attempt and finally, their meeting here tonight.

The governor seemed to be having trouble taking it all in, but when Hernando finished he said, "I will have her arrested."

Hernando put a firm hand on the governor's arm as he made to move away. "Wait until after your party," he suggested. "You do not want to disturb your guests."

The governor stopped. "Yes, quite right. I will have her arrested in the morning."

The governor looked as if he were already planning the confiscation of the rich landowner's properties, but Hernando was just making sure he had enough time to leave port. He could not afford to be delayed as a witness at any future indictment of Isabella. Excusing himself, he and his men returned immediately to his ship.

The young Averra had accompanied them. "God speed, Hernando. I will make your apologies to my father in the morning," the young man assured him as they parted ways.

"Be careful with Isabella," Hernando warned him. "She would gleefully fillet a young man like you. Take some armed officers—do not go alone." Hernando had shared with the son some of what he had told his father on the ride down to the wharf, but he still feared for the young man's safety as he watched him ride away.

"He will be all right, Commander," Wells said quietly, reading the concern on Hernando's face.

Hernando turned to him. "Stow the gear, Wells; I want to make the tide at first light."

"Aye, Captain!" Wells threw a salute into the air and Hernando smiled for the first time after seeing Isabella that night.

* * * *

Hernando was on deck before dawn. As the morning breeze stirred, the crew loosed the ropes and dropped the canvas. Slowly, it embraced the wind. The ship headed for open water, and Hernando moved to the bow to enjoy the salty breeze.

They did not encounter any pirates on the short journey to Vera Cruz. This was a blessing, as they had left the rest of the flotilla back in port to continue loading supplies. The only incident on the trip to Vera Cruz was a sailor sounding the alarm at the sight of a ghost. *They are a superstitious lot,* Hernando thought.

José and Luis embraced on the new pier. Hernando stood uncomfortably by for a few seconds, then spoke up. "You have done a remarkable job here, José." He gazed appreciatively at the fortifications and the nearly completed stone church rising in the middle of the settlement.

"I think my calling is as a builder, not a soldier," José said with a grin, and shook Hernando's hand vigorously.

"Luis, you go and have a visit with your brother," Hernando told them. "You can relate all that has happened in the past year or so since we've last seen him. I will see to the unloading of the ship." Luis hesitated, but Hernando just held up his hand and Luis smiled and turned back to José. The two brothers walked up the pier to the settlement.

"Wells," Hernando shouted, turning only to be startled by the large sergeant standing in front of him. "You get a particular joy out of that, don't you."

"Out of what, sir?" Wells asked innocently, then smirked. "I already gave the orders to unload, sir."

Hernando nodded and turned back to survey the work that had been completed on the settlement. He was amazed at the speed of the transformation, but as he walked toward the gates he noticed large numbers of native workers and realized how José could have accomplished so much. About to head toward the two familiar robed men directing a large work force on and around the church, Hernando paused when he heard voices raised in excitement, back on the pier.

He turned back to see what was happening and even from this distance, he knew what it was. A woman was surrounded by a crowd of men, who were manhandling her off the ship. "Isabella!" Hernando blurted, and headed for the ruckus. Wells got there first and took her roughly by the arm, pushing a sailor away and growling at the rest. Mindful of his fierce reputation, they backed off a bit, but glowered, angry about her being on board, for it was considered bad luck. Hernando reached the knot of angry men and pushed toward her, physically shoving men aside until they realized it was their commander doing the pushing and backed off.

When Isabella saw him, her expression shifted from fear to arrogance. "Get your filthy mob off of me!" she said in loud voice, pretending to be unaffected by her recent treatment. Wells must have tightened his grip, because she winced and looked at him. He was not easily intimidated.

Hernando had regained his composure. He moved in closer. "You keep showing up at the most inappropriate times. This time you should have stayed in Santo Domingo." He looked at his sergeant. "Wells, see if José has built a stockade yet—if not, build one!"

Wells smiled, looking relieved that his commander had not crumbled before her beauty. "She couldn't have stayed hidden for all that time without help," he said in an undertone. "I'll lock this piece up and then set about finding her accomplice." He tugged her away.

Hernando had supper with José and Luis. He introduced his Egyptian companions and explained they were on a mission for the king and Spain, which wasn't too far off the truth. José was disappointed to learn that they would not be here for long; that they would wait for the other two ships to arrive and then take their leave. They talked long into the night, with José regaling them with stories of Cortez's conquests and the riches he'd amassed. Luis was happy he'd decided to remain with his brother in the New World. He laid out the land grants and charters for José to see and explained how they had foiled a plot to assassinate the king. Which brought them to the stowaway. Hernando let Luis explain her participation in the plot and her conviction on treason charges. Hearing someone else talk about her cunning and treacherous nature brought home to Hernando how dangerous she was.

"What are we going to do with her?" José asked.

Hernando shrugged and rose from the table. "That's a question for the bright light of morning, gentlemen. For now, if someone will point me to a bed ..." He was feeling the effects of the port he'd brought for José.

Wells had set up their rooms and taken up residence in the one adjoining Hernando's. Noting that Wells' door was ajar and light flickered within as the servant was showing him to his billet, Hernando called, "Good night, Wells."

"Good night, sir."

Hernando entered his room and flopped down in a large chair crafted of cane and stiff grasses. He kicked off his boots and unclasped the buckle on his sword belt, then stood and removed his clothes. He was dog-tired, he thought as he headed toward the bed. Then he stopped and turned to retrieve the great Saracen sword. "I think you should sleep beside me tonight, Boaz." The thought of Isabella being so close was unnerving. Hernando blew out the light and drew the wool covers up tight around his neck, but he could not sleep.

Sunlight came tumbling into the room as dawn broke. Laocan sat in the big chair with her small brown feet resting on the bed. She poked at Hernando, who'd overslept. She giggled when he opened his eyes. He was about to speak when she jumped into the air and landed on his chest with a heavy thud, knocking the air out of him and squealing with delight. "The great green-eyed god is captured by the Toltec princess," she declared, laughing and smothering his mouth with a wet kiss. "I knew you could not stay away. I have missed you so." She moved down and ground her pelvis into his. He immediately responded. He lifted her small frame and she kicked away the covers; he settled her on his loins and she moved against him. He closed his eyes in enjoyment.

"Sir!" Wells called quietly at the door. "Sir!" he called again, louder, and rapped the door with his callused knuckles.

Hernando opened his eyes. It was indeed morning and sadly, he was alone.

"Sir!" Wells rapped harder.

"Yes, Wells, I guess I overslept," Hernando called tiredly.

"Are you okay?" Wells asked. "I thought I heard a voice—I mean, a female voice. Are you ..." He trailed off suggestively.

"I'm okay, Wells. No one here but us chickens."

* * * *

Wells tipped his head to one side as he pondered the last comment. Shrugging, he left his commander and went to find some breakfast, but not before passing by the cell to reassure himself that Isabella was still locked within. He peered at her through a little window.

"Well, if it isn't Diaz's lap dog," she sneered when she saw him. "Bring me my breakfast, dog! Do you hear me?"

Wells stared at her and she shivered as if she felt a sudden chill. "I would gladly slit your throat and drop you in the sea for the crabs, if it were up to me," he said quietly.

"But it's not, is it?"

Wells smiled. "Not yet. But maybe soon." He turned and strode away to the sound of her cursing him.

* * * *

"I miss my horse, Wells," Hernando said as he and Wells rode through the jungle toward the Toltec village. "Remind me to bring him on our next trip to the New World."

Wells smiled and shrugged. *He probably figures I'm just making conversation to avoid talking about what to do with Isabella,* Hernando thought. He was partly right, but Hernando had made his mind up that he would be back because he felt at peace here.

They were received with great fanfare by the Toltec chief and Hernando wondered how he could have known that they were coming. It was clear that the Toltec king had already been informed that Hernando was back, and equally clear that the chieftain looked forward to seeing him. The fact that Hernando had come to see the great king so soon after his arrival showed his people his great importance in the scheme of things.

They ate after a great hoopla, and Hernando could not believe how many people now spoke Spanish. The great chieftain proudly told Hernando how their lives had changed, and that they had all become Christians. Realizing that this fierce and proud people would never have total control of their land again, Hernando looked about at the smiling faces, young and old, and thought about Laocan.

The chief must have sensed Hernando's sadness for at that point he again offered Hernando a choice of his daughters. Hernando respectfully declined, although one of the daughters was a spitting image of Laocan. The girl lacked Laocan's presence, however, and dared not look Hernando in the eye. This was not Laocan, he told himself, and she could never be. He explained to the chief, when he refused and it seemed that the king was going to take offence, that Laocan lived in his heart and she often visited him at dream time and helped chase away the loneliness. The chief listened solemnly, then smiled and told Hernando that he was a good man.

When they left, Hernando spied the young Laocan look-alike as he was waving good-bye. He smiled she smiled back, then ran away.

Back at Vera Cruz, Hernando passed the days talking to the Jesuits and José about their construction efforts. He found out that the native workers were captives that the Toltecs had sold to them. He often rode up and down the long, white sand beaches with Wells and enjoyed not having a battle to run off to. But he was getting impatient, waiting for the other two ships to arrive.

He did not visit Isabella in the stockade, but had Wells check on her once a day. Sergeant Wells checked more than that, and had the guard changed every day so she could not become too familiar with them.

Finally the supply convoy arrived at Vera Cruz. Hernando had José's supplies off-loaded and said farewell to the brothers at a dinner held for the occasion. "I will miss you both, and I envy the adventure you are about to have," Hernando told them, as always feeling uncomfortable giving a speech, although in the past few years he had been called on to do so many times. He gave them advice about dealing with the Toltecs and told them to stay true to King Charles and Spain. "Cortez is a conquistador and his loyalties may not always rest with Spain," he told them. "Tread carefully when he returns from conquering the unknown lands. You have wrestled civilization out of the wilderness here, and I'm proud of you."

Hernando looked toward the Jesuits, who had consumed large amounts of wine. They nodded to him as if he had acknowledged their achievements. But he was wondering about the fate of the Toltec people at the brown robes' hands. God would watch over them, he told himself.

This is how a proud father feels when his son goes out into the world on his own to make his mark, Hernando thought. But then he realized he too had had too much wine, and sat down. His comrades clapped, stood to cheer, and banged the tables. *Apparently it was quite a rousing speech,* Hernando thought wryly, and smiled. He would miss the New World and all its surprises.

*   *   *   *

By first light they were aboard the tiny flotilla and making ready to sail.

"Commander Calsonia, I am very busy at the moment," the captain started to say when Wells brought him at Hernando's summons. Then he realized something was amiss.

"I have given your quarters to the young lady Isabella," Hernando told him. "She seems to have been comfortable there on the crossing from Spain." He paused as the captain thought hard about his response.

"Sir, she told me you'd be excited to see her and that you would reward me. I had no idea of her involvement in a plot against the king, or of her actions against you. I only learned of these things in the last few weeks. Sir, I'm sorry … I …" He knelt at Hernando's feet, which surprised him.

"Get up, man, your crew can see you!" Hernando hissed.

The captain rose but he did not seem as tall as he had before. Hernando knew how persuasive Isabella could be and that sickened him, for he knew how she got men to do her bidding. "You will have to make sleeping arrangements with your mates. And make no mistake, if you try to see her on the voyage home you will be left in the middle of the Atlantic to swim home. Do I make myself clear, Captain?"

"Yes, sir, completely." He looked at Wells, who had grabbed his arm to lead him away.

Hernando was pensive as the three ships turned on the breeze and headed north. Eyes on the small port, he watched the fourth ship he'd left for José recede as they made for open water. Laocan came out onto the beach and waved. Hernando's heart felt empty. "It must be the sister," he whispered to himself.

The expedition north was good therapy for Hernando. He enjoyed the sea. He could feel the small ship humming the song the wind was singing. Days passed in meetings with the two Egyptians, planning the recovery of the treasure and plotting the next day's heading. They sighted land a few times, which surprised Hernando.

One of the Egyptians shared a chart with Hernando that depicted a huge landmass to the west, one that Hernando could not believe was so large. As far as Hernando knew, no Spaniard was aware of its existence. "How is it that you have these charts and the knowledge of a land we discovered?"

"Many years ago," one of the brothers explained, "a pharaoh came to power—"

"Pharaoh?" Hernando interrupted.

"A king, but much more than that—the people worshipped him as a god on earth. He had enormous power and ruled over a kingdom many times the size of your Spain, a kingdom of immense riches. His name was Akhenaten. Before him, the people worshipped many gods and the priesthood of each of these gods was very powerful—so powerful that nothing happened in the country or its protectorates without their say-so. It is said that the sun god Aten came to Akhenaten and told him to worship one god and only one god. Aten gave Akhenaten and his brother sacred swords with which to rule the empire."

Hernando instinctively placed his hand on the grip of his sword.

"Yes, the very same swords you are now charged to protect," the Egyptian said, seeing his movement. "The various priesthoods were outraged and resisted the pharaoh. He decreed formally that all people would worship the one god and outlawed the worship of all others. The priests had lost their power. They plotted against the throne. Akhenaten ruled for twenty years, then was murdered and beheaded."

"Beheaded?" Hernando questioned.

"Yes. Back then the people believed in an afterlife much like your Heaven, but the pharaoh would not be able to enter the afterlife without his head. The priests severed his head and hid his body and head in separate places. Akhenaten's brother Smenkhkare retrieved his head and sword and fled the country to the land of the Canaans. After a few years there, he fled Judea with a large retinue of Aten believers and priests. The Phoenicians brought them to the New World in their ships."

Hernando remembered the legend that Laocan had told him, claiming that a great hero would return from the east to reclaim the throne of the Aztecs. Cortez had used this legend to undermine the Aztec allegiances.

The Egyptian continued. "So you see, this new land was known to some and the knowledge passed down over the ages to protect Aten's followers. The brotherhood discovered many secrets while on crusade in the Holy Land. The location of the New World was among them. They concealed its location for their own purposes, as you now know."

Hernando was filled with questions but as he was about to speak, an alarm went up. He heard shouts of a sail from amongst the sailors. "Pirates!" Hernando shouted, and grabbed his armour and pistols and headed on deck.

The brilliant sunlight stunned him for a moment. Wells was instantly at his side, directing his gaze. "Port side, two brigantines making straight for us, sir!"

Hernando focused. Sure enough, two ships in close formation were bearing down on them. "They have the wind at their stern," Wells added.

"All hands, battle stations!" the captain ordered. The first mate feverishly signalled the other two small ships, as if they had not seen the danger.

One of the Egyptian brothers turned and headed belowdecks. Hernando finished buckling his armour and placed his helmet on his head, then moved with Wells to stand beside the captain and strengthen his morale. "Load the cannons with shot as they will try to board us," Hernando told him.

The captain hesitated, then gave the order; he looked as though he'd gladly give over control of the situation to Hernando.

"Wells, keep the men low. They will try to strafe the deck to clear it for boarding."

The two ships aimed to slice through the flotilla and separate one ship from the rest. Hernando realized their tactic and hollered orders to the first mate: "Tell the other two ships to stay close! Don't get separated!"

The Egyptian returned from below. "Hoist this flag immediately!" he said, thrusting a cloth bundle at Hernando. "Now!" he said when Hernando hesitated, and shoved it into Hernando's hands.

Hernando ran to the main mast and lowered the white and red standard, replacing it with this new flag. As it unfurled he could see a golden lion on a white background and a golden sun disk above two crossed swords in one corner. *It's a pirate flag,* he thought as he turned to look at the two larger ships bearing down on them.

One of Hernando's ships broke formation and turned, losing the wind. It mired and quickly fell away. The oncoming ships careened off to the port side of Hernando's ship without firing a shot. They circled and dropped some canvas to match Hernando's ship's speed, but stayed out of range of Hernando's smaller cannon. He could feel the crew's tension.

"They must think we loaded gold at Vera Cruz," Wells muttered, nervously looking the two ships over.

"They will not attack us, at least not until they figure out why we have one of their flags," Hernando replied, and turned to the Egyptians. "Why have they not attacked and why are we flying a pirate flag?"

The brothers looked confused, then realized that Hernando was new to the brotherhood and needed a quick history lesson. "The corsairs are members of the brotherhood of light, or at least the captain must be," Hamil explained. "We saw their standard and responded in kind. They are bound by blood oath not to attack us; in fact, it is their duty to protect us."

Hernando removed his helmet and scratched his head. "So what do we do now?"

"They are waiting for us to drop sails and come to," Joseph answered.

"That would make us sitting ducks! I'm not ordering that!" Hernando retorted.

"If you drop a little canvas at a time to see if the corsairs match us, you can be sure they will not take advantage of the situation."

What the Egyptian said made sense, but Hernando was cautious. He'd had run-ins with pirates before. "Make the adjustments, Captain," he finally said, "but tell the men to be ready to ply the canvas back on at a moment's notice!"

All the ships slowed their northerly progress as each ship matched the other. Hernando peered across the closing distance between the two lead ships. A familiar golden-haired figure stared back at him. They both realized they had crossed paths before. *This is the pirate that tried to raid the Alva Cordoba when she was laden with that first cargo of Aztec gold!* Hernando thought. He did not trust this brazen pirate and called for Wells, who, of course, was right behind him.

"Just like old times, eh?" Wells said.

Hernando managed a smile "Take control of the cannons below; aim them at the waterline, and sink that brigantine at the first sign of trouble."

"Aye, sir!" Wells turned and vanished below.

Hernando smiled again. *He really loves the thought of a good scuffle.*

The ships slowed until they'd almost stopped, keeping just enough sail to maintain the heading. The pirate lowered a longboat and rowed across to Hernando, the captain standing in the bow with his yellow hair flowing in the breeze. Hernando checked his snipers in the ship's rigging before moving to the railing to receive this unwelcome guest. No one piped the pirate captain aboard as he and his men climbed the rope ladder that had been lowered for them.

The handsome rogue looked at the captain and then to Hernando. He knew who was in charge—he introduced himself to Hernando. "Allow me to introduce myself: Lord James Atkins of Badennochburn papered English servant of His Royal Majesty King Henry VIII."

Hernando understood immediately that he was a privateer in the service of England, charged with stopping the flow of gold to Spain by any means necessary. "I am Hernando Calsonia, commander of this small flotilla." He stuck out his hand, half expecting the pirate to bite it off.

Lord James took it and shook it in the way of the secret brotherhood. "Is there a quieter place where we can talk, Commander?"

Hernando was a little stunned to think that this cold killer was indeed a member of his father's secret society. "Yes; right this way." He led the pirate, accompanied by his Egyptian friends and Wells—who had reappeared at Hernando's side—to his cabin.

There, before Hernando could speak, one of the Egyptian brothers spoke up. "From what port do you sail?"

"Tyre," Lord James answered without hesitation.

"And what are you seeking?"

"Knowledge and truth," the lord answered obediently.

The Egyptians looked at Hernando. He did not know how to proceed. "All I can tell you is that we are on a secret mission for the brotherhood, one of great importance." Hernando hesitated.

The blond captain spoke. "Then you have my pledge of protection as long as you are in the Atlantic!" He inclined his head slightly to show subservience.

Hernando breathed a sigh of relief. "Stay for supper and we will talk; we have just taken on fresh supplies and our cook is very good."

"Yes, I know you have just left Vera Cruz." He smiled at Hernando's startled expression. "And I would be happy to join you. Let me signal my ships so we are not delayed, and I will stay as your hostage!"

Hernando was taken aback, then realized that the pirate had a good sense of humour. He poured some of his best port and they settled into a long discussion of history and politics. Hernando was fascinated with the stories Lord James recounted, particularly the story of the Templars escaping the pope's attempt to round them all up in one big sweep supported by the king of France, and how they had spirited away the great riches and knowledge they had amassed.

"I even know to where you are headed," Lord James continued, "for my ancestors were the Knights of Malta, the name they took after Black Friday to hide their Templar origins. They brought the treasure you seek to the hidden shores."

Hernando was astounded. "How is it possible that, of all the pirates out here—no offence—we run into you?"

"It is not coincidence, Hernando, it is the hand of God guiding you," The Egyptian Hamil said. "The treasure we seek is not riches in gold but riches in knowledge—the knowledge that proves that the Muslims, the Christians, and the Jews all worship one god, the same god. That knowledge has been kept from the people by Egyptian priests, Catholic clergy, and Islamic clerics since time began. We will restore the truth and the light."

Hernando sat in quiet thought for a moment. "So it is up to us, then." He raised his glass. "To success!"

"To success!" the others echoed.

They spent most of the night talking and planning. Hernando rapidly grew fond of Lord James. Their conversation eventually drifted to the open seas and pirate life.

"It is all changing," Lord James complained. "It's getting crowded out here; getting so as you can't even go a week without running into another ship. It's fortunate that you intend to recover the treasure now, for soon even I would not be able to protect you out here!"

As he watched the longboat return the lord back to his ship, Hernando had a different opinion of pirates—or at least this one, he thought.

Chapter 24

The privateer's two ships escorted Hernando along the coast of some unknown land until they arrived at the coordinates the Egyptians had given the ship's navigator. The Egyptians checked the progress of the ships against the stars every night and were convinced this was the location of the treasure. Hernando realized why his ships had been chosen for this mission as they scouted around for an island—their smaller size was perfect for this. Lord James' larger ships circled offshore like a couple of hungry sharks.

Just a few leagues farther north, they found what they were looking for: an oak-blanketed island with two bays. Hernando thought it looked like every other island they had seen, but they dropped anchor and sent ashore an exploration party headed by Hernando and Wells.

"Keep your eyes peeled, Sergeant," Hernando said as they walked along the sandy beach toward some large boulders. "The Egyptians say that the Templars had some problems with the Indians."

"Maybe I can find a hornet's nest to poke!" Wells grinned and took two men to look about.

The Egyptians found three inscribed stones that apparently were the corners of a triangle, though Hernando could not make out the shape. They pointed and jabbered away in a language that grated on Hernando's nerves, so he went to see to the unloading of the supplies and men.

The miners that they had brought from the Spanish tin mines were relieved to be on solid ground and anxious to get to work, for they had been promised a fortune for their part in this enterprise. Teams of men set up camp, cleared trees, or hewed timbers. Hernando was impressed with all the activity, but didn't really have much to do. He and Wells wandered the edge of the small island under the pretext of watching for Indians.

"What would you like to do when we are finished here, Wells?" Hernando asked.

Wells, who was out in front actively looking for an enemy of some type, stopped and turned. "Haven't given it much thought. I just assumed we'd go back to Spain and soldier for your friend the king."

Hernando thought for a minute as they continued on. "Maybe we should protect our shipping interests—from the pirates, I mean."

"Well, that yellow-haired rogue seems to think that the waters are going to get crowded out here, so maybe that's a good idea." Wells sounded tentative, as if he wondered why Hernando was thinking about this now.

Lost in thought, Hernando walked right into Wells a moment later. "Shh," Wells whispered, eyes scanning the area. "I thought I heard something."

Hernando quickly came back to his senses. They stood quietly for a moment, the only visible movement the sun sparkling on the surface of the placid stretch of water separating the island from the mainland. Then Hernando heard it: faint splashing. Just around the next curve, something or someone was in the water. They crouched in unison and Hernando quietly slid Boaz from its scabbard, the steel hissing at its release.

Wells moved soundlessly forward through the underbrush and Hernando followed. They paused at the forest's edge and peered through the foliage at a party of men getting out of three small boats. "About ten of them," Wells whispered. Hernando nodded.

They were armed with spears, clubs, and bows. Their faces and parts of their upper bodies were painted with black and ochre pigments. Hernando did not think they were here to talk. They looked like a scouting party. There was probably a much larger collection of trouble waiting on the mainland. Reaching forward, Hernando tapped Wells' shoulder and motioned to retreat when Wells looked at him. They quietly moved away and headed back to raise the alarm.

"To arms, to arms!" Hernando shouted as soon as he broke out into the open area where his men were working.

His men reacted instantly, reaching for their weapons. Hernando quickly formed a line of musketeers and placed his pikemen behind them with their long poles thrust through the front line to deter anyone brave enough to get through a volley of shot. They waited, but no one came.

Hernando looked at Wells. "Take the men into the forest, Wells! Stay together and move slowly."

"Yes, sir!" Wells turned and bellowed at the men, "Okay you riffraff, let's see if you remember how to fight. Keep your eyes peeled!" The group moved into the forest, picking their way through the undergrowth.

* * * *

They encountered no one as they made their way down to the shore, where three flimsy boats were pulled up and hidden in the brush. "Where are they?" Wells wondered aloud. "They must have gone around us! Back to the clearing!"

The men turned and rushed back to the excavation site. As they neared, Wells could hear the sound of fighting. When they broke into the open, Wells saw Hernando and a few others locked in combat with the Indians. He paused to assess the situation. The musketeers were useless in this situation—they could not use their muskets for fear of hitting their own men.

He watched Hernando use his blade to deflect a strike from a war club, then counter with a slash to his attacker's ribcage. Bright red blood spewed from under the young man's right arm. Hernando immediately whirled to defend against another attack. A stone spear point tore through his shirt without making contact with flesh. Hernando caught the shaft under his arm and pulled the attacker onto the glistening steel of his Saracen sword.

Wells and his contingent threw themselves into the mass of screaming and shouting Indians attacking Hernando's few remaining men. Seeing Hernando struggling toward the Egyptian brothers who were struggling with their own attackers, Wells raised his pistol, knowing he was too far off to get a clean shot. Hernando was stopped by a blow from a fearsome-looking warrior. As he tottered, Wells fired; the bullet grazed the warrior's shoulder and seemed to get his attention. As Hernando went down, the warrior looked about and shouted orders to what was left of his men. They melted into the bush.

"Take the men back to the boats and stop their escape!" Wells shouted at his corporal, his eyes on Hernando, who lay in a heap on the ground.

Wells fell to his knees and rolled Hernando over. Hernando feebly tried to stick his sword into Wells' big barrel chest. Wells pushed it aside and looked at the nasty gash on the side of Hernando's head. "I thought you might need some help so I came back to see …" His voice trailed off—Hernando was unresponsive. Wells grimly began wrapping Hernando's head in a strip from his shirt.

The Egyptians came to his aid, and the trio carried their unconscious commander to a makeshift hut that was only half built. They laid him on a canvas bed. As Wells straightened, his corporal entered and snapped off a salute.

"Report, Corporal," Wells said.

"Our men made their way back to the enemy craft as quickly as possible, but the Indians had already launched two of them and were paddling madly toward the other shore," the corporal said. "I ordered the musketeers to open fire and two more of the invaders were killed before they paddled out of range. Four escaped, sir. I left a small guard."

"How many?"

"Five."

"Double that."

"Yes, sir." He looked past Wells to the commander, his eyes wide with concern.

"He's tough; don't worry," Wells said tersely, watching the Egyptian brothers trickling some oriental tonic down his throat. Hernando relaxed; he looked like he'd fallen asleep.

"Let him rest now," Joseph said to Wells, and the pair went outside to speak to one another in low tones.

Wells felt guilty for not being at Hernando's side when the attack came. He knew the feeling was silly for Hernando would never blame him, but his mother would—he had promised the countess he'd protect Hernando. He shook off the feelings and went outside.

The Egyptians had already sent the men back to work. Wells pulled up a crate to the doorway and sat quietly in the shade to watch. Judging by their excitement, the Egyptians had located something. When they saw Wells watching, Hamil trotted over to elaborate.

"We have encountered one of the two elaborate traps that the Templars had set to protect the treasure," Hamil reported. "It consists of a tunnel that runs from the bay that will fill the excavation over top of the treasure with sea water, if not properly blocked. We will slide a large rock slab into position to block the sea from rushing in at the sixty foot level."

"And that's it?" Wells asked.

Hamil hesitated. "There is one other such tunnel in the opposite bay. There are many entry points, covered with coconut fibre and hidden from detection by gravel and stones. The only way to stop up the tunnels is to find the proper places designed for doing so, as with the stone slab."

Wells studied the working men. Then he glanced back at Hernando, and shrugged. "Get to it, then," he said. "We won't be going anywhere for a while, by the looks of it."

A day later the Egyptian brothers found the other tunnel and set the miners to digging a large shaft. The miners did not take long in sinking a shaft; every ten feet they encountered oak logs laid across the disturbed soil. At the sixty foot level water started to rush in, and the miners quickly exited the shaft. When the water stopped rising they bailed it out without any further infiltration. At ninety feet they encountered the last oak platform and underneath they found a natural cavern in the bedrock. A week had passed.

Hernando had awakened off and on during this week. The Indians had kept their distance. Wells had had Isabella moved off the ship to the relative comfort of a hut, where he could keep an eye on her.

On the ninth day of digging, a miner shouted from the pit that they had found some chests and kegs. Everyone crowded around the rim of the excavation to watch as the sailors helping pulled on the manila ropes. Large casks came slowly into the light. The Egyptians directed that the chests be piled together and immediately set a guard on them. Large terra cotta pots and carved wooden boxes came up next.

Wells checked on Hernando to find him propped up on one elbow, craning to see what was happening. He slowly lifted his other hand to cradle his head. "It's ringing like the bells of a cathedral in there," he complained as he lay back down. "What did they find, Wells?"

"Looks like pirate treasure, sir. How are you feeling?"

"Like someone hit me in the head with a club." He smiled wryly at Wells.

Wells smiled back. "I'll have some food brought for you."

When it arrived, Hernando ate heartily. "Deer meat?" Hernando questioned around a mouthful.

"Yes; one of the men saw it on the opposite shore. It was so tame they rowed up and shot it from the longboat."

"Good," Hernando declared; "I was sick of fish." The fishing was so good here that the men had been eating fresh fish for a couple of weeks, and drying and smoking many others for the trip home. "Have you heard from the Indians?" Hernando asked.

"No, not since their first raid—although one of our pickets thought he caught a glimpse of some men in one of those tiny boats. It was only for a second, though, and much farther up the coast."

"So they are keeping their distance," Hernando mused. "That's good. I don't think my head could take another encounter with one of those war clubs!" Hernando set aside his plate and rubbed his temple. They'd cleaned away the dried blood matting his hair, but the stitches where Wells had sewn him up were still there. Hernando's fingers gingerly inspected the spot. "Ah, your handiwork, I imagine." He looked at Wells.

"We don't need to be telling your mother, do we?"

Hernando laughed. "We'll keep it just between the two of us, Wells."

*   *   *   *

Hernando managed to rouse himself and visit the excavation site. The two Egyptians joined him when they saw him. "How is the head?" Joseph asked.

"Fine," Hernando replied shortly, uncomfortable about being fussed over. He looked past the Egyptians at the beautiful woman brushing her hair in the warm sun, pretending not to see him. He looked at Wells, one eyebrow raised in query.

"I thought it was better to have her where I could watch her," Wells explained.

Hernando scowled, but he knew Wells was right—better to see the storm than have it brewing over the horizon.

They spent the next two days loading the ships with the treasure—all but a plain wooden box, which the two Egyptians carried with them wherever they went. As they oversaw the filling of the pit, Hernando thought this was a tremendous waste of time, but the Egyptians were adamant about covering their tracks. He was curious about the box, but was sure they would share its secrets with him once they were underway.

On the last day, as they were cleaning up the site and removing the shelters, a brewing storm picked up. Hernando looked to the southwest, where the sky was ominous, with looming black clouds towering into the heavens. Lightning flashed from their bottoms to the sea. He ordered the small flotilla to the lee of the island.

They had just finished preparations for the storm when it hit with all its fury. The men battened down to wait it out. In his cabin, Hernando and Wells listened to the wind raging against the small ship's rigging. The large oaks on the island took the brunt of the winds, but the rain hammered across the decks and soaked everything.

The Egyptians, also present, huddled over the box, which Joseph clutched to his chest. He looked up at Hernando. "This box contains the severed head of the Pharaoh Akhenaten."

Hernando gaped. "His real head?"

"Yes."

Hernando was quiet, expecting more enlightenment. Sensing Hernando was not satisfied, Joseph continued. "Remember we told you that the pharaoh's head was severed to stop him from entering the afterlife?" Hernando nodded. "When we reunite the head with the body that awaits us in the British Isles, then the great lord can continue his journey to his resting place."

Hernando eyed the box skeptically. "Are you sure it's in there?"

"Yes, we used the key from the grip of your sword to check." Hernando maintained his doubtful expression. "It is packed in natron, a salt used by the ancients to preserve the body for its journey to the afterlife."

Hernando remained quiet. In the silence, they noticed that the wind's howling had lessened; the storm was dying down. The Egyptian sighed and placed the box on the table. Hernando handed Joseph Boaz. The Egyptian manipulated the pommel and a strange key appeared. Joseph turned with it to the box. The lid groaned as he opened it. Hernando leaned forward.

The box was filled with scaly chunks of a white, chalky substance, which the Egyptian carefully removed and placed on the table. He then swept aside a white powder to reveal the top of a wrapped object. Carefully removing the package, he set it on the table, as gingerly as if it were Venetian glass. The tension in the small cabin was palpable as Joseph unwrapped the head with all the care a mother uses on a newborn infant.

Hernando expected a skull, but a leathery face appeared, staring at Hernando with half closed eyes. Around its brow was a simple golden crown, merely a band with what appeared to be two serpents intertwined on the forehead. He felt a chill wriggle up his spine. He could easily make out the royal features of this long-dead king.

The two Egyptian brothers knelt and bowed deeply. They remained prostrate for so long that Hernando grew uncomfortable and looked at Wells, who shrugged. Hernando was about to say something when they stood and began talking quickly to each other in Egyptian. Hernando looked back at the head, struck by Akhenaten's unusual features. The skull seemed to have been stretched along a line running from the top of his skull to the tip of his proud chin, and the nose was large and hooked. Hernando recognized some of the same features in his modern-day guides, who were still jabbering in excitement.

Joseph continued in Spanish so Hernando could understand the significance of what his brother was saying. "The prophecy clearly states that when the two are reunited, the great pharaoh will walk among us again, that after going to the afterlife for a short period, he will join us here in this world."

"And bring peace and concord to all men," Hamil continued in Spanish for Hernando's benefit.

"You're saying that he is going to come back to earth?" Hernando exclaimed. "And be alive?"

Hamil nodded. "We take the prophecy to mean he will be resurrected, yes. And that he will bring the knowledge of the true light to mankind. That—"

Shouts on deck interrupted him, followed by musket fire. Hernando and Wells made for the stairs as the Egyptian brothers quickly wrapped Akhenaten's mummified head and packed it back in the wooden box.

Hernando and Wells burst onto the deck. The wind was still strong and the rain came at them sideways. Hernando grabbed one of his men who was about to fire a shot over the gunwale into the darkness. "What is it?" he shouted.

The soldier hesitated for a moment, then he recognized his commander. "Indians, sir; they boarded the ship. We chased them off, sir, no problem," he added.

Wells had gone off to see to security and was already returning with another soldier. He was wounded, his shoulder bloody. "I am sorry, sir. We lost the woman," the man reported. Hernando could only stare, dumbfounded.

"The Indians, sir—they took her!" Wells added.

For a moment Hernando still did not understand, then it sank in that they had taken Isabella. Why would they do that? *It must have been someone else, an escape plan perhaps, or ...* "Wells, see what in God's name is going on here!" he barked.

Wells dragged the soldier away for more questions and Hernando went to the captain's cabin to ascertain if Isabella had indeed vanished. Outside her door, her guard was seated on a stool, propped against the wall, dead where he slept. The blood was still bright red as it ran from his sliced throat.

Hernando entered the cabin. She was not there. Her clothes and jewelry were still there, though. *She would never have left without her jewelry,* he thought. The chair at the small writing table was tipped over. A book lay open and a quill had fallen to the floor next to the table leg. Hernando stooped and picked it up and placed it on the table. *She had been writing when she was abducted.* He bent to read the words, but Wells came in, interrupting him.

"It does indeed seem that we were boarded by a small party of Indians and the woman was taken away," his sergeant reported.

"I don't understand, Wells," Hernando said, straightening to face the other man. "Why would they take her? What reason would they have? How did they even know where to find her?"

Wells motioned to the large windows in the stern of the ship behind Hernando. "Anyone could see a writer at this desk from the water below."

It was too much for Hernando to take in. "What have I done, Wells? I should have taken her back to Santo Domingo. I should have—"

"Begging your pardon, sir, but she tried to kill you. And she's the one who wouldn't leave it alone; she's the one—"

"Yes, yes, Wells. But I ..." He grew decisive. "Form up a search party. Have them ready in fifteen minutes."

"Sir, it's still storming," Wells reminded him. "It's dark, and we have no idea which way they went."

Hernando hesitated. "First light, then."

Wells left the room shaking his head and muttering about having to rescue a woman who kept trying to kill them.

Chapter 25

▼

The wind subsided as dawn was breaking. As they pushed off the longboats and headed toward the shore, Hernando could see the Egyptians' angry faces peering down from the side rail. They had argued hard in favour of leaving, saying that this rescue would jeopardize the treasure and the pharaoh's head.

Hernando sent the other of the two longboats south along the shoreline. His would go north. They traveled miles, checking the beaches for any sign of a craft being pulled out, but saw no trace of the raiding party. At last Hernando looked at the sun; it was low on the horizon. Soon it would be hard to see anything, let alone someone who was very good at not being seen. He ordered his men to turn and head back; maybe the other boat had had more luck.

It was very dark when they finally reached the ships. There was no moon, and thick clouds still lingered from the storm. His men boarded, but left the longboat tied to the ladder. Hernando went below, thinking to catch a few minutes' sleep while he waited for Wells to return.

He woke in the morning to learn that Wells and his men still had not returned. He was about to order his soldiers back into the longboat when a lookout called from the rigging. Hernando followed the sailor's pointing finger and saw Wells' boat, just barely visible as it poked out of the morning mist. He waited impatiently for Wells to arrive, then climb the ladder to the deck.

"Did you find them?" he asked the moment Wells' head popped above the railing.

"Not a sign, sir," Wells announced as he finished climbing aboard. "We rowed for miles and stopped at anything that looked as if it may have been them. But nothing!"

Hernando stood there for a long moment. He knew what he had to do, but he hesitated. "Stow the longboats, Sergeant. Let's see if we can't find our way back to Spain."

The men cheered. "Aye, sir!" Wells acknowledged, whirling to shout orders. Men jumped to the work.

Hernando looked at the two Egyptians and they nodded their approval. He didn't feel like conversing with them, so he wandered to the bow of his little ship. The other two ships were already dropping canvas and turning to open water. Hernando looked to the mainland, as if he might just spot Isabella running to the beach. He felt sick as he imagined what might happen to her. He had no way of knowing that the natives regularly abducted women from their enemies; in fact it was a great mark of courage amongst the tribes.

The mighty oaks of the treasure island slid away. As Hernando was staring at the spot where it had been, Wells came up to him.

"Don't imagine it will go good for her," the sergeant observed, "but she tried to kill you many times, and—"

Hernando cut him off. "It's just that I feel I failed to protect her, that it was my responsibility to take her back safely to answer for her crimes. I do not think God would approve of this end for her."

Wells shrugged. "She made her own bed."

Wells was correct, but it did not ease Hernando's stomach. He went to his cabin, where he remained, staring at his log, trying to write down events but mostly listening to the creaking of the ship's timbers as the captain pushed the little flotilla toward the British Isles.

Two days out, Hernando heard shouts of a sail from the lookout. He assumed it was Lord James finally locating them in this vast ocean, and went topside to have a look. The captain and first mate were peering through their telescopes. Hernando shaded his eyes and squinted toward the horizon. Two tall ships were fast gaining on them. The hair on the back of his neck prickled as he realized what the captain had already.

They were not Lord James' ships.

"Sound general quarters," the captain ordered.

"Aye, sir." The first mate shouted the alarm and vigorously rang a brass bell.

"Signal the other ships to stay close and to put on as much canvas as possible." The captain looked to the east, as if seeking a glimpse of the coast.

Hernando and Wells put on their half-armour and discussed strategy. "They will strafe the decks and try to board us," Hernando said.

"Pirates," Wells sniffed. "No imagination; always the same tactics." He was smiling, pleased that someone he could work out his frustrations on was closing on them in a hurry.

His quip cheered Hernando a little, but he knew this was a dangerous situation. They were seriously outgunned; their only hope lay in keeping the ships together and not shooting each other.

The two pirate ships closed swiftly. Soon they were looming over them. The little flotilla hung together, but one of the larger ships edged between them, actually careening off one of Hernando's ships. The pirates fired deck guns and muskets as the ships scraped past one another.

Hernando kept his men down except for a few sharpshooters in the stern of his ship. They kept the pirates from taking their time in aiming by landing a ball here and there.

The other pirate ship had managed to draw even with one of the other ships. It opened fire. Sharp splinters of wood and burning shrapnel sliced through the deckhands before they had a chance to duck.

Hernando kept his eyes on the ship that was almost riding up on their stern, but the sound of dying and maimed men carried easily across the short distance from his ship's sister. The first volley had greatly damaged its rigging, and with the subsequent barrage, the smaller ship began falling behind. The ship haranguing Hernando pulled up and grappled the crippled ship. Hernando's ship pulled away.

"Captain, turn the ship and attack the pirate on the starboard side," Hernando called.

The captain hesitated. "We must run while we have the chance!"

Hernando placed the tip of his sword against the captain's chest. He immediately backed up—right into Wells, who was standing behind him. Capitulating, the captain shouted orders and the little ship almost rolled over with the sudden turn.

"Wells, take charge of the cannon," Hernando ordered. He'd already turned and waved his sword over his head. "Take her in very close, Captain. I want my men to have easy shots."

The other ship turned as well and headed back toward the fracas. Hernando held his men from shooting until the very last moment. The pirates, concentrating on boarding the little ship, were taken completely off guard by the stiff opposition. Hernando's cannons tore through the sides of the much larger ship. The pirate captain stood on the railing and threw obscenities at the small ships speeding by. Only a few of their cannons answered fire.

Hernando saw that the other of their three ships had also inflicted damage on its much larger adversary, but it had sustained heavy damage as well and was limping off to the north with the pirate in pursuit. Hernando called to get the captain's attention and pointed toward the other ship.

The captain shouted orders to the first mate. The smaller ship cut across the stern of the pirate and opened fire, trying to stay out of range of the pirate's much larger cannon. Although they opened up the rear of the ship, it only seemed to anger the pirate, who answered from all ports.

Hernando was blown to the deck. He quickly stood and looked about. The captain and his bridge were missing; the wheel spun out of control. Hernando lunged for it but one of the Egyptians reached it first, stopping its wild spin. Hernando slapped him on the shoulder. Hernando turned. "Take up that slack, you men—hard to port!" The Egyptian spun the wheel as if it were his rightful occupation.

The pirate could only follow one ship. Angry at Hernando's ploy, he chased his ship down.

"Stay in front of him," Hernando shouted. "If he gets beside us he'll cut us to shreds. Hard to starboard! Let's get another shot at that one before we go down!"

The smaller ship was more maneuverable and turned a tight circle, heading back toward the two ships grappled together. Hernando saw black smoke belching into the sky and knew that his other ship was on fire—she would be of no help.

As they raced back to his ship's sister, Hernando could see knots of men fighting on the deck of the smaller ship. "Take her straight on—let's not give her anything to shoot at," he told Joseph.

The small ship sped toward the side of the pirate ship. The pirate was ready this time, and opened up with its bigger cannons. Great plumes of seawater jumped into the air on either side of Hernando's ship. Planning to turn at the last possible moment and give the pirate a broadside, Hernando murmured, "Hold it, hold it, not yet ... Now!"

The Egyptian spun the wheel with all his might. The ship slowly turned, so close that those below could see nothing but oak planking out of their portals.

"Fire you, scum!"

Hernando heard Wells' shout faintly from below. Seconds later, the deck rumbled under Hernando's feet and cannonballs hit one after another, tearing the guts out of the larger ship moments before the two ships collided. Planking was stripped away as if it were balsa wood. Water poured into a gaping hole just above the waterline as the larger ship shuddered, rolled, and then righted itself.

The pirate captain stood frozen on the deck as the faint rumble of an explosion carried over the water. *The powder room,* Hernando realized.

Hernando's ship pulled away from the pirate, but it was a sitting duck. The other pirate slowed to strafe its decks from a distance. The first volley tore apart the rigging and sails. The second sent hot grapeshot bouncing around the deck, looking for flesh. Hernando knew that they would be boarded soon and hoped there were enough men left to put up a fight.

"Keep your head down," Laocan's voice spoke in his ear, *"help is on its way."*

Hernando snapped his head sideways to see his beautiful princess, but she was not there.

He heard heavy cannonfire. The pirate stopped strafing the deck long enough for Hernando to have a look. Through the grey smoke, Hernando made out a golden lion—Lord James had arrived—late, but arrived he had.

Lord James' cannons blew large chunks of the enemy ship clean away. It looked as if the lord had no intention of trying to take these ships as prizes. Hernando heard a great explosion in the direction of the other ship and whirled to look. Its powder magazine had erupted. Forgetting their foes, all hands on the pirate ship jumped across to the other, where sailors and soldiers alike were frantically chopping away the ropes entangling the two. If the larger ship sank it would drag down the other or, worse yet, the flames could join them in their dance on deck.

Hernando watched the pirate ship being set adrift, with men still jumping off. On this side of his ship, the lord was still pounding an already sinking pirate. Hernando grinned. Lord James was late, but greatly appreciated. Lord James left the burning wreckage to put his ship in next to the one that still had fighting on board. They mopped up the pirates with ease.

Hernando and Wells saw to their wounded. Later, Lord James came aboard. He tracked Hernando down in the doctor's cabin, where he was holding a man down as the doctor tied off and cauterized the saw cut on his newly amputated leg. The man screamed and passed out. Hernando released his hold on him and turned to face Lord James.

"Commander, I must apologize for my tardiness. We were pushed off by the storm and only now found you again."

"And we are grateful that you did, Lord James!" Hernando held out a blood-soaked hand and the lord did not hesitate to clasp it.

"My other ship is scouting to the north, but will have seen the smoke on the horizon; it should be here soon."

They repaired the ships as best they could during the next two days it took to limp into a Scottish port, where the Egyptians took their leave. Hernando sent most of his men with them for protection. They did not tell Hernando where they were off to, and he did not ask.

"Thank you for fulfilling you mission, Hernando," Hamil told him. "You will be remembered in history as the man who brought God back to life!"

Hernando raised his eyebrows and looked at Wells and Lord James, who both mockingly bowed toward him. Hernando smiled, for he knew that at least this part of the adventure was over.

- End -

978-0-595-45113-5
0-595-45113-6